Kokomo

Victoria Hannan

hachette
AUSTRALIA

hachette
AUSTRALIA

Published in Australia and New Zealand in 2020
by Hachette Australia
(an imprint of Hachette Australia Pty Limited)
Level 17, 207 Kent Street, Sydney NSW 2000
www.hachette.com.au

10 9 8 7 6 5 4 3 2 1

Copyright © Victoria Hannan 2020

This book is copyright. Apart from any fair dealing for the purposes of private study, research, criticism or review permitted under the *Copyright Act 1968*, no part may be stored or reproduced by any process without prior written permission. Enquiries should be made to the publisher.

A catalogue record for this book is available from the National Library of Australia

ISBN: 978 0 7336 4332 3 (paperback)

Cover design by Alissa Dinallo
Cover photograph courtesy of Chantal Convertini
Author photograph courtesy of Meredith McHugh
Text design by Bookhouse
Typeset in 12/18.2 pt Simoncini Garamond by Bookhouse
Printed and bound in Australia by McPherson's Printing Group

MIX
Paper from responsible sources
FSC® C001695

The paper this book is printed on is certified against the Forest Stewardship Council® Standards. McPherson's Printing Group holds FSC® chain of custody certification SA-COC-005379. FSC® promotes environmentally responsible, socially beneficial and economically viable management of the world's forests.

Mina

One

MINA KNEW IN THAT MOMENT what love is. She saw it in vivid colour, saw that love is being inside each other. Love is being turned inside out together, all that pink splayed and splayed, everything on show for one another.

She knew that showing love is letting someone inside you or being let inside someone. Inside and outside, in love and out of love.

She looked at Jack, at his penis, so tall and pink, a soldier standing to attention, a ballerina in first position. It was tipping its hat to her, inviting her to dance.

Mina saw herself as a sailor lost at sea and Jack's penis a lighthouse alerting her to the presence of land, to the presence of safety. I am a hiker who has lost her way, Mina thought, and this penis a cooee heard deep in the bush. Mina felt ready to call back, to respond to love.

The second thing Mina knew, that she was sure of, was that this was the nicest penis she had ever seen. Both on the internet and in person. She watched Jack as he began to touch it. His fingers wrapped around the base of it, how you might hold a rolling pin, a truncheon, if you were about to brandish it as a weapon, thwack it down hard on a skull. He moved his hand up and down, that calf-leather softness pulled taut over all the veins and spongy flesh, all the spouts and tubes.

Soon, all of it would be inside her, then outside, then inside again, making its way through the entrances and exits of her body one by one then back again. This was love, she thought, and her heart felt stretched wide open and ready to receive it.

Jack looked at her while he touched it. There was a darkness in his eyes she'd never seen before, that she knew now in this moment – knew for sure! – to be a love so deep it lived in places the sun couldn't reach, down there where the fish had evolved to be too ugly for the light. Love wiped clean. A blank slate. Love as darkness, she understood this now. Love as shadow. Love as shade.

'Come here,' he said, and she shuffled up the soft grey cushions of the sofa, almost on all fours, a kitten padding towards milk. She smiled; wet lips, no teeth.

'Come here.' He grabbed her arm just below the elbow and guided her hand towards him.

She could hear her heart beat, a hollow gerdunk, gerdunk inside her chest like a drum. She was aware of her body; it felt suddenly that her skin was covered in feathers being ruffled by the wind, that she had the backcombed fur of a dog. The sound, the beating, the thud, thud, it was below her, outside of her.

It was not her heart, she realised, but her phone vibrating against an empty, forever-yellowed Tupperware container in her bag.

'Leave it,' Jack said, trying to pull her closer.

But her hand reached down, fingers touching the corner of the cool plastic box, feeling the urgent vibrations of it.

'Leave it,' he said again, the darkness of love in his voice too.

She found it, she pulled it out, she looked at the screen. She answered it.

'Mina, it's your mum,' Kira said. 'She left the house.' Then Kira said it again, as if she didn't believe it either. 'She left the house.'

Two

MINA WAVED AT THE BLOOD red hatchback as it crept along the passenger pick-up lane. Kira grinned at her from the driver's seat, waved back. Without indicating, she pulled in to the kerb almost at a right angle, blocking in a family in an SUV the size of a tank.

'You're here,' Kira yelled, waving with cartoon-like excitement as she climbed out of the car.

'I'm here', Mina said, and Kira wrapped her long arms tightly around her, locking Mina's in place by her side.

Kira released her, pulled her in again. Mina relaxed into it this time; let herself be held up, held tight, close. She stretched her arms around Kira's back, felt Kira's sharp shoulder blades, her ribs through her jumper. Her black bob smelt like apples.

It started to spit with rain.

'You smell terrible,' Kira said as she broke from the hug.

Mina laughed. 'It's good to see you too.' She let Kira wheel her suitcase out onto the road then lift it with ease onto the back seat of the car. Kira smiled at the family in the SUV and the driver smiled back. Mina watched him watch Kira as she jogged around the car and slid into the driver's seat. Mina could tell he was looking at the way her legs moved inside her jeans, that he was thinking about his dry, rough skin touching her perfect soft skin.

Mina sat in the front passenger seat, squeezing her backpack in by her feet. The floor was carpeted with parking fines, dog-eared audition sides, cheeseburger wrappers.

'Sorry,' Kira said as if she was seeing the mess for the first time. 'Just put your feet on it, it's all old.'

She put the car into reverse, then drive, then reverse, then drive, inching backwards and forwards until they were driving out past the airport hotel, past the long-term car parks and into the damp grey Melbourne morning.

'Did you sleep on the plane?' Kira asked.

'Not really. But I'm not a good sleeper these days.' Mina watched the tall white trunks of gum trees whizz by through the beaded curtain of rain on the window.

'It's good you came,' Kira said. Her eyes flicked from the road to Mina and back.

'I don't know that I had much of a choice.' Mina felt the heaviness in her chest, her stomach, like she was submerged in something thicker than water. She reached forward and turned on the radio. The saxophone bit of 'Careless Whisper' oozed out of the car's crackling speakers. 'They look good, by the way,' Mina said, glancing at Kira in profile: the full lips and high cheekbones, the skin that was exactly the same colour on every part of her, save for a light dusting of freckles across her nose. Now the perfect C cups, pointing upwards, everything impossibly in proportion.

'What, these old things?' Kira moved a hand around her breasts like a model on *The Price is Right* showing off a ride-on lawnmower.

'Do they still hurt?' Mina asked.

'A bit when I run, otherwise all good.' Kira cupped one of them instinctively. 'Did they feel fake when we hugged?'

'They felt firm,' Mina said. 'But I've never touched fake ones before.'

'Give them a go,' Kira said and pushed her chest out. Mina poked one, then cupped it, bounced it once, twice.

'They're great,' Mina confirmed. 'But they were great tits before. Just for the record.'

'Well, now they're working tits,' Kira said, smiling. 'Just an ad. Well, a series of ads,' she said. She sounded nonchalant, but Mina could tell she was proud. 'I have lines, though.'

'I'm so happy for you,' Mina said, punching her on the arm. And she was, she was. 'Ads for what?'

'Argh.' Kira scrunched up her face. 'It doesn't matter.' She turned up the radio.

'Tell me,' Mina begged. 'I promise I won't laugh.'

Kira indicated left off the freeway, everything lined by high concrete walls, hard and grey and tall.

Kira groaned. 'It's panty liners.'

'That's great,' Mina said, and the concrete turned to brick, red and cream against a flat white sky.

The traffic up ahead slowed and stopped at the dull, heavy ding of a level crossing. The lights flashed and the arms dropped.

'When do you shoot?' Mina asked.

'This week. So I won't be around much for a couple of days.'

'Oh God, you're abandoning me.' Mina leant forward and cradled her face in her hands, the seatbelt cutting into her neck. She felt trapped. She pressed her eyebrows with her index fingers, hard down on the pressure points, round in small circles, along her eyebrows to her temples.

'You're one to talk. Don't worry, I'll be done in a week.' Kira reached over and rubbed Mina's back. 'Plus you've got Mum. And there's always Shelly.'

The train honked ahead of them, a blur of blue carriages, the silhouettes of passengers facing forwards, facing backwards. Mina looked sideways at her.

'Come on, you two are still friends, right?'

'Of course we are. We just haven't spoken in ages. Our lives have gone down very different paths.' Mina sat back and closed her eyes. 'It's just a few days,' she said. 'Just a few days.'

They passed the Dimmeys, the window stocked with high-vis vests and pants. Mina noticed that, yet again, someone had tried to deface the sign that advertised adult circumcision 'for all reasons'. The graffiti had been scraped off but the faint outlines of the letters were still there. Mina let herself think about it for the first time since the plane; she let herself think about the penis. The Georgia O'Keeffe pink of it, the way it stood to attention, pinged right out of the fly of his boxers.

Mina felt the flight – two middle seats and a four-hour layover – all over her, cramped and heavy and long. There was so much distance and time between her and Jack. Between her and her real life. She made a list of things she'd give to go back in time (an arm, a leg, two feels of Kira's new tits, one of her old ones) and not notice her phone, not answer it. She should've put the penis in her mouth, let it burrow deep inside her, make a home and live there forever. If she'd done that, she would be in London, she would be in love. She would not be driving over the squeaky tramlines in

Melbourne, not driving towards whatever awaited her at home. She would not have this dull ache of dread inside her and the feeling of something unfinished between her legs.

'Nearly there,' Kira said, and they crossed a bridge over the dirty brown swill of the creek that bubbled and gushed, snaking its way south to meet the Yarra.

Mina looked at the gum trees dancing in the wind, at the expanse of sky that was too wide, too open, big enough that it could all just fold in on itself at any moment, swallow them whole.

'Have you seen her?' Mina asked finally.

'No, I just know what Mum told me.'

The car slowed, turned. Mina nodded and took a deep breath in, out, another and another, as they pulled into the sloping driveway of Kira's childhood home.

THE SMELL OF the Chengs' house rushed at Mina when Valerie opened the door. It smelt like fabric softener on just-washed sheets, a hint of incense.

'My baby girl,' Valerie said, wrapping Kira in her arms. 'Still so beautiful.'

Mina stood behind them as they embraced, as Valerie took her daughter's face in her hands and kissed each cheek four times.

'Mum, you saw me yesterday.' Kira pushed past her, kicked her shoes off and wandered through the living room to the kitchen at the back of the house.

'Jasmina, welcome home.' Valerie opened her arms and waited for Mina to step forwards into them. Mina let Valerie envelop her in silk and perfume. The smell was so pungent Mina could see it:

a sunset of whipped egg-white clouds, a field of foxgloves, pink on pink on pink on pink.

'You look so good,' Mina said as Valerie held her at arm's length and inspected her from head to toe.

'You look tired, girly,' Valerie said, tapping her on the cheek before trotting off towards the kitchen. She was wearing a silk shirt, a pencil skirt and a pair of pink fluffy slippers. Mina smiled. You could always count on Valerie Cheng to look glamorous, even at seven-thirty on a Monday morning.

As she took her shoes off she examined the Chengs' living room. Except for a couple of Keep Calm and Carry On throw pillows she'd not seen before, it looked the same, it felt the same. Maybe it was good to be home? She studied the family portrait still hanging above the TV and remembered the day it was taken, how she'd sat and watched Kira get ready, she and Loretta in matching red velvet dresses, Brendan fuming about his red velvet waistcoat. 'I think you look good,' Mina told him out of earshot of his sisters. 'That's because you're an idiot,' he said and stormed out to wait in the car with his dad. Mina's cheeks burnt the colour of the waistcoat, of the dresses. She'd longed for a family like the Chengs back then; the five of them sitting together in their matching outfits against the mottled blue background. She was jealous of all of them, of the cheeks that Valerie prayed Loretta would grow into, of the ease with which Brendan moved through life: just handsome enough, popular enough and smart enough for everything to seem easy. Most of all, Mina envied the way they jostled each other for space in the car, the noise of a full house. That feeling, the want, it growled and stirred deep down inside her even now, waking from its long slumber.

'Come on, slow coach,' Valerie called from the kitchen.

Mina walked down the long hall lined with framed family photos.

There was a pot of tea and a plate of biscuits on the kitchen table. Kira sat looking at them longingly.

'Mama,' she whined, a teenager again, dramatic. 'Why do you tempt me so?' She licked her finger and dabbed at the crumbs on the plate.

'You're too thin, baby,' Valerie said and poked a bony finger between her daughter's ribs as she squirmed. 'We need more healthy girls on TV.'

Mina took a biscuit, dunked it in her tea, let the soggy crumbs tumble into her mouth.

'Good thing Mina knows how to eat. You always were my favourite daughter.' Valerie gave her an exaggerated wink.

'Ha ha, very funny.' Kira rolled her eyes. 'I've got to go to work.' She leant over and kissed her mother on the cheek, and Mina stood.

The two of them hugged, Mina holding on the tightest this time.

'Thanks for coming to get me,' she whispered.

'Of course.' Kira held the back of Mina's head in her hand. 'I hope it's okay over there,' she said as she pulled away. 'There's a party on Friday night. Come stay at mine after.' She spun her car keys around on her finger. Mina nodded.

'Love you, baby girl,' Valerie called down the hall after her.

They heard the front door shut and Valerie shifted her gaze to Mina. 'You look pale.' She reached over and pinched the apples of Mina's cheeks a few times between her thumb and forefinger. 'Better.' Lifting the pot, she refilled their cups. There was a moment of silence that marked the end of one topic and the start of the next, the unavoidable one.

'It's good you came,' Valerie began, holding her cup in both hands, the steam rising and fogging up her red-rimmed cat-eye glasses.

'Have you seen her?' Mina paused. 'Since?'

'I popped over for a cuppa yesterday, but I didn't mention it,' Valerie said. 'I didn't tell her you were coming. She seemed fine, though.' Mina sensed that Valerie had been on the verge of saying 'normal'. 'She's the same. She's your mum.'

'And it happened on Saturday?' Mina felt like a cop on a TV show, checking to make sure the witness's story hadn't changed.

'Saturday morning. She was just up the street.' Valerie pointed north, in the direction of the over-priced corner store.

'And it was definitely her?' Mina needed to be sure.

'After all these years,' Valerie said, her brow furrowed. 'Who knows if it was even the first time?'

'Fuck.' Mina sighed and flopped back in her chair. 'Sorry for swearing, but Jesus.'

'No, baby, this deserves a fuck.' Valerie reached across the table and squeezed Mina's hand. They both laughed a little, as much as they could manage.

Maybe I could stay in the Chengs' house forever, Mina thought. Take Lottie's room.

She sat forwards, finished her tea.

'I guess I'd better go.' She pushed her chair out, stood. Her body felt heavy, tired, like she couldn't remember how it worked. She had to tell herself to lift one leg up, then the other. To remind herself how to walk. She caught a whiff of her armpits: Kira was right.

Valerie stood too, shuffling through the house behind her, ushering her towards the door. A photo on the hall table caught Mina's eye: it was Brendan in a tuxedo on his wedding day.

The same cheekbones, the same perfect skin as Kira. Next to him, Kylie beamed, blonde and beautiful, her huge teeth bared, a sign of true happiness.

Valerie saw her looking. 'Look at my handsome boy.' She picked up the wedding photo and looked lovingly at her eldest child.

'He's got good genes,' Mina said.

'Just a shame his wife's a bitch,' Valerie said and flicked Kylie's face through the glass. 'She's threatening to leave him. I told him: "Let her go, find a better one," but he's moping around all sad about it.' She put on a comically sad face and pretended to cry. 'Boohoo!' She put the photo back in its place on the table and opened the front door as Mina squeezed her feet back into her shoes. 'I'm always here if you need me. Give Mummy my love.' She kissed her hand twice and blew the kisses to Mina before swiftly closing the door behind her.

Mina looked across the street to number ninety-eight. She'd avoided looking at it from the car when they pulled in, when Kira dragged her bag up the driveway to the brown brick porch, as though not looking would make it disappear. Would make all of it go away.

From here she could see the ivy had grown, spreading and tangling itself across the length of the low wooden fence that sloped even further to the right now. It had been white once, but had since dimmed and dulled into a dirty cream, like soured milk. The front gate was still missing a slat of wood and it leered at her with its gap-toothed smile as she wheeled her suitcase towards it.

She pushed the gate open with her foot. The lone tree in the front garden, a tall green pencil pine, now had a single branch splintered off at an angle, sticking out like a welcoming arm or perhaps a crooked warning sign. She dug around in her backpack for her keys, unlocked the front door, wheeled her case in behind her.

'Mum?' she called down the dark hall, the only movement her own shadow. If this were a bad movie there would be a creak of floorboards, a grandfather clock ticking to mark the passing of time. Mina heard nothing but the gentle coo of a spotted dove, a dog barking somewhere nearby. 'It's me.'

She felt the silence draw up around her like floodwater. She waded down the hall. The striped green wallpaper dotted with pink roses gave her the impression she was in a prison designed by Laura Ashley. The walls were bare of photos, bare of art, missing any evidence that this was a home, that a family had lived here once.

The curtain was drawn in Elaine's room, the floral embroidered quilt Mina had sent home from Turkey one Christmas was spread neatly over her bed. Mina felt a little flicker of something – pride maybe, smugness – at seeing Elaine using something she'd sent her. At seeing how much it brightened up the room, just as she'd hoped it would.

Moving down the hall felt like swimming against the tide. She walked past the bathroom, past the kitchen, all the rooms to the left of her hanging from the hall like clothes from a washing line, grapes from a vine. Lopsided, uneven, until the end of the hall where the house opened up. Light flooded the living room through two big sliding glass doors; beyond them, the green mess of a backyard glistened with the residue of the morning's early-spring rain. Mina stood in the entrance to the living room where Elaine sat at the dining table, hands clasped, among piles of books and papers, a cup of tea cooling beside her. Her hair was pulled into a small bun at the back of her head, low and tight, the blonde losing its fight with grey.

'I'm here,' Mina said.

Elaine looked up at her daughter, her expression unchanged. 'You're here,' she said.

Three

MINA SAT ON THE BACK step in the cool, pale light that rested over Melbourne like a sheet on a freshly made bed. She'd woken at four, tossed and turned, given up trying to sleep at six and now nursed a milky, sugary mug of instant coffee in both hands, cursing it, her jet lag, her life with every sip.

She surveyed the garden, remembered it was loved once. For a few good years there were flowers, a vegetable garden by the back fence with green beans, tomatoes and lettuce. It had been Mina's job to wash the lettuce free of bugs before it went in the salad. She'd stand at the kitchen sink and squeal at the tiny caterpillars that writhed in the cold water as they drowned. She wanted to think that now she'd save them, let them worm their way across her hand while she carried them outside to find a leaf on which to set them free. She wanted a lot of things: to believe the best of people; all that pink; for this to go well, be easy.

The places where the garden beds used to be were now indiscernible from the sea of overgrown grass and tall weeds that stretched from the deck to the broken back fence. Mina slouched a little to look through the two gaps where the slats had snapped in the middle.

The house back there used to be rundown and mildewed, full of students, the bass vibrations of their parties shaking until three in the morning. Mina would sneak out and tuck herself in between the tomato plants and the fence to watch couples smoke and kiss. Through the gaps in the wood she got to hear the types of things people say to each other when they think no one's listening. Through the fence now she could see a new back deck and a huge barbecue, curvaceous in its winter coat. The kitchen light emitted a golden glow in the early morning. She imagined a couple lived there, that they were well off, her age but fitter, better-looking, making the world better in some small way, happy. Mina shivered in the morning chill with the envy that ran cold through her veins. Envious people are cold-blooded. She stood and walked to the end of the deck and threw the rest of her coffee onto the grass.

Back in her bedroom, Mina tried to think of something to do. She wondered how long she could just stand there. Ten minutes. An hour. All day. From dusk until dawn. Just standing. She looked around the room. It looked the same as when she'd left. She'd thought it would be dustier but that must've been one of the ways Elaine filled her time. Sitting, staring, reading, dusting. Mina had been in the house for twenty-three hours and she was already bored, her arms and legs crawling, restless. She had no idea how her mother could've done it for twelve years.

The white gauze curtain that hung at the bay window rippled in an invisible draught. There were still some framed photos on top of the chest of drawers. She and Kira and their dates at their year eleven formal – Kira with Tim Gardner, the best-looking guy at school; Mina paired up with Tim's much smaller friend, Paul. Poor small Paul, Mina thought, looking at the photo of him now; the professional photographer's big studio lights shining off his braces, off the glint of grease across his spotty forehead.

Beneath her feet, the light pink carpet was still worn in all the places it used to be worn. Everything changes, nothing changes.

Mina looked out the window to the quiet street. No cars passed, no sirens blared off in the distance, there was no whirr of a double-decker bus as it slowed to a stop. It was still as a corpse, deathly quiet inside and out.

She collapsed onto the bed and unleashed her phone from its charger. She hoped the twenty minutes she'd spent without it had rendered her suddenly popular. She opened her email and pulled down the screen to refresh. It checked and checked, perhaps taking its time to download something important. *Updated Just Now.* There were no new emails. She opened Instagram and scrolled down through the posts. She saw a baby she didn't know, a stack of books on a bedside table, a photo of a bird, another photo of a bird. She saw Busy Philipps wearing camouflage shorts, Alexa Chung at a wedding in Greece. A stranger's child got her first ballet shoes. She double-tapped a few photos, she watched all the new stories in a row: someone was at the beach, someone got a dog. All these things happening to people she vaguely knew, people she felt like she knew, complete strangers she had no idea why she followed. She searched for Jack's name, just in case she'd missed a post but she hadn't missed a post. She looked at who'd tagged him in photos but no one new had tagged him. She scrolled back through his grid: there were dozens of pictures of him drunk, one from a lads' trip to his family's villa in Majorca, one of the two of them in accidental matching outfits at the office. We look good together, she thought. She zoomed in on her face, on her thighs, she wished she was thinner, she wished she had a long face instead of a round face (she would even settle for a heart-shaped face), that her eyes were just a millimetre closer together. She wished she'd washed her hair that day, she wished she hadn't answered the call, she wished he was beside her, inside her. She chewed on the inside of her cheek and scrolled down through the activity of the people she followed. A freelancer from work had liked four pictures of women in bikinis an hour ago. Kira's ex-boyfriend's housemate, whom Mina hadn't seen in eight years, had liked nine pictures of Kira in a row. Didn't people realise that everyone could see everything? Maybe they didn't care. Jack hadn't liked anything. Maybe Jack didn't care. Where are you? Mina asked silently. Where are you?

She checked her texts again, just in case the flight, the time zone, her roaming, something wasn't working and he'd texted her. But he hadn't texted her. She opened her work email and looked at Facebook while the emails downloaded. The news was never good anymore; there were hurricanes everywhere, wildfires in California, someone had another ill-informed opinion about Brexit, a woman from school was pregnant again. She let herself wonder, just for a second, if anyone had even noticed she'd left London. If anyone would notice if she left the world. Lucy would notice if she failed to pay her rent. Kira would notice, she thought. She opened Instagram, typed Kira's name in and looked at her feed: eighteen thousand followers. Dozens of people Mina didn't know left comments on Kira's photos telling her she was stunning, she was hot. What was her secret, what was her diet, how, how, how could someone be that beautiful? It was the same question Mina had asked herself their whole lives. How was it fair? When she'd told Jack about her best friend, he'd scrolled through pictures of her. He liked seven of them in a row, followed her immediately. He liked every picture she posted. He was a good friend. Mina was sure he was just being a good friend. She shivered, her skin prickled.

There was a ping as new work emails downloaded. There was another message about the state of the men's toilets; a drunken, accidental reply-all that someone would be kicking themselves over for days; an all-staff email from her boss, George. *Mina MIA* was the subject line.

Morning team,

Mina Gordon's had to go back to Australia for a family emergency. We're not sure when she'll be back in the office but Jack will sign off all creative while she's gone. Copy-specific questions can go to Lizzie.

George

She'd put her out-of-office on at the airport so any client or production questions could be addressed by other people. She counted back on her fingers: it'd been twelve hours since George sent that email. She knew they all checked their emails on the weekend but none of her team had emailed to check if she was okay, no one had texted. Jack hadn't written to see if she was okay. Jack hadn't texted. She threw her phone down on the bed and thought back through everything that had happened before she went to his flat, before Kira called, before Heathrow and the four hours she spent pacing around Singapore airport, before she was here. She thought about his penis again, how his head cocked towards her, his lips tight as he unzipped his fly.

THE MINUTE SHE'D met him, she knew she was in trouble. The way he laughed at her jokes in his interview, held her gaze for just a second too long, rolled his eyes at just the right time. He wasn't the best-qualified candidate for the job but she didn't care. He was a good fit for her, they'd make a good team. He had the right kind of fire in him – a desire to do well but the cynicism to call bullshit when necessary. She saw it right away.

She knew she wasn't the only one at Peach who liked him. Loved him. There was that word again. She knew it in his flat and she knew it now. The word made her stomach flip over itself and her body turn inside out. She swam in it for a moment, weightless in the thought of the feeling, in the feeling itself.

She thought about how he walked through the office. There was something magnetic about him; the way his body moved made people's heads turn, eyes glued to him as he walked back from the kitchen with two cups of tea.

The account teams stopped by the office more often after he started working there. They stayed longer. He'd muck around with them, promise them the world, and then grimace at Mina once they'd gone.

No one had what they had, and she knew the other girls in the office watched them as they headed out to lunch together, as they sat whispering and giggling on the long benches at the pub. It was just the two of them. It had been the whole time. She couldn't remember the last person who had found her so funny, who had made her laugh like that. Not Ben, not really. Mina would sometimes look up from her huddle with Jack and catch the others looking at them. They were jealous. Mina didn't think anyone had ever been jealous of her before. She liked it, wore it like a cape, like a new leathery skin.

The night before she left was different, though; from the start it felt different. She had stood on the footpath outside The Sun and 13 Cantons with Lizzie and Danny, celebrating their promotion from junior to midweight creatives – a promotion she'd fought hard to get them. She could see Jack through the pub's wide windows: he had one empty glass next to him at the bar and the pint he held was not far behind. He looked up, saw her watching him and stared, turning away only to order from the spiky-haired bartender, necking the last of his second drink before the next one arrived.

'Mina?' Lizzie nudged her. 'Pay attention to my funny story.'

'Sorry,' Mina said, 'I'm listening,' but she couldn't look away from him. She watched him scull his third pint and weave his way out of the pub to where they stood on the footpath. He hailed a passing black cab and practically barrelled Mina into it, a half-full pint glass still in her hand. Before they drove away, Mina saw Danny raise an eyebrow, lean over and whisper something to Lizzie. She knew there were rumours, she liked them.

She turned her attention to Jack. 'What's up with you tonight?' she asked.

'Nothing,' he said and took her pint glass from her, drank the last of the warm pale ale, then put it on the seat between them.

They sat in silence as the cab stopped and started, caught behind two 38 buses plodding their way up Theobalds Road.

'We're making two stops,' Mina said to the driver as they pulled up to Jack's flat. His parents had bought it for him six months earlier, after he and Mina had traipsed around half of Hackney looking at flats for sale, Jack laughing it off every time an estate agent referred to them as a couple, Mina trying it on for size, liking how it felt. In every flat they looked at, she imagined her life there too.

He had eventually settled on half a terrace house just down the road from her, so they soon started sharing Ubers home to his place, where they'd stay up late and talk, not really watching whatever was on his huge TV. They'd sit close on the sofa. Once he fell asleep with his legs draped over her lap. This is it, Mina had thought, this is it. And she watched his chest rise and fall for an hour, wondering if his heart beat like hers. Wondering if his heart was hers.

'No, just the one stop,' Jack said to the cab driver, and he clambered out, paid through the window, held the door open for her.

She followed him silently through the gate to the front door, into the kitchen where dirty dishes filled the sink.

He sniffed a few times, scratched at his nose, his whole body seemed to twitch. He pulled two glasses from a cupboard and poured them both a drink.

'Jack,' she said as he passed her a glass.

'Jasmina,' he said and clinked the heavy base of his glass against hers before swallowing the contents in one gulp and pouring himself another.

She took a big mouthful of whisky and let it burn her tongue, felt it as it warmed her throat, travelled down through her chest. She took another big sip and held her glass out to him to refill.

She followed him upstairs and sat beside him on the L-shaped sofa. His drink was gone in another gulp and he put his glass on the coffee table without looking at her.

Mina folded her legs under her and sat facing him.

'You're being weird tonight,' she said.

'You're always weird,' he said, and he turned to look at her, to really look at her, as if he'd never properly seen her before. He breathed her in with four deep breaths. Mina felt the space between them fill with something, the air shift as it does before rain turns to sleet, turns to snow.

'What if –' he said and stopped himself.

'What if what?' Mina could feel every inch of her skin suddenly, as if an electric current was passing over her.

She saw his hand moving back and forth, up and down on his crotch, his fingers unfastening the top button of his jeans.

MINA SCROLLED BACK through Jack's messages. She started to type but didn't know what to say. Just say what you feel, she thought, get the idea down first – that's what she always told junior copywriters. She typed: *I like you*. She deleted it. She typed: *I love you*. She deleted it. She typed: *I love you. I should've stayed, I wish I'd stayed*. She deleted it. She wished she'd touched it. If she'd touched it, things would be different, better, good. That's all she wanted, for things to be good sometimes. She slipped a hand down beneath the elastic of her pyjamas and between her legs.

She moved her fingers as though he was on her, in her. His eyes looking into her eyes, his lips on her lips, his tongue intertwined with hers like two snakes, her mouth on him, her hands on him: a handshake of sorts. Sealing the deal, binding them together forever with a human glue.

She slid her hand out of her pyjamas, wiped her fingers up her stomach, onto her pyjamas. She felt a stillness, a calmness in her brain, in her body, like the power had been cut, the radio lost its signal. Five, ten seconds of calm until it wedged in behind her shoulder blades, at the base of her skull. It was back. It wasn't a pain, or a twinge, but the feeling of air between her brain and her skull, a big man's hand on the back of her neck.

She picked up her phone again and looked at the time. Seven. Only seven. She felt the time pass with exquisite precision. Wound up tight like a clock, Mina could account for every second. She imagined her life in time lapse, shadows moving in circles away from the sun, the stars scattered like glass from a broken window, flowers wilting, a dead fox decaying in the forest, babies being born in a gush of blood, the whole world moving on while she stayed perfectly still in that house. That fucking house.

She opened Instagram and pulled and pulled at the screen to refresh the feed. She sat up; Jack had followed someone named LenaSeraphina. Lena. Who the fuck was Lena? Her body twisted itself. She threw her phone down on the bed. She picked it up again and tapped on the profile picture. LenaSeraphina's account was private. Mina stared at her tiny photo. Tall Lena; Mina could tell Lena was tall. Long-haired Lena. Lena who would touch it. Lena who would not answer her phone, Lena who would let him inside her. Lena with the long face. Lena with the twigs for thighs. Mina threw her phone. It hit the pink carpet with a thud. She flung her head back on the pillow. This fucking house.

She heard Elaine stirring in the next room, the thin walls disguising nothing of the sounds people make. The door of the bedroom next to hers opened and Elaine shuffled down the hall. The toilet flushed, a tap ran, a door opened and closed. Mina waited until she was sure Elaine was in the kitchen, then she darted from her room to the bathroom. She showered quickly under the lukewarm trickle that her dad, then later Elaine, had promised to fix, and ran back to her room, a rough beige towel barely wrapped around her wet body.

She assessed the mismatched clothes she'd packed in a hurry, drunk, at two in the morning. Four bras, six pairs of underwear, two summer dresses. She put on the jeans she'd travelled in, the t-shirt that smelt slightly of sweat, sprayed herself with deodorant and perfume. She scrabbled in her backpack for her wallet, took her phone off the floor and listened for Elaine in the hall. Nothing. Just muffled silence, as though they were living under water.

'I'm just popping out to get coffee,' she yelled down the hall and then slipped out the front door.

MINA FELT UNTETHERED the second the door shut behind her. She walked down the street that stretched in a straight line east from the creek. The street that in late summer sizzled with the little red and pink fireworks of the flowering gums, but in early spring was a pastoral of damp leaves and dewy grass, trees bulked up with chocolatey gumnuts.

The rain had brought the smell out and the air was soggy with eucalyptus, wet with the smell of a home she barely knew anymore. These streets hadn't changed much: they were still lined with small brick bungalows, the maroon Ford Falcon that had been parked in the same spot for seven years was still there, bark and leaves collected at its wheels, rust caked around its edges. She wanted to walk, to keep walking, to never stop walking. Anything to avoid that house.

Mina and Elaine were engaged in a duel, moving around each other in a silent dance, trying to avoid the sharp point of the other's foil. Adulthood is just getting used to the things you can't avoid, Mina told herself as she walked past tall wooden fences, low white ones, manicured lawns of verdant green.

'I guess you know why I'm here,' she'd said the day before as she pulled out a wooden chair to sit opposite Elaine at the table.

'Why don't you tell me,' Elaine said, her voice taut.

'Mum . . .' Mina studied Elaine's face, her long thin nose, her cool blue eyes; she looked older, tired, just as sad. She wanted to hug her mother but instead she reached over and put her hand on Elaine's hand. Her skin felt cold like paper. They sat there for a minute in silence, their hands touching. 'Are you –' Mina started, but Elaine stood.

'You must be hungry,' she said, pulling her hand out from under Mina's. She walked into the kitchen.

Mina followed her and stood at the kitchen door, watching her mother move around the room in a tight circle. She took two slices of white bread from the freezer and put them in the toaster, slamming the lever down twice before they stayed put. The microwave flashed three zeros.

MINA SAT ON a high stool at a communal table in a cafe on High Street hunched over a hot black coffee. She counted the hours back in London time. If she were there now, she'd be lying in her bed with her laptop, listening to Lucy coming home, listening to her talk to Oliver on speaker phone in her room, listening to her laugh in the kitchen while he cooked for her, listening to them fuck (not on purpose: Lucy's bed squeaked with every thrust – slow first, then faster and faster until it was over, thankfully, a few minutes later). The sound of Oliver's voice through the thin walls made Mina's skin crawl. Not just because she didn't like him, but because his presence made her even more aware of all the time she spent alone, all the things she went without. Once she'd heard him grunting and imagined him on top of her, his long body at odd angles with her short body. She put her hands on her skin as though they were his.

'Sorry if you can hear us,' Lucy said one morning after Mina had listened to giggling give way to the sounds of sex: silence first, then movement, short breaths, a moan.

'I was fast asleep, didn't hear a peep,' Mina lied and Lucy sighed with relief, smiled sheepishly.

The coffee was working now, too well, and Mina caught herself scraping her top lip out and in again along her bottom teeth. She tried to steady her breathing. She counted in, two, three, four, hold, two, three, four, out, two, three, four, picturing her breath as a square like she'd seen on YouTube. She wanted a drink. A massage. She wanted to go to work and see Jack and be near Jack. She missed the smell of him. She longed for her bed in London now, for Oliver's moans, for the foxes that ripped open the bin bags they left at the bottom of the front steps, their screeches piercing the night. For something more than this, something bigger. For a different mother. A different life.

She finished her coffee and watched as a blonde woman dressed head to toe in Lululemon entered the cafe, a toddler at her heels. They locked eyes before Mina could look away, look down.

'Oh my God,' Shelly shrieked and the cafe din quietened for a second, heads turned. 'What are you doing here?'

Mina slid from the stool and the two of them hugged, Shelly's hard, round pregnant belly pressed against her soft belly.

'Look at you!' Mina said. 'I didn't know.'

'Well, it's been a while. How long have you been back?'

'I just got here,' Mina said. 'Very last minute. I was going to let you know.' She was mesmerised by the way Shelly stroked her stomach from top to bottom, round and round, over and over.

'Mum okay?' Shelly asked as the toddler hugged her leg before letting out a bloodcurdling scream. 'Jason, come on. That's not a very nice way to say hello to Mina.' Shelly tousled his hair encouragingly and he screamed again. 'Watch him while I order?' Shelly didn't wait for an answer, she just walked to the counter.

Mina squatted down next to the boy.

'Hello, Jason,' she said, her voice automatically shifting an octave higher than usual. 'Nice to meet you.'

He looked at her, narrowed his eyes, then screamed again before running to hide between Shelly's legs at the counter.

'Where's Mason?' Mina asked when Shelly returned, the boy squirming on her hip.

'He's in the car with Justin.' Mina looked out the cafe's big windows. A black BMW idled at the kerb. 'He's on the way to work, and we're off to the park. Justin can only handle one of them at a time.' Shelly shook her head. 'And it was his bright idea to have another.' She looked at Jason then kissed his cheek, and he giggled. She kissed him again and again, seeming to lose herself in the boy's chocolate-stained face, his almost white-blonde hair, before turning her focus back to Mina. 'How long are you here for?'

'Just a quick trip, I think,' Mina said as the boy's smile turned to a scowl at the loss of his mother's attention.

'Why don't you come over during the week and see the new house? We're just down the road.' Shelly gestured vaguely.

'Okay,' Mina said as the barista called Shelly's name.

She collected two coffees in a tray, pausing to kiss Mina on the cheek on her way out.

'I'll message you.' Shelly smiled. 'It's really good to see you.'

'You too,' Mina said and watched Shelly leave.

'Shit,' she whispered under her breath. She finished her coffee, paid, then walked out into the street. Standing on the footpath, she took her phone from her pocket, pulled down, pulled down, pulled down. This place, the past – it's inescapable, she thought. She pulled down again. A message from Shelly already.

So excited you're here!! Tomorrow?

She breathed in and out. She considered putting her phone away without answering, to avoid seeing Shelly's perfect life with her own eyes.

Tomorrow's great, she wrote instead and walked home.

When Mina let herself back into the house she could hear the TV on down the hall. Elaine was watching one of the morning shows, the presenters' voices smug and shiny. It was up loud enough that Elaine didn't hear her coming so, for the second morning in a row, Mina observed her mother from the doorway. Elaine sat on the sofa in her dressing-gown, a cup of tea on the table beside her. Her hair was in a neat plait. Mina wondered who cut her hair. Did she get someone in? Did she do it herself? Maybe that's why she had left the house: she was sick of dealing with her split ends. She looks so alone, Mina thought. She imagined her doing this every morning. Sitting here on her own as the world moved on around her.

'Do you remember when I used to insist that plaits were pronounced plates and I didn't believe you or Dad when you tried to convince me otherwise?'

Elaine's eyes didn't move from the TV but her body stiffened a little in acknowledgement of Mina's presence.

'Not really,' Elaine said, and Mina screamed silently behind her.

She walked over to the sofa and perched on its arm. 'Can we talk?' she asked.

Now Elaine looked up. 'If you insist,' she said. Her hands curled in her lap. She kept her eyes on Mina.

'Can you turn the TV off for a minute?' Mina leant over her for the remote.

Elaine snatched it and turned the sound to mute. Onscreen, four people sat behind a desk. The women wore tailored dresses, perfect bobs. The men, a light dusting of silver through their wiry hair, wore suit jackets with checked shirts underneath, the top button undone. A uniform repeated on all morning shows the world over. Elaine returned her gaze to Mina.

'Watching this shit will rot your brain,' Mina said.

'I didn't ask you to come.' Elaine glanced back at the soundless TV, distracted by the ticker of headlines that ran along the bottom of the screen.

Mina's whole body sagged. She wished the ground would open up and swallow her, spit her out somewhere in the middle of the Atlantic.

'Can you just tell me why?' Mina begged. 'Why now?'

Elaine's eyes flicked to Mina then back to the TV.

'It's not important,' Elaine said and turned the sound back on.

'Not important?' Mina paused, took a deep breath. 'Okay.'

She stood and walked back to her bedroom, closed the door and sat on the corner of her lumpy bed. She looked at the time. Nine o'clock. She let her body convulse on the bed in a mock seizure. Then she curled into a ball, uncurled, and eventually tumbled into an anxious, restless sleep.

MINA WOKE TO a dull dusk, an incoming rain shower, the lights of a car and the purr of its engine stopping across the street. She sat up and through the darkness saw a new car in the Chengs' driveway. The lights cut out and she watched a figure emerge into the spitting rain. He opened the boot and took out a small suitcase, a duffel bag. Valerie was waiting at the front door, and when he reached the porch, she hugged him for a long time. Valerie shepherded Brendan inside and closed the door behind them. Their house glowed golden, warm light beaming from all the windows.

Mina sat down on the bed, picked up her phone. She looked up Brendan Cheng on Facebook. There were photos of him on a boat, photos of him in New York. Photos of Kylie kissing his cheek. They looked happy. Mina followed the trail, looked at Kylie too. She was skinny, pretty but in an obvious way. Mina looked her up on Instagram. She scoffed at the hashtags on their wedding flashbacks: #bestdayever #loveubabe #myforever #husband #myhusband. Mina kept scrolling. She wandered through all the scenarios that could've led to Brendan moving back home. Maybe she'd cheated (with someone from work; a guy at the gym; Brendan's best friend), maybe he'd cheated (over a desk in the office; for twelve hours straight in a sticky, dingy hotel room; worse, in their bed, king-sized, Egyptian cotton sheets, ten or twelve decorative cushions that had to be removed every night and replaced every morning). Maybe she really was a bitch, like Valerie said (maybe she nagged and nagged, put him down in front of their friends).

Mina sat in the dark room. She hadn't eaten all day but she'd rather stay hungry, starve to death, become a sack of bones, than go back out there and face this new version of her mother. It was bad enough before. But now Mina faced an even more evasive, even more frustrating version of her. Elaine 3.0. She lay back down and listened to the sound of her stomach churning and rumbling like clouds before a storm.

Four

IT STARTED IN THE DAYS between his death and the funeral. Long, bright sunny days; one of Melbourne's scorching heatwaves, the high-sun summers that are hot when you wake up and hot when you toss and turn, doze restlessly, sweating through a thin cotton sheet, praying into the darkness for respite in any form.

The heat spread to every corner of the house. Night after night Mina found herself hamstrung in the long stretch of time, of darkness and still, hot air, her eyes unable to focus on anything except the sharp point of his death. On the fact that her dad was dead. Dead. Dead. It would show up in the darkness, show up in the light, it would poke her again, pricking her skin, never enough to draw blood but enough to hurt. To remind her constantly that he was dead. Dead. He was dead.

Arthur drove them home from the hospital and they all filed into the Chengs' house. Arthur sat on the sofa, his head down, his hands together between his legs in a kind of inverse prayer. Valerie led Elaine upstairs, where she climbed into the single bed in Brendan's old room with her shoes on, with her clothes on.

Mina plonked down on the edge of Kira's bed, and Kira sat down beside her.

'I don't know what to do,' Kira said. 'Tell me what to do.'

'Just being here is good,' Mina said and lay down.

'I don't really have a choice, because you're in my house, but okay.' And Kira stretched out beside her, their bodies touching at the hip.

When Mina woke, Kira was gone; a blow-up mattress made up with a pillow and sheet lay on the floor. She was dressed in a t-shirt of Kira's, her clothes from the night before folded in a neat pile at the end of the bed. She hoped she'd slept for weeks, months. Maybe a year had passed, maybe two, maybe she'd go downstairs and find Elaine sitting at the kitchen table drinking tea with Valerie, Arthur cooking breakfast. Like one of those coma patients who wake up and have to learn who the prime minister is, what the internet is.

'Good morning, sleepyhead,' Elaine would say, the tight rope of mourning loosening around her, around all of them.

What was life but a series of hypotheticals anyway? Mina wondered. No one ever really knew how things were going to turn out.

She walked across the hall to the bathroom, sat on the toilet and listened to the music that filtered through the wall from Lottie's room; the steady bang of a kick drum made her heart beat faster as if trying to keep up. After splashing cold water on her face, she opened the mirrored cabinet and punched four ibuprofen from their plastic pockets. She washed them down with four handfuls of water from the tap, the last one sitting like a sugary lump in her throat, then closed the cupboard and inspected herself in the mirror. She looked like one of Francis Bacon's screaming popes: pale-faced, in agony. Mina thought of her dad in the cold darkness, shoved in a drawer like some limp iceberg lettuce, a forgotten carrot, a whole lot of secrets, and shivered, cold on his behalf. She made a vow to herself to try to feel everything on his behalf from then on. To see the world on his behalf. To do the things he would never be able to do because he was dead. Dead. He was dead.

MINA AND ELAINE stayed at the Chengs' for two days: Mina on the sofa watching *Ellen*, *Oprah*, watching *Days of Our Lives*, watching *The Bold and the Beautiful*, Valerie and Kira watching her in shifts, Arthur hovering behind them, not knowing what to do. In the afternoons, when the temperature soared, she'd lie down and let the twitter of voices on the TV, the hum of the air conditioner, lull her into a dreamless sleep. Twice on the first day, once on the second, she mustered the energy to go upstairs and peer through the door of Brendan's room where Elaine still slept, only the rise and fall of her chest evidence that she hadn't died too.

On the third day, Mina stood on the edge of the porch and watched as Arthur and Valerie moved Elaine across the street, from their house to hers. They flanked her, taking small steps, Elaine's body moving like it was filled with air, like she was one of those inflatable tube men that danced their funny dance outside used-car lots. Something had shifted in her; Mina had sensed it at the hospital, witnessed it at the Chengs', and now it felt like fact. Her father was dead and her mother was gone.

Mina followed them inside, watched from the hall as they lowered Elaine down into bed, saw Elaine roll over, settle down into the sheets and fall instantly back into a deep sleep.

'Call us if you need anything,' Valerie said. 'We're here for you twenty-four seven, okay?'

'I will, thank you,' Mina said.

'I mean it, anything.' Valerie took Mina's hand and squeezed it, then took a step back, then another and another, her eyes on Mina until she was through the gate, she and Arthur standing side-by-side on the footpath.

Mina's smile dropped once she'd closed the door. She felt closed off, the house felt tiny: the low ceilings, the narrow hall. A straitjacket big enough for two.

In the days that followed, each so hot and so long Mina thought it might never end, she spent hours hovering outside Elaine's room. She made toast, sometimes with jam, sometimes with peanut butter, always spread meticulously with perfect coverage from corner to corner (as if this was the thing that would bring her back, bring him back), and stood with it at the door until there was a creak of the bedsprings, a muffled break in the pattern of her breathing. In her father's death, Mina found herself acutely aware of her mother's signs of life. As if the quietening of one made the other scream.

Mina put the plate on the bedside table next to a glass of water and shook Elaine's shoulder gently, then more firmly, until Elaine's eyes flickered, her lips twitched.

'Food,' Mina said, and when she was sure Elaine had heard her, she walked back into the hall where she stood still, waiting for something to change, waiting for him to come back through the door, chuck his keys into the copper dish on the hall table, the clink and clang of metal on metal the most comforting sound she could imagine.

ALL THE POST-DEATH tropes rang true. The days blended into one another. Time was marked by people knocking at the door. People she recognised, people she didn't. They all said how sorry they were and asked if there was anything they could do. They spoke in hushed tones but Mina responded loudly, hoping the sound of voices would wake Elaine, would bring her back. Some brought food: casseroles straight from the oven, stews, cakes – cooking that had made their houses hotter, an even greater kindness. She'd slam the door after they'd left, peering into Elaine's room to see if she'd stir, but she didn't stir. The phone rang too, sometimes twice an hour. Mina wrote down names, messages, condolences. After the first few days of answering the phone loudly, Mina just let it ring and ring and ring and ring.

Sometimes people came by but didn't knock. They just deposited things on the doorstep for Mina to find. Anything she got to in time went in the fridge, where it slowly grew a coat of storm-grey fur. The rest went rotten in the hot sun. Mina found the scooping out of rancid, sun-curdled or fridge-rotten casserole almost ceremonial. She washed up each dish and added it to the pile on the dining table. A new daily ritual of mourning, the plastic and glass tower a monument erected in honour of a life cut short.

One morning, Mina woke to hear Valerie pottering around in the kitchen. She moved differently from Elaine, faster, quieter. She heard her knock at Elaine's door, the creak as it opened. Valerie's voice through the wall was patient and kind, but firm too. Mina heard the curtains open, the bashing of a pillow being fluffed.

Valerie knocked and opened her door too. Mina sat up in bed and Valerie sat beside her, held her hand, Valerie's fingers holding all of Mina's fingers, her thumb stroking Mina's palm back and forth. Valerie's hands were cool, somehow.

'We have to go to the funeral home today,' Valerie said calmly. 'Your mum isn't up to it so I'll go with you.' Valerie let go of Mina's hand then leant forward and kissed her forehead. 'We'll do it together. Now get ready and come across the road in half an hour.' Valerie rose and left the house.

Mina was glad for something to do, a way to help. Grieving was a slow and heavy pastime, an unfulfilling hobby. Bill would be proud of her, taking control. She walked to the shower, let the cold water trickle down over her. Dead, she thought. He is dead. She held onto the cream-tiled wall for balance.

IT WASN'T A long drive: a right turn, straight ahead, another right turn. Valerie drove slowly while the radio blared an ad about air conditioners, a department store sale. Valerie didn't turn it down, she just talked louder over it. 'Brendan got the good internship,' she was almost yelling. 'The big firm. My boy is going to be a huge success one day. I'm taking him shopping for suits tomorrow. He'll look so handsome. So grown up.'

She stopped the car outside the funeral home and pulled the handbrake on. Mina thought about Brendan in a suit, his broad shoulders.

'Listen to me,' Valerie said as she cut the engine, the radio with it. 'You know that I grew up in China. I lived with my mum and dad and my baby sister. When I was thirteen they decided to send me to Australia to live with my aunty. For a better education, for a different life. I had to leave all my friends, my school, everything I knew to come here. I didn't get a say. I had to make them proud, make their sacrifices worth it. I cried myself to sleep every night for six weeks, but now here I am. Sometimes we don't get to choose when we grow up. We just have to be strong and make our families proud of us.' Valerie paused for a second, looked at Mina tenderly. 'You understand me, baby girl?'

Mina nodded.

The footpath had sucked up days of sun already, and it shimmered with the heat of it. It felt like the whole world was on fire, as if it was a mountain of rubbish that had caught alight, a forest sparked by lightning. Maybe this is what hell feels like, Mina thought. A hot footpath, a red-brick chapel, everyone dead or gone.

They pushed through the front door. The temperature in the office was twenty degrees cooler than outside. A man stood in the reception area. He was too tall, too thin for this.

Valerie introduced herself. 'We spoke on the phone,' she said as she shook his hand. 'This is Jasmina.' Valerie put her palm in the middle of Mina's back. 'She is the daughter of . . .' Valerie paused, then said tentatively, sadly, 'Bill.'

Valerie gently pushed Mina forwards.

'Bob,' the man said and put his hand out to shake Mina's too. Mina felt the bones in his fingers. 'I'm so sorry for your loss,' he said. 'Please, come through.'

He led them to an office with a desk. There were shelves along one of the walls, lined with urns. Some were silver or brass, with etchings of birds or flowers, patterns like hotel carpet, a few engraved with poems or prayers. There were wooden boxes with decorative fastenings in gold, one shaped like a hand. Mina couldn't understand why anyone would want to keep the crumbs of a person around, the detritus of a body, of a life.

'I have all the certificates and forms you asked for,' Valerie said. She took a folder from her bag and slid out a small stack of papers, lay them out on the desk. The death certificate of William David Gordon, some paperwork with her mother's signature at the bottom, dated that day.

'That's wonderful,' Bob said as he glanced over the forms, checking for signatures. 'Thank you.' He smiled at Valerie and she visibly relaxed, dropping her shoulders.

She smiled back at him then they both looked at Mina.

'So, Jasmina,' Bob said, 'I understand your mother wasn't able to be here with us today.'

'No, she's –' Mina stopped. She didn't have a word for it yet, didn't know how to frame the severity of it, medically, emotionally. 'She's incapacitated,' Mina said. Gone, she thought. She's gone.

The hair on Mina's arms prickled in the air conditioning. Why was death always accompanied by cold? she wondered. The body goes cold, the morgue is cold, the funeral home like ice.

'It was your father's wish to be cremated,' Bob said, scanning the paperwork Valerie had brought.

Mina laughed.

Bob leant forward, confused.

'Sorry, I just,' Mina stopped and smiled. 'I just miss him.'

Bob handed her a brochure with pages and pages of caskets and coffins, boxes in varying wood finishes with silly, masculine names: the Maximilian, the Augustine, the Hyperion in chocolate brown. She wondered what the brief was in the naming of these things: something solid and long-lasting. She probably would've gone historical too. Emperors and kings.

'What's the difference?' Mina asked as she flicked through the pages. 'Apart from price. I mean, aren't they all going to be burnt anyway?'

'Some families like to choose a casket that represents their loved one, that provides an appropriate final resting place. So the quality, type and finish of the wood means the prices vary,' Bob said patiently.

'That one's nice.' Valerie pointed to the Leonardo. MDF with a walnut finish, a three-tiered lid, big silver handles all the way around it.

'It's four thousand dollars,' Mina said. She looked at Bob. 'Why not just put him in a cardboard box and set fire to the money?'

'Mina,' Valerie scolded her kindly, 'you don't need to worry about the money, the life insurance will take care of it. Just pick something nice. It's your dad.'

'Exactly. Have you ever known him to spend a cent on himself? He'd be horrified if we spent four thousand dollars on firewood.' She put the brochure back down on the desk and sat back in her chair, folded her arms. 'Are there cheaper ones?'

Bob opened the drawer of his desk and handed Mina another brochure.

She flicked through it and selected one that to her eyes looked just as good as the ones in the first brochure but for a quarter of the price. She chose a song for the start and a song for the end of the service, she put herself down to deliver the eulogy, she requested no flowers, decided on a format for the death notice. She ticked boxes and signed forms, and half an hour later she and Valerie crossed over High Street, riding in the hot car back to their houses.

'Your dad would be proud of you,' Valerie said when she stopped to let Mina out.

'I think he'd be more angry at Mum than he would be proud of me,' Mina said, unclicking her seatbelt.

'Go easy on her,' Valerie said as Mina leant in through the open door of the car. 'She's in shock.'

And I'm not? Mina thought but didn't say. She felt as if there was a brick wall behind her eyes, a pile of sandbags. She felt everything in her hardening, fortifying.

'Thank you for today. I had no idea I was meant to do any of that stuff.'

'I just looked it all up on the internet,' Valerie said. 'Brendan showed me how.' She waved at Mina to signal that it was time to close the door.

Mina watched Valerie park and disappear into the house, then she turned and walked towards her own.

A new delivery, an offering of sympathy on the doorstep, caught her eye. Daisies, their long white petals wilting in the heat. Mina picked them up, inhaled the bitter scent of their bright yellow middles, tiny dying suns. There was an envelope with them, ivory, Elaine's name on the front in a man's careful handwriting. Mina tore into it, pulling her finger through the paper across its top. It took her a second to recognise the scene painted on the front of the card, washed with golden watercolour: the scorched grass, that giant dead tree. Little white dots of sheep scattered around it in clumps. She knew that tree. She pushed back through her brain, waded through the silty water of the last week, a diver searching for a body. It came back to her in glimpses. That one last walk up to the tree before they sold the farm, the dry grass as sharp as glass under the boots they'd made her wear in case of snakes. Bill had knocked on its hollowed trunk for luck before they used a wooden spoon from the kitchen drawer to scoop her grandma's ashes and chuck them into the wind. Mina hadn't thought about the farm in years but there it was, the colour, the heat and the brightness. She opened the card to read the message.

Elaine,
I'm still here,
Jeff

She fished her keys from her pocket and let herself into the house, the daisies leaving a trail of white petals in her wake. She filled a glass with water. It overflowed as she shoved the stems in and then dripped back along the hall. She entered Elaine's room, her mother's body a lump under the sheet. She moved a plate full of stiff, cold toast and placed the flowers next to it on the bedside table. She put the card there too; the picture glowed even with the curtains drawn. She watched Elaine's chest move as she slept, still breathing, still there.

She let her eyes wander around her parents' room. Her mum's room. The plastic bag of her dad's possessions, given to them by the hospital, sat on top of a pile of paperwork on the chest of drawers. She walked over to peer inside the bag: his wallet, his keys, his wedding ring. She could see the second hand on his watch moving in slow circles. She let the name slide through her head: Jeff. Jeff. Jeff.

She left Elaine sleeping, left the door open, walked back down the hall. She let the front door slam behind her, crossed the street, walked up the driveway past Valerie's parked car, the colour of purple jelly beans, and let herself in through the Chengs' front door.

MINA WOKE AT five. She'd forgotten what day it was, forgot just for a second or two what lay ahead of her. The heatwave had lingered, days and nights mired in the white noise of fans oscillating in their cages, sending hot air from one side of the room to the other then back and back. Her body was damp with sweat; it trickled down her chest, sat in puddles under the folds of her breasts.

Valerie had written a schedule for Mina of how the day would go: *Seven a.m. Get up and shower. Get dressed. Eat breakfast. (Important!!!).*

In the shower, she shaved her legs, her armpits, she let the cold water run down her back, over her shoulders, she wet her hair, washed it in slow motion.

She'd taken the tram into town with Kira and they'd tried on black dresses, black skirts and tops at Sportsgirl and Witchery. Kira had looked good in everything. Now Mina pulled on the dress she'd bought: spaghetti straps and a button-down front.

She went to the kitchen and pushed a piece of bread into the toaster, smeared it with peanut butter after it popped up, chewed and swallowed, the thick paste sticking to the roof of her mouth. She crossed breakfast off the list.

Back down the hall, she knocked on Elaine's door. There was no answer, so she entered. The daisies had dropped most of their petals onto the bedside table, their water had browned. The card was gone.

She sat on the edge of the bed. Elaine lay on her back, her forehead and top lip moist with sweat, her eyes closed. Mina was sure she was awake. She shook her mother's shoulder, maybe a little too hard. Elaine's wet blue eyes flicked open and looked right at her. She was there, Mina knew; she was there.

'Mum,' she said, 'this is the last thing I will ever ask of you.' Mina heard her voice crack. 'I need you to pull it together,' she continued. 'Just for today.'

Elaine sat up on her elbows. Her hair was half stuck to her head with sweat, half matted in a straw nest, a tangled, golden crown. She nodded at Mina and Mina nodded back.

A key turned in the front door.

Eight a.m. Valerie arrives.

She swept through the house like a tsunami in a little black dress, Arthur trailing behind her like flotsam. She knocked on the open bedroom door, walked straight in.

'You're up,' Valerie said, and she smiled at Elaine, she smiled at Mina.

Valerie opened the mirrored wardrobe. A black top and a black skirt hung together on the inside of the door. Valerie had organised them too.

'Mina, how about a cup of tea for everyone?' Valerie suggested.

In the kitchen, Mina found Arthur already standing next to the kettle as it boiled.

'Tea?' he asked.

Mina nodded and pulled four bags from the cork-topped jar that sat permanently on the kitchen bench, rested them inside four faded floral mugs, their strings out over the thin ceramic edge. She heard the bath running and she peered around the corner to see Valerie helping Elaine down the hall to the bathroom.

Arthur poured the steaming water into the four cups. Mina was too hot for tea but the ritual was comforting: she could count on the water changing from clear to brown to black. Mina needed all the certainty she could get right now. They stood next to each other while the tea steeped. Mina could hear the hum of the fridge, Valerie's quiet voice one room away.

'You'll be back at uni soon,' Arthur said.

'A couple of weeks.'

Mina took the milk from the fridge and waited while Arthur used a teaspoon to squeeze each bag against the side of the mug then carried them to the bin.

'Your final year too?'

'Yep,' Mina said and poured milk, Arthur beside her, the spoon tinking and tonking against the sides of each mug as he stirred. He wiped the spoon with a tea towel, scooped a spoonful of sugar into one of the cups.

'For your mum,' he said.

'Thanks.'

Mina took a mug in each hand. She walked past the bathroom to deliver them to the bedroom and saw Valerie perched on the side of the bath, lathering shampoo into Elaine's hair. Elaine was hunched forwards, naked, her bare breasts pointing downwards. Her body the body of a mother. Mina had never thought about that before, about her mother's body. The body of a woman, filled and laboured and emptied. Worn down and down. She looked away before Elaine could see her, put the two cups of tea beside the bed and, as she passed the bathroom on her way back to the kitchen, silently clicked the door shut.

Arthur was in the middle of the living room, holding two cups.

'Here.' He passed one to her.

'Thanks,' she said, and they stood near each other holding too-hot cups of tea in the middle of the too-hot living room.

'You know that if you need anything –' Arthur began.

'Actually, there is something,' Mina said. 'Have you ever heard Mum mention someone called Jeff?'

Arthur's brow furrowed. 'Jeff,' he repeated, his cheeks pinking a little. He took a shallow sip and swallowed loudly. 'Not off the top of my head.'

'We leave in twenty,' Valerie called from down the hall. 'Artie, can you make sure the kids are ready, please?'

He swigged a big mouthful of tea. 'Should probably go and . . .' He nodded towards the door, handed the cup to Mina.

The front door closed loudly behind him, Mina tipped both mugs of tea down the sink and listened to the drone of the hairdryer, walked three times around the back garden and then went to wait by the front door.

Arthur pulled the car up out the front, stayed in the driver's seat while Valerie guided Elaine into the passenger seat.

'It's like *Weekend at Bernie's*,' Kira said from the back as Mina climbed in next to her.

Brendan and Lottie were in Valerie's car, which was idling behind them, Brendan behind the wheel. They watched on wide-eyed.

Kira took Mina's hand in hers.

Valerie reached in over Elaine to fasten her seatbelt, then slid into the back beside Mina. She put her hand on Mina's knee – on the bit Mina always missed when shaving.

'You should epilate,' Valerie whispered. 'The hair hardly grows back.' She took Mina's hand and put it on her own leg, moved it up and down. 'See? So smooth!'

Mina nodded, agreeing that it was smooth. She knew that within a week, an epilator would appear in her house as if by magic.

THE SKY WAS perfectly blue, cloudless, the car's air conditioning roared. The backs of their legs stuck to the seat. People milled out the front of the chapel, bunched in small patches of shade. Mina recognised some people from her father's office, some distant cousins. Everyone turned to look when they arrived, watched them walk through the crowd and in through the chapel door as if Mina and Elaine were celebrities, the Chengs their entourage.

Mina stood near the door and greeted people as they filed past her while Valerie and Arthur escorted Elaine to the front pew.

'Thank you for coming,' she said in response to the murmured sympathy. 'It means a lot to us.'

A woman bobbed up to her, her body shaped like a buoy wrapped in navy blue chiffon. 'I'm Marjorie,' she said. 'I'll be taking the service today.' Her face was crinkled like used baking paper.

'Nice to meet you,' Mina said.

'I'm so sorry for your loss.' Marjorie put a hand on Mina's arm. 'It sounds like your father was a lovely man.'

'Thank you,' Mina said, but she couldn't summon a smile. 'Is there any chance we can start soon? I'd like to not be here anymore.'

'Of course, dear,' Marjorie replied and looked at the thin silver watch on her wrist. 'We can start in a few minutes.' She moved to a nearby cluster of people and gently shepherded them into the chapel, her hand to their backs.

What a gift, to know how to touch people gently, Mina thought. She looked into the chapel. The casket she'd chosen, the Tiberius, looked just like any casket, sitting there at the front of the room. She couldn't believe he was in there. This process seemed maudlin, grotesque. She wished they could just let him go already, that he could just be gone.

'I can't believe Shelly brought Justin,' Kira whispered, standing beside Mina. She pointed to Shelly in the third row. 'They've only done it, like, once. Oh God, is she crying?' Kira squinted. 'I think she's crying. Did she ever even meet your dad?'

Mina turned to face her friend. 'I don't know if I can do this.'

'Of course you can.' Kira put a hand on each of Mina's shoulders. 'You danced in front of a thousand people while dressed as a sexy alien at Rock Eisteddfod. This is a piece of cake.' Kira turned Mina around and gave her a gentle push down the aisle between the mourners.

Mina made her way to the front pew, took her seat next to Elaine, nodded to Marjorie for it to begin.

AFTER THE SERVICE, everyone congregated in the Chengs' living room. There were sandwiches on platters decorated with curly leaf parsley and carrots Arthur had carved into flowers. Mina spent the first hour moving from group to group, listening attentively as people told her stories about Bill. The time he impressed some clients, how he was a good storyteller, quick to laugh, loved to argue but knew when to concede defeat. She repeated the words in her head as they were spoken to help her commit them to memory. Good storyteller, quick to laugh. She wanted to make sure she remembered him as more than just something that was missing.

Throughout the wake, Mina watched Elaine on the sofa. She shook the hands that were offered to her, she let people hug her. Sometimes she lifted her arms to hug back. For the most part, she just sat silently on the edge of conversations. Mina would've given anything to know how she was feeling, what she was thinking.

The time dragged on and on. Mina, done with talking, with remembering, edged away from the crowd and into the kitchen.

She was relieved to find it empty. There was a stack of trays on the kitchen bench, scattered stray triangles of bread, separated from their partners somehow. She pressed a finger into the bread; it was almost toasted from the heat. Her stomach churned. She opened the fridge. More sandwiches. More strawberries. Towards the back, a beacon of light: some cans of beer. She pulled one out; the crunch and the hiss as it opened was like music. She took a sip, then another, bigger. She gulped the cold, fizzy beer down and down, it swelled and swirled inside her. It made her feel tired. She was so tired. She leant one cheek against the fridge's cold door, held the can of beer to the other, and closed her eyes.

'Can I get one of those?'

Her eyes snapped open. Arthur stood in the kitchen with another empty tray of sandwiches.

'Of course,' Mina said and scrambled out of his way. 'Sorry,' she said instinctively. She felt like she'd been caught out.

'Don't be sorry.' He put the tray down on the pile and fished around in the fridge for a beer. 'You need one more than anyone.' He tapped his beer can against hers. 'To Bill,' and he took a big gulp, then another.

Mina watched him curiously. He seemed nervous. She'd never seen him nervous before. But, then, she'd never seen him at the wake of a friend before. Maybe she'd never really looked at him before. The only time they were ever alone was when she was in his dentist's chair, his face mostly covered by a white mask and goggles, her mouth wide open. She wondered what he was able to tell about a person by their teeth: the nervous grinders, the meticulous flossers. Maybe he knew her better than she realised.

'That guy you asked me about,' Arthur said between sips. 'Jeff.'

Mina looked up at him expectantly.

'He was here.'

'He was?' Mina tried to recall every face she'd seen but it was just a catalogue of strangers.

'Old guy in a white shirt. Late seventies, early eighties maybe.' Arthur shrugged. 'He said he was a friend of your nan's, from back in Gippsland.'

'A friend of Nan's?' The beer, the day, the heat, turned Mina's head into a swamp. 'I thought he might be an old boyfriend come to win Mum back now his competition was gone.'

Arthur laughed so loudly it surprised them both.

'Apparently your mum invited him,' Arthur told her.

'Did she talk to him?'

'I didn't see, sorry.'

'I guess these things always bring people out of the woodwork.'

'I guess.' Arthur placed the empty can beside the stack of trays on the marble benchtop. 'Better get back out there or Val will come looking for me,' he said, and he pulled another tray of sandwiches from the fridge and disappeared down the hall.

Mina tipped her head back and drained the last of her beer. She put her can next to Arthur's and wandered back out towards the gathering.

'Oi!' came a voice from up the stairs.

She looked through the bannister and saw Kira sitting halfway up.

'This is shit, isn't it?' Kira said as Mina sat on the step below her.

'It's so shit,' Mina said and rested her head against Kira's leg, letting the tears come. 'I'm so hot,' she said as she cried. 'I'm so sick of being hot.'

Kira handed her a tissue from the little plastic packet she'd been carrying around all day, then rested her hand on Mina's head.

The breath shimmied in and out of Mina's lungs as she gulped it down, let it out. 'I think I need to get out of here.' She blew her nose. 'Am I allowed to leave?'

'I've got an idea,' Kira said. 'Wait for me outside. I'll be two minutes.'

No one noticed Mina as she walked past them. She stopped at the front door and scanned the room. Groups of people were bunched together like grapes. Empty glasses and paper plates were scattered on every surface. Lottie, who'd changed into camouflage shorts and a Peaches t-shirt, was sitting silently on the sofa, holding Elaine's hand. If Elaine could tap out of this, Mina thought, so could she. Even if it was only for the rest of the afternoon. She slipped outside into the pummelling heat and shut the door behind her.

Five

SHE BUZZED SHELLY'S FRONT GATE. Who even needed a security gate on a street this nice? Mina wondered, relieved to see that the house still resembled the one she'd looked at on Google Street View – just with a new paint job and a small extension. It wasn't *that* nice, she thought.

The gate clicked open. The front garden consisted of a tiny round patch of pristine white gravel with an ornamental cement urn in the middle of it. On top of the urn sat a sculptural metal ball that looked like a giant cat toy. If she knocked it off she was sure it would jingle as it rolled.

Mina let the gate snap shut behind her and got closer to it. Inside the ball sat a white marble Buddha statue. Mina smiled to herself.

'You're here,' Shelly said from the front door. She held a toddler on her hip. Mina couldn't tell if it was the same one she'd met the other day, though apparently the twins weren't identical. In the photos she'd scrolled past, they both looked like tiny Justins to her: investment bankers with baby bodies.

'I brought cake.' Mina held up the box and hugged Shelly with one arm.

'Hello, Jason,' Mina said to the boy.

He stared blankly at her.

She reached out and tried to ruffle his hair but he pulled back. 'No,' he screamed and buried his face in Shelly's neck.

'This is the other one. Mason, say hi to Mummy's old friend Mina.'

'No!' he screamed. 'No, no, no.'

'They'll be shy for the first couple of minutes and then they won't leave you alone,' Shelly said and stepped aside to let Mina into the house.

Mina immediately knew she'd been deceived by her internet search. The house before her was enormous, light-filled and modern.

Jason tore down the hall towards them and launched himself onto Shelly's leg, took one look at Mina and started crying big salty tears.

'Well, at least you're happy to see me,' Mina said as she followed Shelly through the house, peering into every room they passed, each one nicer than the last.

'You're a sight for sore eyes,' Shelly said. 'All I do is watch *Peppa Pig* and change nappies. I'm desperate for adult company.'

They reached the open-plan kitchen, dining and living area, with two storeys of glass windows, dark wood. It was one of the most beautiful houses Mina had ever seen. Outside, the garden stepped up in levels to create more space. A thin lap pool ran down one side of the house.

'Shit the bed,' Mina said under her breath but loud enough for Shelly to hear.

'I know, it's a bit silly.' Shelly put Mason down and the two boys ran towards the living room screaming. The rug was strewn with wooden building blocks and plastic trucks.

'It's beautiful,' Mina said. 'How? Sorry, that's rude.' But she was desperate to know.

'Justin got a promotion, he's VP now. The youngest in the company's history.' Shelly was glowing with pride.

'Well,' Mina said. 'Well done you.'

'And what about you?' Shelly asked. 'How long are you back for? How long's it been? How's London? I have so many questions.' She paused. 'I know it's not quite midday yet, but what do you say about a glass of wine?'

'Are you allowed to?' Mina pointed at Shelly's giant pregnant stomach.

'I figure he's far enough along not to do any lasting damage.' Shelly patted her stomach.

'Another he?'

'I know, can you believe it? Watch the boys and I'll grab a bottle from the cellar.' Shelly disappeared down the hall.

Of course they have a wine cellar, Mina thought. She looked down at the twins. She'd already forgotten which was Jason and which was Mason. She couldn't believe Shelly had agreed to call them Jason and Mason. She ran through a list of names for the new baby: Grayson, Harrison, Jackson, Justinson.

'Hi,' Mina said, and they stop stacking the coloured blocks and looked up at her.

She sat down cross-legged next to them. 'Which one are you?' she asked the boy closest to her.

His eyes widened and a big strand of thick, milky drool ran down his chin and dripped onto the floor. She used the boy's own sleeve to wipe the drool off his chin. He snatched his arm away from her and screwed up his face. It started turning red, and a guttural noise circled and grew in his throat like an approaching siren. The other one looked at his brother and started making the noise too. They looked like sundried tomatoes in matching Ralph Lauren polo shirts.

'Oh shit,' Mina said, and patted one of them on the head frantically.

His moan turned into a wail. The other one stood and started stamping his feet.

'Shit, shit, no, don't cry. Come on.'

One of them un-scrunched his face. 'Shit,' he said and giggled. 'Shit,' he repeated. 'Shiiiiit.'

'Oh fuck,' Mina said, and the other brother's face turned back to pink.

'Shit!' they both yelled in unison before collapsing in giggles.

One of them pointed at Mina. 'You're shit,' he yelled and they screamed with laughter. Mina felt it cut deep.

'Boys,' Shelly yelled from behind them and they immediately quietened. 'We don't use that language, remember. That's a bad word.'

'Oh my God, I thought I just taught it to them.' Mina laughed with relief.

'No, their uncle did. It was their third word after "daddy" and "dog".'

Mina watched Shelly open the bottle she'd fetched and pour two large glasses of crimson wine. She unboxed the cakes and cut each one in four, hosting with the ease of someone married to someone important.

They sat next to each other on the long sofa, leant in to clink glasses. Mina took a sip; it was the nicest wine she'd ever tasted. She took another just to be sure.

'It's really good to see you,' Shelly said. 'Now, tell me about London. How's work?'

Mina started talking about Peach, the agency she'd moved to London to work for seven years ago. She had a spiel that made it sound much more impressive than it was. She talked about the shoots: one in South Africa, a few in Spain, the ad they shot in New York with Ryan Reynolds. 'We went to his house,' Mina added.

Shelly nodded in all the right places, keeping one eye and half her attention on the twins.

'What was Ryan Reynolds like?'

'He was nice. Very angular.' Mina shrugged. 'No one was allowed to use the bathroom, though. That was weird. I wanted to tell everyone I'd taken a dump in Ryan Reynolds' house.'

Shelly laughed. 'Well, it sounds very . . . fun. I'm jealous,' she said unconvincingly.

'We do have fun.' Mina was laying it on thick now. 'But it's serious too. I'm in charge of a whole team and I'm due for a promotion soon. I'll be joint creative director with Jack.' Mina felt herself blush. She hoped Shelly didn't notice.

'Oh, and who is Jack?' Shelly asked and motioned for the boys to come to the coffee table. She gave them each a quarter of lemon tart. One of them swallowed it down in one mouthful. The other spat it right out, squealed, and then squashed it into the carpet.

'Oh, Mason, honey.' Shelly picked up the soggy crumbs and put them in a pile on the designer coffee table.

'God, look at your life,' Mina said. She glanced at the four designer metal stools perfectly lined up under the designer kitchen bench, at the two children grabbing at pieces of chocolate cake. 'We're a long way from winning those Academy Awards, aren't we?'

'Oh, I never really wanted that,' Shelly said. 'That was your dream.'

'But' – Mina was confused – 'it's all we talked about for our entire degree.'

'I just went along with it because I wanted to be part of your little gang. I thought if I pretended I wanted to be a Hollywood director then you and Kira would let me in. These days I only watch rom-coms and kids' films.'

'But what about those short films we made at uni?' Mina thought about all the film studies lectures they'd sat through, all the plans they'd concocted over long nights at the pub. Mina would write, Shelly would direct, Kira would star. They'd dominate the Oscars every two or three years. A force to be reckoned with.

'This is all I've ever wanted.' Shelly gestured to the twins. 'Family is everything.' Mina felt the pointed jabs Shelly delivered as she spoke. Shelly bent down and kissed the top of Jason's head, nuzzling her face in his hair.

'This life suits you,' Mina said. 'You're great at it.' She poured herself some more wine, held the bottle out, but Shelly covered her glass with her hand, shook her head. 'And you've got great taste in wine.'

'That's all Justin,' Shelly said as one of the twins made a dive for the chocolate cake, knocking the plate onto the floor. 'Jason, baby,' Shelly said in her best soothing mum voice.

Mina wondered how different she'd have turned out if she grew up in a house like this, if she lived a life like this now.

Mason screamed and threw himself onto the floor. Jason screamed too.

'I'm going to put these two down for a nap. Come upstairs with me. You can take a look around.' Shelly manoeuvred a boy onto each hip and walked up the stairs. Mina followed, running her hand up the smooth wooden balustrade.

The boys' room looked like it was straight off Pinterest, everything curated rather than just bought. Even the rainbow mess of toys on the ground looked styled.

Mina walked through to the bathroom – double shower and a clawfoot bath – then wandered around the master bedroom, through the double walk-in robes where Justin's business shirts were lined up in colour order. She knocked gently on a closed door, heard nothing, opened it. A home office.

'Oh no, don't go –' Shelly said, but Mina was already in, face to face with an oil painting of the family, Shelly and Justin sitting in white robes and, floating above them, the twins depicted as winged and haloed cherubs.

'Shelly, what on earth?' Mina laughed. She couldn't stop laughing. She doubled over. She took her phone from her back pocket (no messages, nothing from Jack) and took a few photos of the painting, trying to get the right angle.

'Don't,' Shelly begged. 'It was a present from Justin's mum. It's horrible but we can't get rid of it. We keep it in here so no one will ever see it.'

'The cherubs are really the icing on the cake.' Mina laughed until tears welled up in her eyes.

'That bit was a surprise. God, the artist did make Justin look so handsome, though, don't you think?' Shelly grew doe-eyed looking at him. 'He's a wonderful father. He really takes care of us.'

'Do you ever worry?' Mina asked. 'You know, one person for the rest of your life?'

'I can't imagine loving anyone more than I love him.' Shelly rubbed her stomach. 'You'll understand when it happens.'

Mina thought she did already. That feeling bubbling up under her skin. It was love. She was sure it was love.

She followed Shelly back downstairs. It was quiet in the living room with just the two of them. Shelly poured Mina another glass of wine and she drank two mouthfuls quickly while Shelly got down on all fours and scrubbed the tart out of the rug.

'So tell me about this Jack,' Shelly prompted.

'There's nothing to tell,' Mina said, her cheeks burning again.

'Come on.' She sat up on her haunches. 'I let you see the painting.'

'Not on purpose.' Mina laughed again, thinking about the pink-cheeked babies. 'We work together. He's funny and handsome and charming. I don't know what it is yet, just new and complicated.'

'Have you done it?' Shelly pulled herself up onto the lounge, readied herself for the sordid details.

'We've done it,' Mina stretched the truth. She liked the new shape of it (the colour, the size), and anyway, she'd thought about it so often that it felt like they really had. What was the difference?

'This is exciting!' Shelly said.

'Like I said, it's early days.' Mina took another sip of wine.

'Oh my God,' Shelly shrieked. 'You haven't met Phillip.' She pointed towards a labradoodle licking the glass at the back door. 'He's come to say hi.' She got up slowly, cradling her bump.

Phillip jumped excitedly, a ball of caramel fluff and energy, as Shelly opened the door.

'Who's Mummy's big boy?' she asked in a baby voice, bending over so the dog could lick her face, her cheeks, her lips.

Mina had seen Phillip before: he had his own Instagram account that she'd felt obliged to follow. Each photo had a caption written in Phillip's voice. Most of the posts were photos of Phillip looking cute on a blanket, looking cute with the twins (the caption for one read: *I never get ruff with my brothers*). Mina liked every photo instead of writing to Shelly to ask about how she was, to ask about the boys. A double tap had become an easy substitute for friendship.

'Hello, Phillip.' Mina stood and walked towards him. 'You don't know me but I've seen you on the internet.'

Her voice calmed him a little. He sniffed between her legs, licked her hand, then let out a meaty bark and launched himself onto her. With his front paws locked onto Mina's thighs, he mounted her side on. She looked down and saw the little pink lipstick of his erection on display. He thrust it towards her leg.

'Oh my God.' She tried to push him off but he was strong, determined. She looked to Shelly for help, but she was laughing too hard, one hand supporting her stomach. 'Shelly, get him off me!' Mina gave him a shove and the dog lost his balance and fell back down to the ground before mounting an attack again. Mina dodged him and ran for the back door. She pulled it closed, Phillip on the inside, Mina in the garden.

'I think he likes you,' Shelly called through the glass, still laughing. 'We need to get him fixed but Justin can't bring himself to get it done.'

Mina stood helplessly at the back door.

'Go around the side and let yourself in; I'll put him out again,' Shelly said.

Mina walked along the side of the house and entered through the laundry door. Just as she returned to the living room there was a shriek from upstairs, a loud bang.

'Oh God, I'd better go up.' Shelly headed for the stairs. 'Will you stay a bit longer?'

'I should be getting home – Mum, you know.' Mina motioned to the door.

'It was good to catch up.' Shelly hugged her. 'You'll have to come for dinner before you go. Justin would love to see you.' Then she disappeared up the stairs without waiting for an answer.

'Bye,' Mina called as the two boys screamed in unison. She walked past Phillip at the back door and gave him the finger. He barked at her and charged the glass.

Mina let herself out the front door, feeling grateful for the quiet of the street and a little buzzed from the wine. She wasn't ready to go home, so she made the short walk to the station instead.

When the train arrived, she found a seat facing backwards and pulled out her phone. She checked the time, counted back. It was four-thirty in the morning in London. Where was he? She opened her messages, scrolled down to her last exchange with Jack, looking for the last thing he'd said to her, hoping for a clue, for proof that he loved her too.

His last message was from the night they'd stayed back to finish the pitch, a few nights before the penis.

SHE ARRIVED AT the office at seven-thirty in the morning, having wedged herself into a carriage of businessmen on the Overground from Clapton to Liverpool Street, then again on the Central Line. Most of them got out at Bank, St Paul's, Holborn, in their blue shirts and grey suits, all their personality channelled into their colourful socks.

Mina was always the first one in. She claimed it was because she liked the quiet time to get her thoughts in order, to write, but it was more that she'd wake at five and quickly run out of things to look at on the internet. More that the sooner she got to work, the sooner she'd see Jack, the closer she'd be to things that belonged to him. The closer she'd be to him.

Mina loved the pace of the city, how sometimes she'd find herself jogging up escalators even if she had nowhere to be in a hurry. Living in London was like being carried out to sea in a rip. She knew that if she just kept working, if she just stayed focussed, she'd be too busy, too stressed, to think about Elaine. To think about everything she'd left behind.

The morning before the pitch, she rushed with the scrum through the maze of tunnels under the streets of London, tutting at the slow walkers (mostly tourists) who got in her way, raced up the escalators, through the gates, up the steps and out into Soho.

It was going to be one of the last warm days, a remnant of summer that appeared joyfully in September before the darkness came, before the clocks were turned back. She knew this sliver of morning was all she'd see of it. She bought a coffee from the Scandinavian bakery, two of their favourite cardamom buns, and carried them all through the revolving door at the front of the building.

The office was still dark. She let herself in with her pass and took the lift to the third floor, decorated with dark wood, low-hanging bulbs. It looked more like a high-end burger restaurant than a creative space. She sat in their glass-walled office and stared at her laptop. She started writing. She was good at this. Too good at it. She wished the things she really wanted to write came as easily to her as a funny headline about toothpaste, a script for a car ad, an idea for how to sell ice cream.

She'd finished tidying up the strategy slides and consolidated the idea slides by the time the rest of the team arrived either side of nine. They were a good team, a smart team. Mina rounded them up – all those boys and poor Lizzie. They sat in the breakout space and she assigned them each their tasks for the day, gave them feedback from George, from the strategy team. She felt organised, in control, confident they could get everything done.

All the work was well underway by the time Jack rolled in at ten with a bacon sandwich and the fog of a hangover. Mina watched him from across the studio as he sat down at his desk, popped some painkillers and swallowed them with the dregs of a beer he'd left on his desk the night before, his Adam's apple rippling in his throat. She knew he had a full day's work to do and she knew he knew that the unofficial pitch rule meant no one was going home until everything was finished. She wanted to be mad at him but she couldn't. Not at that curly mop of brown hair on his head, at the strong body she felt beneath his clothes when he hugged her goodbye, hello, sometimes for no reason at all, at the way he looked at her when she spoke: intensely, sometimes for too long. She thought about the gap between his two front teeth. She wanted to lick it. She wanted to take his clothes off, to lie down with him on top of her, him underneath her. She'd let him open her up and put his whole body inside her whole body, to move around and live inside her if that's what he wanted. She'd do anything. All he had to do was ask.

She felt the heat bubbling up inside her, rolling and rolling until it reached boiling point. It pulsed in her wrists, in her toes. She walked to the toilets, unisex and painted navy blue, the stall walls from floor to ceiling. She locked the door behind her, put the lid down, sat down on the seat and unzipped her jeans. Her body was ready for him, her heart. She imagined it was his hands on her, his hands rubbing and rubbing, that her fingers were his tongue, that he loved the taste of her, the feel of her. She rubbed her hand on her leg and pretended it was his leg sliding up and down on hers, slow first, then fast, his breath, his mouth on her, his love inside her.

Her cheeks burnt hot and she sat while she caught her breath, then flushed in case anyone was at the sinks. She flicked open the lock, and looked at herself in the mirror as she washed her hands. She felt a hum inside her chest. Was it shame? Maybe it was love. She leant forward for a closer look at her face in the cold bathroom light, the dark pores dotted across her nose, then scrunched up her face and counted the laugh lines around her eyes.

'That's a cute face.'

She was startled by the voice behind her. She looked at him reflected in the mirror and felt her heart split wide open, felt insects crawling under her skin, fire in her veins.

'Half-day today?' She raised an eyebrow at him and squirted soap into her hands again, ran them under the cold water, anything to cool her down.

'I'm sorry,' Jack said, sidling in too close, squirting soap in his hands too.

The two of them standing side by side: Mina couldn't help but picture them at his house, in his bathroom, her bathroom one day too, the two of them getting ready for bed.

'I was out with George last night and you know how he gets.'

He turned on the tap and she watched his reflection as the soap foamed around his fingers and swirled down the plug.

'You were out with George?' Mina turned to look at him. 'Just the two of you?' She couldn't imagine what Jack and George could possibly have to say to each other.

'And Ian and Sam.' He shook the water from his hands, scrunched the curls on the top of his head.

'Lads' night out.' Mina rolled her eyes. 'What'd you do? Hit the strip clubs?'

'It's called networking, Mina. Team bonding.' He turned to face her. 'You should try it sometime.'

'Someone's got to stay here and do the work,' she said, taking him by the shoulders, turning him around and pushing him out the door. 'We've got a shit tonne of work to do today. I want everything done by eight so we can show George and still get home before midnight.'

'Yes ma'am,' he said and saluted her before marching the whole way back to their office.

Mina couldn't help smiling. She couldn't help the way she felt. She just had to ignore it to get through the day, to get through the work.

For the next few hours, she hovered near him to make sure the presentation stayed on track. Mid-afternoon, she locked his phone in a drawer so he couldn't get distracted. At six, she ordered dinner for the studio, pizzas and burgers, and ate at her desk while he went out to buy beers for everyone. At eight, she offered to go downstairs and check in with George while Jack kept working, kept the team moving. Networking. He was right. She needed George to see that she was in charge, to see that the work was good, on brief, on time, and it was all because of her.

'All you have to do is make sure the copy in the document matches the copy in the designs. As soon as they're finished, drop them into the latest version of the deck,' she said, her laptop resting in the crook of her arm. 'Promise me you'll keep everything moving.' She looked up at him. She liked how tall he was, she liked the space he took up.

'I promise,' he said and went back to work. She wondered if he watched her walk away.

Two floors down, Mina found George with his feet up on his glass coffee table, his phone up to his ear, a half-empty beer bottle resting beside him. He motioned for her to come in and wait while he wound up the call. As he chatted she wandered along the shelf that ran up one wall of his office. There were lions and pencils, all his – the agency's awards were on display in the foyer. She knew they were meaningless, that 'award-winning' work meant nothing to anyone outside the industry, but it didn't stop her from wanting a trophy of her own, wanting a shelf like this in an office like this. Nothing ever stopped her from wanting.

'Mina?' he called.

She went and sat down next to him on the sofa, her laptop open to Keynote.

'Blow me away,' he said, and she started the presentation.

As she spoke, George did what George always did: he picked apart every idea, every iteration across every channel. He challenged every decision they'd made. Mina kept her cool, defended all of it.

'You know I'm just playing devil's advocate?' he said when she clicked through to the final slide. 'The work's solid. You've done well.' He was ordering his Uber home before she'd even closed her laptop.

Relieved, Mina walked into the bowels of the building. The lino on the old stairs squeaked under foot as she took the stairs two at a time back up to the creative floor. She heard the cheering even before she got to the door. Her blood ran cold. Through the porthole window, she saw them standing around an obstacle course they'd set up in the breakout area: sofa cushions as crash mats, chairs on their sides, tables upturned. The pitch was at ten the next day and they hadn't even had a practice run yet. She knew Jack had set this up the minute she left. She knew the presentation wasn't finished. They needed to win this work to reach their targets, to prove themselves as managers. She knew that if they succeeded, the promotion was theirs.

She swiped her pass and entered the makeshift stadium. Rory was up next. He started strong thanks to his little Hobbit legs, running the length of the kitchenette in the middle of the office. Jack was hollering at him to go faster, Danny had his phone on stopwatch, the whiteboard had been rubbed clean of deliverables and turned into a scoreboard. Part of Mina was impressed at how organised they were. The rest of her was consumed with a silent rage.

Rory made it to the crawl – six chairs lined up that he had to shimmy through like a tunnel. His legs got stuck in the legs of the first chair but he kept going, each chair banging into the next until they all toppled over with a crash. He looked like a fat cat marooned half in and half out of a cat flap.

Jack noticed her from across the room and raised his eyebrows a few times as if to say look at what I'm capable of, look how clever I am, isn't this fun?

Mina walked past the carnage and back to their office.

She knew everyone saw her as the serious, killjoy manager, while Jack got to be the fun guy, everyone's favourite boss.

'They'll love me so much they'll never want to disappoint me,' he'd said when she broached the topic of their different management styles a few months after he started. 'It's classic good cop, bad cop.' He'd nudged her under the table. 'Female cops are hot,' he said and smiled that smile at her. She'd dropped the subject. She let him win like she always did.

Jack's screen was asleep. She moved his mouse to wake it, entered his password. The presentation was open, at least, but nothing had been added.

She heard a cough, a shuffling of feet. Lizzie loitered at the door, holding a can of beer.

'Hey,' Mina said.

'They tried to get me to do the obstacle course,' Lizzie said as she stepped into the office. 'But I just said I had my period.'

'Fail-safe get-out-of-obstacle-course-free card,' Mina said and laughed.

'That and diarrhoea,' Lizzie agreed.

'Do you know where they got up to?' Mina asked.

Lizzie sat beside Mina and took the mouse. She flicked down through the pages of the presentation. 'The copy's wrong in these three slides.' She hovered over the three key-idea pages. 'I told Jack but he said you'd sort it out when you came back up.'

Mina sighed and shook her head.

'We all know,' Lizzie said, and the blood rushed out of Mina's whole body and pooled in a puddle at her feet.

'Know what?' Mina said, acting coy. Of course they all knew how she felt. That there was something going on. If they all knew then it must be real.

'That you do all the work,' Lizzie said, and Mina exhaled.

'We're a team,' she said, then whispered, 'but thank you for noticing.'

Lizzie laughed.

Mina looked at her, said, 'I really want to get out of here. Shall we try to finish this?'

Lizzie nodded and the two of them got to work, Mina fudging through it in Jack's Photoshop, Lizzie dropping the saved files into the presentation.

Half an hour later, when the final loud cheers erupted from the breakout space, they saved the presentation, exported it and emailed it around. Mina gave her permission to come in late, even though she knew Lizzie wouldn't. Then they joined the rest of the team while Jack gave out prizes he'd stolen from other people's desks to the first, second and third place times. Arjun belched loudly from the back of the group.

'Thanks everyone for staying late. Lizzie and I finished the presentation so you can all go home,' Mina announced and everyone cheered. 'Rory, Danny, can you be in by eight in case there are amends?'

They groaned in unison. 'Then you can leave at ten,' she said, and they cheered again. Jack just stood beside the whiteboard. Mina could tell he was at least three drinks in. He beamed at her. She loved and hated him in equal measure. He rendered her powerless, pathetic. She walked back through the kitchen, around the banks of desks to their office. She closed her laptop and rubbed her hands over her face. It was half past ten, and she hadn't left the office all day. She wondered about all the other things she could be doing with her life if she wasn't babysitting these boys every day, every night, worrying about them, worrying about work on the weekend. Maybe she'd have written something real by now: a screenplay, a novel?

'Don't be mad,' Jack said from the door. He walked over to her and shook her chair so her whole body vibrated. 'It was a bit of stress relief.' He stopped shaking and put his hands on her shoulders. 'They needed it.'

'And what about what I need?' She swivelled her chair around to look at him; their knees were almost touching. 'I got here before eight to make sure all my work was done on time. We could've had this finished hours ago if you hadn't messed around all day.'

'Hey, hey,' he said calmly, putting his hands on the arms of her chair. 'That's what makes us such a good team: we pick up each other's slack.'

Mina rolled her eyes dramatically enough for him to notice. 'I don't have any slack,' she said.

'If it wasn't for me, half of those guys would've left six months ago.' He kneed her gently, pressed his weight further and further against her.

She knew he was right. Morale had been better since he started.

'C'mon, admit it. We're a good team.'

She kicked him off her and turned her chair around. They played this game every time. She felt his hands on her shoulders again, this time his thumbs needling into the tight muscles that clumped like grapes around her collarbone.

'Fine,' she said. 'I admit it.' She sank into it, and he brushed a finger against her neck.

She felt his hands on her the whole way home on the Tube.

Later that night, she was in bed when her phone flashed. She held it above her head in the dark and smiled when she read:

Thanks for tonight. You're the best and everyone knows it. X

She was gone. Gone.

MINA WATCHED THE trackside prickly pears whizz past, the graffitied fences, a heavy rain lashing the train's windows. She noticed a couple a few seats away had started fighting, tiny whispers spat venomously. Mina couldn't make out what they were saying, just the anger with which they were saying it. The woman got up and moved seats, and he followed, sitting next to her in silence. When the train pulled into Flinders Street, Mina walked past them and saw they had already made up and were kissing, their tongues in each other's mouths. Mina's body throbbed at the sight of it. She thought back to the last time someone had kissed her like that, kissed her at all. It was Dave. Dave from that weird club near Liverpool Street that used to be an old Turkish bathhouse. It was the night they went dancing for Alice from work's hen do. Dave who danced close to her; Dave from Manchester who unabashedly declared that he hated Paris; Dave who was five centimetres shorter than her; Dave who persisted until she gave in and let him kiss her with all tongue straight away. He tasted of Jägerbombs. He put his hands on her hips and pulled her against him.

He had a City jersey hanging on his bedroom wall, his flat ex-council and mouldy in the corners. He took her clothes off methodically, from top to bottom. She unbuttoned his shirt, undid his belt, let him do the rest. She thought about Jack while Dave plunged his fingers inside her. She wondered if the news would spread around work, if there were photos of her locked mouth to mouth with a stranger, if he'd be jealous. She stayed over but she didn't sleep. She just imagined it was Jack snoring softly beside her. Jack's body and her body, bonded together.

In the morning, she'd counted eight empty bottles of body wash in the shower. He asked to see her again, she put her number in his phone. He kissed her goodbye.

On the way home through grubby Shoreditch, through Hackney's backstreets, Mina hadn't given Dave a second thought. She daydreamed of Jack's hands on her, Jack's mouth. Jack. His name sung in her head as she crossed the canal with its floating sheet of neon-green duckweed, again as she smelt the chlorine of the lido walking through London Fields. She was in trouble, she knew she was, but she liked it. Jack. His name again. She liked it.

Mina stopped in the middle of the concourse at Flinders Street station. People rushed in all directions around her. She pulled out her phone and started typing.

I'm doing fine down here, thanks for asking. How are you? x

She made the little x a big X, deleted the x altogether, put the big one back. She pressed send, put her phone on aeroplane mode to make herself ignore it, then put it back in her bag.

Six

MINA PUT HER LAPTOP INTO her tote bag along with her work pass, her purse, phone, notepads and pens. Jack didn't bring anything but his phone and his wallet, with the company credit card tucked inside one of its leathery folds. They had been given one when he started a few weeks earlier. Technically only he was given one, but they were a team; it was theirs. They walked down the back stairs, out the fire exit and into the blustery autumn afternoon. Mina loved London in the first few weeks of autumn, when the warmth lingered in the air until late evening, when the golden sun cast long shadows. Not these though, these blustery days when the leaves sat soggy in the gutter, blocking the drains. These long weeks of shorter days, this steady decline to winter and the slow ascent out of it made her homesick. Or maybe just weather sick. She wasn't really sure where home was, what it meant, not anymore.

'Where do you fancy today?' Jack asked, standing in the middle of the footpath on Brewer Street, his arms spread wide as though London were his and his alone. 'Crown?'

'Crown smells like piss,' Mina said. She watched a woman pushing a pram tut as she squeezed past him, almost losing a wheel off the kerb and upending in the gutter. Jack didn't notice. 'So does The Duke.'

'John Snow?'

'There must be somewhere else good around here.' Mina chewed on the inside of her lip as she ran through all the pubs she knew, desperate to think of somewhere that would impress him. He folded his arms and waited. 'Follow me.' She marched past him into the throng of people crowding the footpath, sure he'd follow her to the pub, hopeful he'd follow her anywhere.

They passed Soho's sex shops and restaurants, the streets jammed with white vans and black cabs. They crossed Oxford Street as the red man stopped flashing, running a little to avoid the 55 bus that sped towards them. At the door of The Champion, Mina turned to face him.

'Bloody great choice.' He brushed past her to get inside just before the tumbling clouds above them gave in to rain. He held the door for her to follow, bowed as she passed like a footman at a ball, a real gentleman.

The pub was mostly empty, except for the regulation old man with a newspaper you could find sitting in the same spot at the bar in every pub across the country. It was almost as if they came flat packed as part of the fit-out.

Mina chose one of the intricately carved, curved wooden alcoves and started unpacking her things. She watched Jack up at the bar, his back to her, his long legs in those skinny black jeans. How could legs be that long? How could jeans fit that well? She wasn't sure she'd seen anyone look so good, ever. He turned and saw her watching. She mouthed, 'Hurry up,' and he smiled, turned back to the bar to tap the credit card on the machine.

She looked around at the pub's stained-glass windows. She couldn't believe it the first time she'd seen them: intricate depictions of top cricketers, the first person to swim the English Channel, Florence Nightingale, all resplendent in colourful glass. The curved wooden bar was like something out of a BBC show. There were pubs in Melbourne, of course, but there was nothing like this. She loved that about London: how everything was bigger, better, older, more important (looked better in black jeans).

Jack placed two pints and the number nine attached to a long silver pole on the table.

'Figured you'd want some chips too.' He sat down next to her and picked up his pint.

'Thank you,' Mina said, lifted hers.

'To the champion copywriter who's going to nail this brief.' He clanked his glass against hers, spilling beer on her leg. They both drank, him half the pint in three big sips. She took a few small ones, put her drink back down on the table and finished unpacking her pens from her bag.

'Oh God, you actually want to work. I thought we were just going boozing,' he said.

She gave him one of her best death stares.

'I'm kidding.' He reached over and patted her knee where the beer had darkened her jeans in splotches. 'I'm just kidding.'

Under his hand, she felt the way a body looks in a house of mirrors. Part of her hoped he couldn't tell; the rest wobbled and warped and hoped he could.

They talked through the brief. Mina didn't know anything about sport but she knew how to sell sportswear. She gave him background on their past campaigns and all their pain points. She listed territories that were tried and tested, good ideas the client had previously rejected. She gave him a rundown of the team, the way you had to make every idea you presented seem like it was the marketing manager's. And then her crowning glory: she told the story she wasn't meant to tell about the time the ex-creative director put one of the new sports watches they were trying to market on his penis and dropped his underpants in front of one of the client's senior strategists.

'Do you think it can track this?' She delivered the punchline in her best northern accent.

'No,' Jack said, his face in his hands in horror. 'He didn't!'

'I saw it with my very own eyes.' Mina laughed. 'And you can never un-see something like that.'

The barman brought the bowl of chips to the table, took the number away. Jack took the biggest chip from the top and dunked it into the pot of sauce, breathing through his teeth as he chewed to cool it down.

'Did he get fired for that?'

'No, he got fired for stealing stuff from around the office to pay for his coke habit.'

'Wow,' Jack said. 'Old school.'

'But that was only after they'd already paid for him to go to rehab.'

'Bloody hell,' he said through a mouthful of chip and sauce. 'So as long as I keep it in my pants and don't develop a coke habit, I'll be fine.'

'Isn't it a prerequisite that all men in advertising in London are high-functioning coke addicts?' Mina asked, smiling wryly.

'God, you're cynical. I love it.' He laughed. 'If you hate it all so much, why are you here?'

'Here in London or here in this job?' Mina asked, popping a chip in her mouth.

'Both.'

'You want the long or short version?'

'Both,' he said. 'Tell me everything.'

She told him about her first job, how they kept giving her more and more responsibility but without the title, without the money, then hiring or promoting men over her. He nodded sympathetically.

Then Mina went back to the point when her dad died, when Elaine barely got out of bed. When, during those days between his death and the funeral, she had to grow up, put her own grief aside and just get on with it, because other than Valerie there was no one else who would. If she hadn't kept moving, then everything would've stopped, everything would've fallen apart.

'So how's your mum now?' Jack asked, leaning forward, so close to her.

'Still inside,' Mina said, knocking back the last warm sip of her pint. 'You want another?'

She stood and took his glass up to the bar, ordered two more. She didn't look back at him while the barman poured one, stroked his moustache, tipped the glass and poured another. She just hoped Jack was looking at her the same way she had him.

She handed him his fresh pint, sat down next to him. Their knees touched; he didn't pull away.

'Wait, so when did your dad –' He couldn't say the word.

'Eleven years ago,' she said.

'Shit. So your mum hasn't left the house in eleven years?' He was flabbergasted. 'That must've been so hard.'

'It was hard. It is.'

An old man opened the door, shook his umbrella off, took his spot at the bar three stools down from the other guy. They nodded to each other, didn't talk.

'Do you know why she won't go out?' Jack asked. 'Is it – what's it called – agoraphobia?'

'I don't know. Maybe she's scared something bad will happen?' Mina picked at some imaginary lint on the sleeve of her jumper. 'It's like her feet were stuck in concrete or something. She wouldn't budge.'

'It must've been a tough decision for you to leave.'

'Yeah,' Mina said meekly. 'She's the only family I have. But she left me first. She left me to grieve on my own. And then I spent five years' – Mina's voice faltered a little; she'd told this story so many times, but for some reason, this time felt important – 'I spent five years in that house trying to help her. I did everything I could think of: begged, pleaded, staged an intervention, suggested counselling, begged some more.'

'Jesus,' he said. They were silent while he took it all in, drank his beer. 'So you gave up and came here?'

'I didn't give up,' she said defensively. 'I still try. I try to show her how good it is to be out in the world, show her everything she's missing out on. But it's not enough. Nothing I do is enough.'

Jack reached out, put his hand on her shoulder, squeezed it once, left it there.

'Then one day my boyfriend made some joke about how if we got married, we'd have to do it in the backyard of my parents' – she stopped, corrected herself – 'of our house, Mum's house. And that was when I knew I had to go.'

'Boyfriend?' he asked, eyebrow raised.

'Ex-boyfriend,' Mina said, trying to hide her smile by taking a sip of her beer.

'So how often do you go back?' he asked.

'I don't. I mean, I haven't.'

He exhaled in a whistle.

'I've always said I'd go back if she left the house. That's what it'll take.'

'God, you make so much more sense to me now,' Jack said. Mina couldn't tell if he meant it in a good way.

'Shut up,' she said.

'No, I mean, you're so strong, you don't take any bullshit, you're kind of terrifying. It's amazing.' He smiled at her, took his hand off her shoulder. She wished he'd leave it there forever. 'Everything you've been through makes my mum's mild alcoholism seem like a walk in the park.'

'Ooh!' She rubbed her hands together. 'I want to hear all about that.'

Jack stood to go to the bar and get them another drink, one more while they settled into this game of get-to-know-you. Mina looked down at her phone, saw a message from a number she didn't have saved:

Turns out Danny DeVito is actually five cm shorter than his wife and they've been happily married 30+ years. I had fun the other night. We should do it again sometime.

Dave. She read the text twice, deleted it and put her phone back in her bag.

MINA EXITED THE station onto St Kilda Road and walked in the rain over the wide brown river. At the entrance of the big gallery, she passed the long pools full of silver coins thrown by people hopeful that was all it took for wishes to come true. Mina knew nothing came that cheap.

She walked through the arch, past the cascading water wall, tourists posing for photos in front of it, through it. The light in the cavernous foyer always stopped her in her tracks: it flooded in from the glass ceiling, made her feel like she was in a cathedral.

On the second floor, Mina headed for the international collection, where people flocked to see the pink Rothko, the pastel colours of the Monets. But the one she wanted, the one she needed to see, sat flush against the back wall of the first room. Lee Krasner's *Combat*, swirled and jagged with pink and orange. It was just as big, just as violent as she remembered. It commanded the room. It still took her breath away.

The first time she'd seen it was on a year eleven excursion. Kira had rushed through the painting section with Tim Gardner to find a place where they could make out, out of view of the chaperones. Mina dawdled through the pottery, through the landscapes; she was bored by the gums and the squalling oceans, the reclining women, the pastorals. None of them made her feel anything. Her mother had always said the purpose of art was to make you feel something, anything at all. When Mina walked into the room and saw *Combat* on the wall, it felt as if she'd shifted out of her body for a split second, as though there'd been an earthquake. She walked up close to it, took in the juxtaposition between the pink circles and the jagged edges, between the softness and the hardness. Mina read the label. *Lee Krasner.* She wrote it down in her notebook then took three steps back and let the painting wash over her again.

'Mr Moss.' Mina waved her art teacher over. 'Who's Lee Krasner?'

'She was Jackson Pollock's wife,' he said. 'Come on, we need to get going. We were meant to be outside two minutes ago.' Mina wrote the detail about Jackson Pollock's wife on the piece of paper but it wasn't enough. She took one last look at the painting. It made sense to her that it was painted by a woman, the violence and the softness of it.

At home that night, Mina described the painting to her parents while Bill gnawed at his lamb chops to get the last of the meat off the bone.

'Mr Moss said she was Jackson Pollock's wife,' Mina said, breathless with enthusiasm.

'Yes, she was married to Jackson Pollock,' Elaine said, putting her fork down. 'But she was so much more than that. The patriarchy is alive and well.'

'I don't understand,' Mina said.

Bill was interested now too; he put his chop down.

'There were some incredibly influential female painters in that era, all doing inventive, ground-breaking work, but the men got all the credit. They mostly still do.' Elaine took a sip of wine.

'That's so messed up,' Mina said.

'That's the way the world worked back then,' Elaine said. 'Still works sometimes, I'm afraid,' she added, and placed her knife and fork neatly on her plate. Then she and Mina looked at Bill.

'Don't look at me, it's not my fault!' He laughed nervously.

'Down with men,' Mina joked. She threw a piece of lettuce at him, Elaine nudged him with her elbow.

But Mina couldn't stop thinking about what her mum had told her. She didn't stop thinking about it for weeks. She went to the library and searched for references to female abstract expressionists from that time. She stayed behind in art class one day just to tell Mr Moss what she'd learnt about Helen Frankenthaler, Elaine de Kooning, Alma Thomas, Georgia O'Keeffe, Joan Mitchell.

'Elaine de Kooning was married to Willem de Kooning,' Mr Moss noted, which made Mina's blood boil.

'For fuck's sake, Mr Moss,' she yelled. 'Not every woman is defined by the man she's married to. You need to stop with this misogynistic bullshit.' And she stormed out.

When the principal phoned later, Elaine took the call wearing a wry, proud smile. Mina stood in the kitchen listening nervously.

'Mm-hmm,' Elaine said. 'I will talk to her about the swearing, but you must agree she has a point about the rest. What kind of message is he sending the girls?' She paused, listened. 'Yes, of course I'll talk to her. Thank you, Mrs Hellier, goodbye.'

Elaine hung up the phone and took her daughter's face in her hands.

'Next time, don't swear at your teacher, okay?' She kissed the top of Mina's head.

Standing in front of the painting again, Mina felt the tears well in her eyes at such a rate and with such force that she was powerless to stop them. They surged up and over, down her cheeks, gushing out of her like a waterfall, dripping off the hard line of her jaw and down the front of her jumper. She knew now that this painting was a representation of grief. An expression of everything Lee Krasner had given up and everything that'd been taken away from her. Now, it represented everything Mina had lost too. She gasped, shocked by her tears, desperate for air in her lungs. A security guard who'd been sitting in the next room stuck her head around the corner to see where the noise was coming from.

'You okay?' she asked.

'I'm sorry.' Mina laughed a little through her tears. 'I don't know where that came from.' She wiped her face with her sleeve, put her hands on her hips to look casual, as if that might steady her or stop the tears.

'Normally people cry in front of the Rothko,' the security guard said, pulling a crinkled tissue from her back pocket. 'It's clean,' she said and returned to her post guarding the Cézanne, the Pissarro. Mina dabbed at her eyes, blew her nose, took one last look at the Krasner.

In the bathroom, she wiped her nose on the rough paper towel, wet a piece of it and held it up to her eyes. She looked at herself under the fluorescent light. She wondered when everything was going to stop feeling so hard here, when she was going to start feeling like she was *home*. She wondered if she'd been wrong to come. The light made her eyes, the muddy grey to Elaine's ice blue, look even more puffy and bloodshot. She thought about Shelly's full life in that huge house, already all tied up, framed neatly in gold leaf, the next twenty years all mapped out. She'd never wanted that for herself; at least, she didn't think she did. Now, all she really knew for sure was that she didn't have a clue.

She dug her phone out of her bag and turned it off aeroplane mode. The message to Jack had been delivered. She stared at it, willing a reply, but there was no reply. A message from Kira dropped down from the top of the screen. She opened it.

We finished early. Fancy a lil drink? 👀

She replied straight away:

omg yes yes yes. Please. Anywhere, asap.

'THANK CHRIST.' MINA kissed Kira's cheek, sat opposite her on one of the high stools. She looked at her friend, at the thick swoop of eyeliner over her dark eyes, at her perfect red lipstick. She thought she looked beautiful, as always. 'That is a look,' Mina said.

'Oh boy.' Kira turned her phone camera on and looked at herself. She screwed up her face.

'I meant it's a *good* look,' Mina said. 'It suits you.' And it did. Of course it did.

'I look like a doll.' Kira took a napkin from the silver napkin holder in the middle of the table, spat into it and started wiping the red from her lips. It hardly budged.

'Wow, this pub.' Mina turned to look around the main bar. She hadn't been there since she graduated, but before that it'd been a

Carlton stalwart for them. She'd probably spent four afternoons (that slowly turned to evenings, hazily to mornings) a week drinking in its corners, shouting over bands playing, legs sticking to the vinyl-covered stools no matter the weather. It was where she'd first met Ben, where she, Kira and Shelly made their plans.

'The studio's just down the road so I thought we'd take a little trip down memory lane,' Kira said, watching her.

'I've been doing a bit too much of that lately,' Mina responded. She picked up the pint Kira had bought her before she arrived. 'To ghosts from the past.' Mina clinked her beer against Kira's and took a long sip. 'Carlton Draught?' She laughed, sipped again.

'Memory lane.' Kira lifted her drink in another toast, smiled.

'I don't remember it tasting like popcorn,' Mina said and took another sip. 'Disgusting.' She took another, then another. 'How's the shoot going?'

'Fine,' Kira said unconvincingly. 'It's fine.' Her phone vibrated on the table. She turned it face up. 'Shit, I need to take this. It's my agent. Sorry.' She slid off the high stool and answered the phone, walked through the pub's doors and into the street. Mina watched her pace on the footpath, her face animated as she listened, as she talked.

The only other people in the pub were a guy in a denim jacket flicking through the songs on the jukebox and a barman staring at his phone, his elbows pressed into the soggy beer mat. It hadn't changed much: the same worn, sticky velvet-upholstered booths, the same stools lined up along the bar. The stereo blasted on: a Queens of the Stone Age song. She couldn't help but smile.

'Nothing changes, does it?' Mina said, more than half a pint down, when Kira climbed back onto the stool opposite her.

'Apart from the speed at which you can drink a pint,' Kira observed, 'nothing at all.'

'I'm a Londoner,' Mina said in a half-baked Cockney accent.

'You haven't got any better at accents.' Kira laughed. 'Remember when we used to sit over in that corner booth and make plans to take over the world?' She nodded towards the booth in the corner where the guy in the denim jacket now sat rolling a cigarette. He licked the length of the paper, sealed it, rolled it back and forth between his fingers.

'We were going to live these big lives,' Mina said wistfully.

'At least one of us made it,' Kira said.

'Who? Me?' Mina blew air out of her nose. 'I think Shelly's doing the best out of all of us.' She turned the glass around in her hands, picked it up and finished it in two sips. 'I saw her today,' she said. 'She's so happy.'

'She's a Stepford wife in activewear.' Kira groaned.

'No, it's not like that. It's more like she's bursting with love or something. Full to the brim.'

'She's just busy, that's a different thing,' Kira said. 'Plus, it's not normal to be happy all the time. It's the greatest lie of the twenty-first century.' Kira took a sip of beer, her face starting to flush red. She pressed the back of her hand to her left cheek, then the palm to her right.

'After big tobacco and the moon landing,' Mina said and laughed, remembering the nights they'd spent around the Chengs' dinner table while Valerie explained her newest theories about 9/11, the Middle East.

'Oh boy, when you see Mum next, ask her about climate change. She has some thoughts.'

'I bet she does,' Mina said. 'God, I love your Mum.'

'Everyone does.' Kira drained her glass. 'Another?'

Mina stood at the bar while the barman poured two pints. To her right was the spot where she had first met Ben, near where they'd met for the second, then third time. In the booth in the corner, he'd held her hand while she told him everything: the whole story from start to finish.

'So she hasn't been outside since the funeral?' Ben shook his head in disbelief.

'For six weeks,' Mina said, and she felt the tears come, up and over, streaming down her cheeks. 'I'm sorry,' she said and his arm was around her, pulling her close into his chest, her mascara leaving black smudges across his white *Unknown Pleasures* t-shirt, his hand in her hair. When she'd stopped crying he got her a drink and some napkins from the bar and handed them to her one after another as she blew her nose.

'I want to know about your dad,' he said. 'Tell me what you love about him.'

Mina smiled at him. She had never known such kindness. She felt something blossoming inside her.

'He always had a stupid joke up his sleeve,' Mina said through sniffles.

'Oh, so that's where you get it from.' Ben smiled.

'Shut up.' Mina smiled too, hit his arm playfully. 'Once we were eating peas at the dinner table and one fell on the floor and he said, "Oh no, we have an escapea."' Mina chuckled through the last of her tears. Ben laughed too.

'Terrible.' He shook his head, held her tighter against him.

'He really loved Mum,' she said. 'It seemed to come easy to him. He'd just do what she said, gladly. Like she could do no wrong. He was very sensible. Maybe sometimes too sensible. But if you ever needed someone to talk you through the logical solution to something, he'd be there. He preferred margarine to butter.'

'Weirdo,' they said in unison.

'He was just there when I needed him to be,' she said. 'He'd always show up when he said he would – if not on time, then early. He used to say: "To be early is to be on time." He hated wasting people's time. He knew time was valuable and precious. He made me promise never to waste it on people who didn't deserve it.'

Standing at the bar now, Mina thought about the people who deserved her time, thought about Jack. Her dad would've hated him. He would've made her make a pros and cons list about him.

Pro: Beautiful penis, handsome, made her laugh, thought she was funny.

Cons: Cocky, lazy, selfish, moody, too good-looking, had never kissed her, didn't love her, didn't care about her, hadn't written to her. Where was he?

But then she thought about his hand on his penis, his eyes on her. She couldn't shake it, couldn't step out of it. She felt like she was in a cocoon, bound tightly with wool that she didn't know how to cut through, how to escape.

'That's twenty-two.' The barman's voice snapped Mina's attention back to the pub. She carefully carried the two drinks to the table.

'Did you ever even like Shelly?' Mina asked Kira as she sat down.

Kira smiled, like she'd been waiting for this question for years.

'Of course I did.' She took a big gulp of her beer. 'I was just petrified she was going to steal you away from me.'

'Come on.' Mina laughed. 'Really?'

Kira shrugged, smiled sardonically.

'I'm not going anywhere.' Mina reached out and squeezed her hand.

'That's not true,' Kira said. 'You left me for London.'

'I didn't leave *you*, I just left.'

'Same difference,' Kira said, her face still pink. 'Stupid Asian flush.' She reached down and pulled a script from her bag and fanned her face with it.

'I only left because I couldn't stand how bad you are at drinking,' Mina said and smiled at her, taking one of the pieces of paper from her friend's hand to fan her other cheek.

On the street, Kira clumsily put on her helmet, a high-vis vest. She swung one leg over her bike, unsteady, tipsy.

'Don't forget, party on Friday night,' she called as she wobbled, pushed off. 'Love you,' she yelled over her shoulder.

Mina watched her go, waited until she was out of sight, then walked towards Carlton Gardens. She knew she couldn't avoid it much longer, she felt hemmed in, trapped by it too, but she would feel that way forever if she didn't at least try to get to the bottom of it. Passing the grand dome of the Royal Exhibition Building on the tram, she came up with a plan.

MINA OPENED THE front door, kicked her shoes off in her room, dumped her bag, put the groceries she'd bought on the way home on the kitchen bench, then grabbed her laptop. The house was still, quiet. Elaine's bedroom door was closed. Mina loaded the recipe she'd found and started pulling pans out of the backs of cupboards, raiding the spice basket in the back of the pantry, separating spices past their use-by dates from those still edible. She moved methodically around the kitchen, following instructions, chopping, stirring, repeating. It felt good, like a kind of poetry, and soon the whole house felt warmer, lived in again.

Elaine shuffled out of her room and stood at the door of the kitchen watching.

'I'm cooking us dinner,' Mina said. 'A tagine.' She pointed to the cast-iron pot bubbling away on the stove.

'You sent me that,' Elaine said, as though Mina mightn't recall that she'd lugged it all the way from Marrakesh to Hackney, then spent eighty-five quid shipping it home.

'I got it in Morocco,' Mina said.

'I remember.' Elaine turned to walk away.

'I saw Shelly today,' Mina said, and Elaine stopped, turned back. 'Her house is huge. It must be worth a fortune.'

Mina lifted the lid of the tagine with a tea towel. Elaine stood on her toes to look inside it; vegetables bubbled in the sauce.

'She must be due soon,' Elaine said.

'How did you know she was pregnant?' Mina asked, confused.

'Facebook,' Elaine said, and she turned and left the kitchen.

Mina let the lid fall with a clunk.

Seconds later, she heard the TV click and buzz and come to life in the living room. She followed the sound of a studio audience clapping.

'You're on Facebook?'

'Isn't everyone?' Elaine said without turning around, without shifting her gaze from the patterns that danced on the screen.

'Why aren't we Facebook friends?' Mina sat down on the arm of the sofa.

'You're my daughter.' Elaine picked up the remote and started flicking through the channels.

'Hey, do you think maybe you could turn that off and talk to me?' Mina said.

'My show's on soon.' Elaine kept flicking, quiz show to news and back again.

Mina snatched the remote from her. With a press of the red button, the screen went black.

'Please don't,' Elaine begged, reaching for the remote, but Mina held it tight, her body stiffening on the arm of the sofa. Elaine paused for a second, then grabbed for the remote, but Mina held it out of arm's reach. Elaine stood and grabbed at it again.

'For fuck's sake, Mum,' Mina snapped, and Elaine froze.

'Jasmina, language,' she said sharply.

'You haven't seen me in seven years. Seven years. Your only daughter. Your only family. And all you want to do while I'm here is watch TV.' Mina was surprised to find she was yelling.

'It's just there's a show on that I watch every week.' Elaine seemed shaken. Mina didn't know if it was because of the yelling or because her being there had disrupted her mother's schedule, thrown everything out of whack. Mina didn't know anything about this person.

'Okay, fine, watch your show.' Mina let the remote slip out of her hand. It hit the floor with a crack, its batteries spilling out and rolling under the sofa. Mina watched Elaine get down on all fours to retrieve it and she felt so tired. She felt suddenly and thoroughly exhausted.

'All I want is to talk, Mum. I don't think that's too much to ask.'

She watched as Elaine scrambled on the floor, trying to put all the parts of the remote control back together. Mina sighed, got down on her knees. She stuck her arm under the sofa, dug around until she found both batteries and handed them to Elaine. The two women knelt on the floor facing each other.

'I didn't ask you to come back,' Elaine said.

'But aren't you glad I'm here?' Mina asked.

Elaine looked at her, breathing heavily. She didn't say anything, but Mina took it as a no.

'Okay, just tell me one thing and I'll go,' Mina said, her voice getting away from her. The wobble before a fall. 'Did you really go outside?'

Elaine lifted the remote and turned the news back on, and they sat and watched it in silence, a half-time break. On the screen there were more hurricanes, storms surging towards islands, heading for coasts. It's too late for sandbags here, Mina thought. She wished for a rescue boat to come and get her, a helicopter to airlift her out of there.

'Can you please take the tagine off the stove in half an hour?' Mina asked. 'I'm going to bed.'

In her room she climbed into bed without undressing and pulled the sheets up over her head. She unlocked her phone, opened her messages.

She looked at the message to Jack again. *Delivered*. Ignored. She knew his phone was never out of reach, that he slept with it under his pillow, that he looked at it when he woke up, in meetings, constantly. He must've seen her message. He must've. This was the longest they'd gone without talking since they started working together just over a year ago. She reread the message. Maybe it was too cold.

I'm too cold, she thought. I'm a bitch. I should've said something cute, something sexy. It should've been a small x, two? One big, one small. I've fucked it all up.

She read it again. It was playful, it was fine, she decided, and as she watched the screen three little dots appeared in a grey bubble underneath it. He was typing. He was replying. She watched them move, a gradient of storm clouds. She thought she was going to be sick. They stopped moving. They started moving. She watched the little dots, one two three, one two three, his fingers typing, his fingers, his fingers.

The dots disappeared. She stared at her phone screen until it went dark. She pressed the home button and it woke again but there was nothing. Nothing but this rising tide, this howling wind.

Seven

MINA WOKE WITH HER PHONE still in her hand, the sheets still up around her head, her clothes on, her body heavy, her head throbbing. It was almost eleven. She'd never slept so much in her life. She wondered if her jet lag was made worse by her dread, by seven years of unresolved tension, by regret, by love unconsummated. Her stomach rumbled. It was eleven already, and Thursday. Somehow it was already Thursday. Almost a week since she answered her phone, stood up, picked up her bag, walked down the stairs, out of Jack's front door. If she really loved him, she would have stayed and let him comfort her, let him help her pack, let him drive her to the airport. What is love if not a lift to the airport?

Instead, she'd gone home, packed a suitcase and spent the hours until dawn on Saturday trawling flight aggregation sites. Where had the time gone? There was a point – it was around four in the morning, just before she gave in and bought the flight that would take her, via a four-hour stopover in Singapore, to Melbourne – when she considered not coming at all. When she considered closing her computer and walking back around the corner and climbing into Jack's bed. But instead she'd booked the flight and flown more than twenty hours to the other side of the world. For this. This return on investment would get a big black cross next to it on the end-of-campaign report. She sat up. The house still smelt like paprika and cinnamon, like onion and turmeric. The smell of failure, the smell of regret. She was starving.

She opened her bedroom door. She could hear Elaine down the other end of the house, moving things around from place to place, doing whatever she did hour after hour alone. Mina had always wondered how Elaine spent her time in the house; now she was desperate to know how she spent her time out of it. She thought about how much easier her life would be if she didn't care at all. But what is love if not the inability to abandon hope?

In the kitchen, she saw the tagine still on the stove. Or back on the stove. It was bubbling again. There was couscous, freshly made, next to it. The living room was quiet, the TV off for a change. Elaine was standing on the little brown square of deck, looking at the garden. Despite every brick wall she'd hit over the last few days, Mina still felt something. Pity. Sadness. Love?

Mina stood on the cusp between the inside and outside, the metal railing of the sliding door digging into her bare feet.

'Good morning,' she said.

Elaine turned around. 'Good morning,' she said. 'I thought you might be hungry when you got up.' She motioned to the kitchen, started moving towards the door.

'I'm starving,' Mina said and let her mother brush past her.

'Can you have tagine for brunch?' Elaine asked.

'I don't see why not.' Mina noticed that the table had been set. She wondered how long Elaine had been waiting for her to get up.

'Tea, coffee?' Elaine called from the kitchen.

'Tea, please,' Mina called back. She sat in the same place she'd sat on the day she arrived, across from her mother, their hands touching.

Elaine brought out two plates of steaming tagine.

'Did you try some last night?' Mina asked as Elaine put the plates in front of them.

'No, I wasn't very hungry.' Elaine sat opposite Mina. 'It smells wonderful, though. I don't think I've ever eaten anything like this before.'

'Well, bon appétit,' Mina said.

They both began to eat, Mina sneaking looks at her mother to see if she was enjoying it.

She thought back to the two weeks she and Kira had spent travelling through Morocco, all the hours she'd spent trying to choose a gift for Elaine before at last deciding on the burnt orange ceramic tagine on their last day in Tangier. She went through the same agonising routine every time she travelled somewhere new: a tradition fuelled by guilt, by the desire to bring a piece of the world into Elaine's life.

They didn't talk while they ate. There was just the excruciating scrape of knives and forks on plates, there was chewing, swallowing.

'What did you think?' Mina asked nervously when their plates were clean.

'I thought it was very nice,' Elaine said. 'Thank you.'

'You're welcome,' Mina said. She fell quiet, stayed sitting. Maybe there was more? At some point, Elaine had to speak to her. Mina waited and waited, the pressure to break the silence building and building inside her.

'You were always very good at trying new things,' Elaine said at last. 'Even as a kid. You never seemed scared of anything.' She didn't look at Mina while she spoke.

'That's funny – these days I feel like I'm terrified of everything,' Mina said, releasing a breath she hadn't even realised she was holding.

'I understand,' Elaine said, then quickly: 'What are you going to do today?'

Mina shrugged. 'I don't know. Maybe I'll go for a walk. Honestly, I don't know how you haven't gone mad cooped up in here for so long.'

'Who says I haven't?' Elaine smiled and stood to take the plates to the kitchen.

'Well, you're welcome to come with me,' Mina suggested tentatively.

'I can't today,' Elaine said, already walking away. 'I'm waiting for something.'

'Okay.' Mina decided not to push it. She could feel Elaine softening, the gap between them closing.

In the shower, she let the hot water stream over her face. She closed her eyes and tried to think of a time when she'd felt fearless, felt brave. Mostly she just felt like she was in survival mode, like she'd never been given the choice to fall apart, to stop, to ask for help. She wondered now if things would've been different if she had. Maybe if she'd climbed into bed and refused to get out for two weeks. What would've happened if she'd turned down invitations one after the other until people stopped asking? If she'd stopped attending lectures and tutorials, failed her final year, dropped out of uni? Would Elaine have stepped up and taken over, snapped out of it – whatever *it* was – to help?

MINA CUT DOWN the alley between the two red-brick walls. Up ahead, the creek bubbled, swollen just over its banks and gushing south. She followed the flow along the path lined with tall-trunked eucalyptus trees and fuzzy yellow wattle flowers dancing in the breeze.

A magpie bounced across the path in front of her, another in a tree nearby sang its strange strangled song. Melbourne was putting on a show for her and, for the first time since she'd arrived, she let it feel good to be there. She'd been away so long, she'd forgotten what it felt like not to be from somewhere else.

She crossed a main road, followed the path further and further south. She watched a few men in lycra ride their bikes around a velodrome, pedalling as though their lives depended on it. She followed one of the streets west and found herself in a familiar part of the neighbourhood. Kira had lived around here, in one of those dirty student houses.

She turned left, then left again, and there it was. It'd been painted, gutted probably, renovated, and would now be worth millions. It was valuable to Mina back then, too, despite the spots of mould on the walls, despite the thick grime that smoked every time someone turned the oven on. For a while, it'd been another home to her, a refuge. None of Kira's housemates cared how often she was there. After a while, they were surprised when she wasn't, would ask Kira about her, include her in their group emails as if she lived there too. This house gave Mina an escape; an opportunity to leave home without ever really leaving Elaine.

Mina stood in the street, staring through the gate, remembering the spots where she'd thrown up – at least once there in the gutter, twice in the front garden. Back then it was just a jumble of grass and weeds. She remembered that one morning Kira had to sit her in the shower with the water running until there was nothing left inside her to come up.

'I'M DYING,' MINA said as she lay with her head in Kira's lap. It was May, and somehow warmer outside than in, so they sat on the sofa on Kira's front verandah.

'You just need a Coke and three slices of pepperoni pizza and you'll come back to life, I promise.' Kira stroked her hair, whispered, 'It'll be here soon.'

'It hurts to talk,' Mina said and closed her eyes. 'Tell me a story.'

'Once upon a time' – Kira put on her best storytelling voice – 'there was a young woman who didn't know when enough was enough.'

'Fuck you!' Mina laughed then clutched her head. 'Ow.' Laughing sent pain rippling through her skull. Something rumbled deep down in her guts. 'I was celebrating.'

'I know,' Kira said. 'I'm so proud of you. You're going to get paid to write for a living.'

'I still can't really believe it.' As far as she knew, Mina was the first person from her graduating year to get a job relevant to their arts degree. She'd heard about some working in admin, data entry, but she was a junior copywriter now. She wished she could tell her dad about it. He'd be proud of her too.

'Now you have a job, maybe you can move out,' Kira said. 'I could get out of this shithole. We could get a shithole together.'

Mina opened her eyes and looked up at her friend.

'You know I can't leave her.'

'Why not? It's not like you're not going to know where she is at any given time.' Kira forced a laugh.

'It's not even been eighteen months,' Mina said. She thought she might be sick again. 'And it's not funny.'

'I know, I'm sorry.' Kira put her hand on Mina's head again. 'I just think you deserve a life too.'

'I'm living my best life right now,' Mina said, motioning to the pizza delivery driver pulling up in front of the house.

She knew Kira was right. Mina was twenty-one, she had a job. She wouldn't be earning much but it'd be enough to get by. She should move out, leave her mum to wallow in the house forever, moving quietly from room to room on her own as she'd done every day since her dad's funeral. But how could she? How could she even broach the subject? In the same way Elaine was stuck inside, Mina felt stuck right there with her.

Mina had tried everything she could think of to get Elaine outside. She'd suggested counselling, they'd staged an intervention, in which Mina and Valerie had sat with Elaine and talked about all the things they missed doing with her. But Elaine had just sat there, glassy-eyed, cold as ice. Mina had tried crying. She tried yelling, begging, but it was no use. Nothing worked. It was like her mother had shut down.

Mina watched the pizza delivery driver flirt with Kira, give her too much change.

'Holy shit, I just remembered – I do have a story to tell you,' Kira said, walking back to the house with a bottle of Coke under one arm and a huge pizza box in her hands.

Mina sat up so Kira could put the box on her lap. The hot steam warmed her legs through the cardboard. She opened the lid.

The sight of the pizza made her realise she was ravenous. She took a slice and folded it in half, the cheese dripping back into the box, squelching through her fingers. Kira seemed to have paused for dramatic effect.

'I'm listening,' Mina said, shoving as much of the slice into her mouth as she could.

'So I was at Mum and Dad's yesterday, and Lottie was acting extra emo . . .'

'Like when she accidentally squashed her class hermit crab level emo?' Mina had been there when they found her sobbing over his tiny crushed body. 'God, she cried so much.'

'Mum told her not to sleep with it under her pillow. What did she expect?'

'Rest in peace, Hank.' Mina sighed, wiped the pizza grease from her chin.

'So anyway, she pulled me aside and was like, "Kira, I have to tell you something. It's really bad." So apparently, at your dad's wake' – Mina shifted uncomfortably at the mention of it, of him, the nausea back suddenly, ferociously – 'Lottie was talking to your mum and told her that Brian Wilson from the Beach Boys was a recluse for three years and then went on to make a bunch of music once he'd got help, and that if it was okay for Brian Wilson, your mum should just take all the time she needs. Except he was also a heavy user of heroin so she shouldn't do that.'

'Oh my God,' Mina said, as she realised what Kira was saying. 'Lottie thinks this is her fault?'

'Yeah, and also that Elaine is going to just snap out of it after three years.'

'And then maybe release a psychedelic pop album.' Mina was laughing now.

'She's been feeling guilty this whole time.'

'Oh God, the poor thing,' Mina said. 'I'll talk to her.'

'Yeah, might be a good idea.' Kira opened the bottle of Coke, took three big gulps, passed it to Mina.

Mina felt better after the pizza settled, after her headache subsided. Still dressed in Kira's leggings – so long they were scrunched at the ankles and pulled up over her belly button – she slowly made her way home. Through the park, along the creek, moving at a snail's pace. She thought about Lottie, dwelling in that guilt for all this time.

She wished there *was* someone to blame, wished it could be explained that easily. She thought about what she'd give to understand this, to fix it, make it better, easier, for everything to go back to how it was. She felt drained, as if soon her reserves (energy, patience, resilience, sympathy) would be running dangerously low. She wasn't sure what would happen when she hit empty, or if she was even going to stick around long enough to find out.

'CAN I HELP you?' A voice pulled Mina back to the cold early-spring morning, the blustery east Brunswick street. A woman was standing at the door of the house Mina was staring at.

'Sorry, I got lost down memory lane. A friend of mine used to live here,' Mina called to her, sheepishly.

'The Johnsons? They moved out last year,' the woman wiped her hands on her flour-dusted apron. Mina guessed she was in her late fifties, her hair cut into a perfect silver bob.

'No, about a decade ago,' Mina said, 'long before it looked like this.'

'Ah well, the neighbourhood's changed a lot in the last few years.'

Mina smiled, waved to the woman in lieu of a response. She walked back towards the creek, towards Elaine, still with a little energy, patience, resilience and sympathy in the tank, but just a little, she thought. Just a little.

Eight

'SO WE'RE SPECIFICALLY GAY UNICORNS, not just unicorns?' Mina asked as she, Kira and Claire walked through the streets around the back of Edinburgh Gardens. They were dressed in identical faded American Apparel *Legalize Gay* t-shirts with horns on their heads made quickly, shoddily, from rolled-up cardboard and stapled-on gold pipe cleaners. 'I just need to know in case someone asks.'

'It's to show our support for gay marriage,' Claire said.

'And it's extra funny because there's three of us,' Kira explained. Then whispered, 'just go with it.'

Mina had met Kira's housemate that afternoon, the three of them sitting in the kitchen downing pre-game tinnies, then cosmos, at Claire's insistence. Claire was from Kira's acting class. She was beautiful in a different way from Kira. She was the type of woman who looked destined to become an artist's muse, her long brown hair falling naturally in loose curls over her bare breasts as she posed casually, artfully, on a chaise longue.

'So whose party is this, anyway?' Mina asked, shivering in the damp night air. She felt nervous about not knowing anyone, nervous about not actually being invited, nervous that it wasn't a dress-up party at all.

'It's James from our acting class,' Kira said. 'He's the hot one I told you about.'

'And you're sure it's alright if I come?' Mina asked.

Kira waved away her concern. 'It's a house party, dummy. It's fine.'

'Relax and have some of this,' Claire said, and she pulled a joint out of the gold bumbag she wore low and loose around her waist. Claire lit it, inhaled the hot smoke and held it in her lungs as she passed the joint to Mina.

Mina hesitated for a second but took it from her, put it to her lips and inhaled. The smoke hit the back of her throat and she coughed a little but managed to keep it in. As she exhaled, the smoke disappearing into the clear night air, she noticed the stars, a few silver dots, scattered and sparkling.

They passed the joint between them until there was nothing left but filter. Claire chucked it on the ground and stepped on it, the tiny light extinguished under her heeled boot.

Mina spotted a small group of people standing on the street outside an old white cottage. She could see someone dressed as Superman and breathed a sigh of relief. They walked through the gate; the front door was open, the hall full of people in costumes: a guy dressed like He-Man, another with a Granny Smith apple hanging down in front of his bowler hat – a living, breathing Magritte painting. Mina was impressed. The three of them squeezed through the doorway. Inside, a Beyoncé song played but Mina didn't know which one. Kira and Claire forged their way through the crowd. Mina heard one of them squeal. From the entrance to the living room, she watched a man dressed as a long Tetris piece smother Claire as he hugged her. Another Tetris piece, an L-shape, kissed Kira on both cheeks.

'And this is Mina,' Claire said to the two pieces. 'She's Kira's oldest friend.'

Mina shook hands but they didn't tell her their names. The long piece just took the six-pack from Kira and added it to a big tub filled with ice.

'So, what are you ladies meant to be?' the L-shape asked, looking Claire up and down.

'We're gay unicorns, obviously,' Claire said and slapped his arm.

'Amazeballs,' he said. 'I love it.' He fist bumped her. Mina hated him instantly.

'Come on, let's take a turn around the room,' Kira said. They linked arms and the two of them swept around the living room. They used to do this at high school parties; join forces to see who was there, who was interesting, who was worth their time, who Kira would try – and succeed without much effort – to make out with.

Kira led her into the backyard.

'Everyone here is so good-looking,' Mina said, pulling the tight t-shirt down over her stomach. 'Are they all actors and models?'

Kira surveyed the scene. 'Mostly,' she said. 'One of the Tetris pieces was in *Neighbours* for a while but they killed him off. Aladdin over there was in an episode or two of *Rake* but now he deals cocaine.'

'In which show?' Mina asked, and Kira just shook her head. Mina laughed. It felt good to be back by her friend's side. 'I had no idea there were so many aspiring actors in Melbourne.'

'There're also a lot of baristas. Pretty much everyone here works in hospitality.' Kira spotted a man dressed as Hillary Clinton, holding court and surrounded by four women. 'Oh, there's James.'

She made a beeline for him, Mina following. He kissed her on the cheek, and Kira introduced Mina.

'I'd shake your hand but we're about to have some picklebacks. Grab some shot glasses,' James said. He had a bottle of whisky in one hand and a jar of pickles in the other. Kira reached over and took four shot glasses, handed two to Mina, ignoring her objection.

'Right,' James said, 'who's ready to get their Hillary drinkonnn?'

All the girls in the semi-circle around him screamed 'Wooooo!' except Mina.

He poured whisky into seven shot glasses, pickle juice into the others.

'Pickle juice first, then whisky straight after,' he instructed.

'This seems like a reaaaally bad idea,' Mina whispered to Kira, but she wasn't listening.

'One, two, three,' James chanted and they all shot back the pickle juice and then downed the whisky in one go.

THE ROOMS WERE packed with bodies, the music loud enough to make the windows shake. Mina felt too high and too drunk to get the words out fast enough to be funny or interesting to a group of strangers, so she just stood on the sidelines of conversations, picked the label off the beer bottle she'd been nursing since the third round of shots. She moved from inside the house to outside the house and back inside; none of the rooms seemed to have definite edges anymore. She found Claire in the kitchen and watched her trying to make a shape that fit perfectly between two of the Tetris pieces.

In the living room, she found Kira doing a do-si-do with a man dressed as Steve Irwin. She sat on the sofa and watched them spin around, Kira laughing so hard her head was all the way back.

She noticed a guy hovering next to her dressed as a big grey blob.

'Cloud?' Mina asked him.

'Stingray,' he said. 'The one that killed that guy.' He nodded at Steve Irwin, and Mina noticed the big wound in Steve's chest, complete with protruding barb and fake blood.

'What are you?' the ray asked, edging closer. 'The Eiffel Tower?' She could smell beer and cigarettes, pizza on his breath.

'No, I'm Kim Jong Un,' she joked and stood, desperate for air.

Outside, she found Hillary Clinton smoking on the front step. Mina sat next to him.

'Did you know that when Hillary was a kid she wrote to NASA and asked how she could become an astronaut?' Mina asked. Without waiting for him to respond, she continued, 'But they wrote back and told her that girls couldn't be astronauts.'

'They should've told her girls couldn't be president either,' he said through a mouthful of smoke.

'Ouch,' Mina said. 'Did you ever want to be an astronaut?' She turned towards him slightly. Their knees touched.

'No,' he said. 'I wanted to be in Jurassic Park.'

'The movie?' Mina asked.

'The actual park. I loved dinosaurs.' He stubbed his cigarette out and flicked the butt into the garden bed.

'And now?'

'Now I'd kill to be in a Spielberg,' he said. 'What about you?'

'Oh, I'm not an actor,' she said and looked at her feet. She felt him turn to look at her properly, really take her in.

'I didn't think so.' He put another cigarette in his mouth. 'But what did you want to be?' He lit it with a hot pink lighter and held it between two fingers.

'A writer. I wanted – *want*,' she corrected herself, 'to write a screenplay.' She thought of all the blank documents she'd opened, the cursor blinking at her. She'd write a line or two, then get distracted by YouTube videos or Instagram cats. She saved some of them: Screenplay1.docx, Screenplay1.1.docx and on and on. 'Failing that, I'd like to be happy,' she said.

'How's that going for you?'

She chewed on her lip and looked right at him. He adjusted his position a little, turned and leant towards her. Mina wondered if he was going to kiss her but he just took another drag and rolled the smoke around in his mouth. He blew it out and it shrouded them both, Hillary Clinton and a gay unicorn, suspended in white smoke, floating in space.

'Can I ask you something?' he asked, asking her something.

'You have the floor, Madam Secretary.'

'Cute,' he said. Mina thought his gaze felt romantic, had a hint of something more. 'Did Kira say anything about me?'

Mina's guts twinged a little. Of course, she thought.

'She refers to you as the hot one,' Mina said, and watched Hillary Clinton scramble to his feet and walk inside, his body immediately swallowed by the throng of beautiful people.

Mina shuffled forwards, bent over the front garden bed and spewed, covering the neat row of pink and purple petunias with pickle and cranberry juice, whisky and beer. It tasted briny and bitter. She wiped her mouth with the back of her hand.

She got up and went inside. The heat in the house made her dizzy, all those bodies. She'd forgotten the heat that bodies could make. She found the bathroom, shut the door behind her. She ran the cold tap and bent down to drink directly from it, her unicorn horn knocking a plastic cup of toothbrushes and a bottle of mouthwash onto the floor.

'Shit,' she said, pulled the horn off her head and chucked it in the bath. She picked up the cup, threw as many toothbrushes back in as she could find, took the lid off the glacier-blue Listerine and swigged a mouthful into her cheeks, to the back of her tongue, then spat. She gulped more water from the tap, and then looked at her face in the mirror. This is how I look at thirty-two, she thought. Bloodshot eyes above dark, puffy semi-circles. She pulled her hair out of its ponytail and let it flop, mousy and limp, on either side of her head. Behind her, the door swung open. A man in a cockroach suit pushed in, all gangly arms and legs.

'Sorry,' she said instinctively.

'Shit, sorry,' he said, his human hands up as if shielding himself from seeing too much. He was about to turn and slip back out the door when he stopped still. She looked at the heavy brow beneath the brown lycra hood that covered his hair, those big eyes.

'Ben?'

'Oh my God.' He bounded over to her, all his arms and legs jiggling, and hugged her, picking her up off the ground. She'd forgotten how tall he was, how strong. 'What are you doing here?' He put her down but kept his hands on her, kept her close.

She shrugged. 'I'm back.'

'For good?'

'For a bit. I thought you were in Paris?'

'Visa run.' They stared at each other a bit too long, like they were relearning each other's faces. 'I need to piss so badly. Can you help me get out of this stupid thing?'

'Turn around.' Laughing, Mina unzipped him.

He wriggled his hands free and started to fold the costume down to his waist. 'Oh my God, that feels better.' She noticed that his chest glistened with sweat. He fanned himself with one of his thin fabric roach legs.

'I'll leave you to it,' she said, heading for the door.

'Don't go anywhere,' Ben said. 'I want to know everything.'

'Meet me in the kitchen.' She closed the door behind her and floated on the sea of bodies towards the kitchen. She passed Claire on the stairs. Her tongue was in the mouth of a woman dressed as a narwhal, their horns banging wildly against each other.

Mina searched the kitchen for a clean glass, a cup, any receptacle for water. She found one under the sink, rinsed it out three times, then drank three Vegemite jars of water, took two stray Heinekens from the fridge and opened them just as Ben came into the kitchen in search of her. She handed him one, they clinked bottles, drank.

'Can you zip me back up?'

He turned. His costume was unzipped all the way down to the crack. She felt the sharp stab of a feeling that was not love, it'd not been that for a long time; more like the feeling that something she'd been missing had just found its way back to her. A lost book, an old photo, a favourite scarf.

'I can't believe you're here,' Ben said, turning back to face her. 'Why didn't you tell me?'

'I didn't know *you* were here!' she said, laughing. 'Why didn't *you* tell *me*?'

'How long's it been?' He rested his back against the kitchen bench.

'Too long,' she said. She'd missed his big face, his huge smile. 'You look great, by the way – all those extra legs really suit you.'

'Do you think my thighs have got fatter?' Ben waggled one of his cockroach legs at her and she squeezed it.

'Maybe you've filled out a little,' she said and he laughed. She remembered how much she liked making him laugh. She felt the breath return to her lungs, the haze lift from around her.

They moved outside to the front of the house for air and sat with their backs against the dusty white weatherboards.

'Looks like someone can't hold their liquor.' Ben pointed to the contents of Mina's stomach in the front garden bed. 'Remember the way you used to spew every single time we went out?'

'Not every time,' she protested. 'You'd hold my hair up and rub my back.'

'A proper gentleman,' he said.

'Always.' She smiled at him just as two sparkling unicorns and Hillary Clinton came tumbling out of the front door.

'Found her!' Claire yelled and pointed at Mina. She was clearly wasted.

'Is this cockroach bothering –' Kira squinted at him. 'Ben?' She shrieked and jumped on him. 'What are you doing here?' She was so drunk her words were almost indistinguishable.

A car honked on the street. 'That's our Uber, we gotta go.' Kira ran out the front gate and launched herself headfirst into the back seat. Hillary Clinton followed her, Claire squeezing into the back beside them.

'Wait, doesn't Hillary Clinton live here?' Ben asked.

'Nah, this is a white house.' Mina gurgled a stupid laugh.

'Good to see you're still an idiot,' he said, and they stood up and hugged.

'Can I see you before you go?' she said into his chest.

'I leave on Tuesday,' he replied. 'Message me.'

The honk of the car's horn and Claire's holler from the back seat separated them.

Mina hurried over, got into the front seat and watched Ben watch her drive away.

MINA STARED UP at Kira's living room ceiling. It was after three, creeping towards four. Orange light from the street and the strange sky shone in beams across the room. Cars passed and their headlights flashed through the curtains, their tyres swished on the wet road. Mina could hear Hillary Clinton panting in the next room, four grunts and a moan, a bedframe banging against the wall. A few minutes earlier she'd heard him start chanting, 'You're so hot, you're so hot.' Kira shushed him and giggled. Mina imagined him on top of Kira, still in his wig, his bare chest sweaty, his penis a long thin pencil poking in and out of her.

Mina turned on her side and picked up her phone from the floor. She and Ben didn't follow each other on Instagram; his account was private. She searched for him on Facebook and realised they weren't friends there anymore either. She wondered when he'd unfriended her, though she understood why: she had left. She requested his friendship (that's all she wanted, she hoped he knew that), then she searched for Elaine and requested hers. In the next room over, the grunting started again. She scrolled down through her feed. Jack had liked a meme about Brexit two hours earlier. It was about seven-thirty last night in London. Mina imagined him getting ready to go out on the pull, finding someone to fuck at The Scolt Head or The Fox or The Talbot. One of those girls who'd just moved to Dalston and lived in the new apartments above the Overground station. That's probably what he thought his type was: young, pretty girls who weren't funnier than him. Mina was sure he'd think of her when he was inside the unfunny girl, on top of the pretty girl. When he noticed a wonkily put together IKEA bookcase holding a half-read copy of *The Corrections*, he'd remember that Mina's furniture was all mid-century, bought from that expensive Danish shop near the Pembury. He'd think about Mina then, she knew it.

'I want to fuck you forever,' Hillary Clinton yelled from the next room.

She felt like she was being punished for something – for leaving, for coming back, for leaving it so long before coming back – and now she'd have to lie there and listen to this forever.

She picked up her phone, a Facebook notification lit up the screen: *Ben Farley has accepted your friend request.*

Going out with Kira, seeing Ben, made it feel as though no time had passed at all. Life felt mostly the same: hard sometimes, fun sometimes. The difference was that here, she had people who looked out for her, people who tried to help her forget how bad things were.

Hillary Clinton screamed as he came then, through the wall, Mina was sure she could hear him saying, 'Thank you, thank you,' over and over.

She stifled a laugh, put her phone under the pillow, pulled the blanket up over her head and tried to sleep.

Nine

MINA WAITED OUTSIDE THE CHENGS' house for Kira. Despite the hair-dryer hot air, the sweat that flooded her top lip, getting away from the mourners, away from Elaine and away from the weight of all that grief made Mina feel instantly lighter. Escape, she was realising, was a soothing balm.

She flapped her dress to let the air in, got a whiff of anxiety sweat, adrenaline, the only thing that had kept her upright during the funeral, in the whole week leading up to it.

'Hey.' The voice behind her made her jump.

Brendan stood against the wall, smoking. 'It's pretty heavy in there, huh?' he said and offered her the cigarette.

She took it, held it between her fingers and brought it up to her lips. She took a puff but the tobacco made her woozy, made her stomach churn. The blood rushed to her head. She coughed the smoke out of her lungs and reached a hand out to steady herself on the bricks.

'Whoa there.' Brendan caught her, his arm around her waist, her dress damp from the sweat.

'I'm fine,' she said, leaning her back against the wall.

He released her and took back his cigarette.

'Sorry,' she said, too embarrassed to look at him. 'I'm fine.' Out of the corner of his eye she watched him wipe his hand down the leg of his black pants. 'Not a great day for wearing black, is it?' she said. 'Sorry.'

'Jesus, stop apologising.' He threw the cigarette on the ground and stubbed it out with the toe of his Doc Martens, his old school shoes.

'Sor—' She banged her head back against the wall. 'Okay.'

'I'm sorry,' he said. 'About your dad. I always liked him.'

'Thanks, me too.' Mina looked at Brendan. This was the first real conversation they'd had since he hit puberty, got too hot and too cool to talk to her.

'Your mum's a mess,' he said and turned to face her, getting closer, his shoulder against the wall near her shoulder.

'She's in shock. Apparently, she just needs time,' Mina said. 'I hope she just needs time.' She felt Brendan's eyes on her. On her arms, on the bit of black lace bra visible from the side of her dress.

'Time heals all wounds,' Brendan said and leant in a little closer.

Mina thought that was just about the deepest, smartest thing she'd ever heard.

Kira burst out the front door and Brendan took a step back from Mina.

'Come on,' Kira said. She had two towels over her shoulder and car keys in her hand. 'I'm breaking you out of here.' She clomped down the front steps.

'Where are you going?' Brendan asked.

'None of your business, dipshit,' Kira called from the driveway. The lights of the Barina blinked twice as she pressed the button.

Mina shrugged at Brendan. 'See ya round.' She followed Kira to the car.

They drove east and north, where there was more space between houses, more sky.

There was a brand-new ute with the number plate M1UTE in the car park but it was otherwise empty. It was too hot to be outside, too hot for swimming, too hot for a funeral, too hot for all of it. They walked along the path that circled the lake. The gravel crunched underfoot, the ground uneven, eroded over time by rain. Mina peered over the edge at the deep green water, at the drop, the white-trunked gums that seemed to grow right out of the rock.

They laid their towels out in the dappled sun and stripped down to their underwear. Mina waded in up to her knees; the water was cool but not too cold.

'That's not very funeral-appropriate underwear,' Kira called. She was already submerged, her long limbs floating in the murky water.

Mina looked down at her body, at the gentle slope of her hips, her breasts that would turn downwards one day. She wondered if her body would end up like the one she'd seen in the bath that morning. If it would ever be useful to anyone but her. She saw a few dark curls of hair had escaped from the sides of her hot pink undies.

'Do you think I should've chosen something sexier?' she said, then she dived headfirst into the water. She kept her eyes closed and kicked her legs. She wanted to live down there, to learn to breathe and eat and sleep down there. She broke the surface and wiped the water from her eyes. 'This was a really good idea,' Mina said. 'Thank you.' She turned onto her back and let herself float, let her body relax. The sun beat down on the quarry, on her face.

She felt light. Lighter, anyway, than at any other time in the last ten days. Cleansed.

On the bank, Mina lay on her towel as the sun dried her. Silt from the water clung and crisped in her hair; her skin mottled, pinked. Kira walked up the bank and sat down on the towel next to her.

'My mum reckons your mum blames herself,' Kira said, wiping the drops of water from her body with her fingers, then wringing out her hair. 'And that's why she's such a . . .' She paused.

'A mess?' Mina lifted herself up onto her elbows and looked at her friend.

'Yeah. I didn't want to say it, but she really is a fucking mess.' Kira lay down on her stomach, her head turned towards Mina.

'Maybe the fact that it was nobody's fault makes it worse. If he was in a car accident or something, then at least we'd have *someone* to blame.' Mina sank back onto on her towel. 'It's hard to be mad at a blood clot.' A trail of little black ants made their way across her arm. She let them be, willed, dared them to bite her.

'I guess,' Kira said. Her face was squashed against the towel, against the ground, but even then, still beautiful. 'I'd kill for your tits, you know.'

'Shut up,' Mina said, and rolled self-consciously onto her stomach. 'What am I going to do?' She sighed. 'I miss him so much already.' Tears dripped over the bridge of her nose and pooled on the towel, soaked through into the cracked dirt.

'You're going to take a deep breath and just keep going.' Kira reached over and squeezed her hand.

On the walk back up the hill, Kira collected as much rubbish as she could carry: Corona bottles with labels faded and browned, half-full cans of sun-cooked lemonade.

Mina felt giddy with the sun, giddy with the day. In the hot car, she made a mental list of everything she was going to do to take control of this, to fix it. She knew she had to be there for her mum, to do everything she could to make this, if not better, then bearable for the pair of them. She was going to be strong, be a good daughter, help her mother get back on her feet. It's what her dad would've wanted.

She wound the window down and the breeze made her feel that it was possible; that some of it, at least, was possible.

SHE FOUND BEN sitting out the back of the pub, pint in hand. He stayed sitting while she hugged him, long and hard, apologetic. It was after nine-thirty already, but she was thankful to hear from him, thankful to have been drawn from her hungover hatewatching of rom-coms.

She sat down next to him with a gin and tonic. He was wearing a nice jumper. She wanted to feel it, rest a cheek against it.

'How's your hangover?' he asked, his long arms stretched halfway across the table.

Mina shrugged. 'It's okay. I think Kira and I ate enough carbs today to soak up whatever was left in our system. Yours?'

'I woke up feeling great. I think I sweated all the alcohol out of my body and into that cockroach suit.'

'Gross.' Mina laughed. 'I hope you disposed of it immediately.'

'Mum's going to wash it for me.'

'Of course she is.' Mina sighed. 'How is Sharon?'

'She's good, limber. She's retrained as a yoga teacher.' Ben smiled. 'She says hi.'

'Tell her I miss her,' Mina said, and she did. Lovely Sharon Farley, the nicest woman in the world, all sinew and essential oils. Welcoming, warm, sweet Sharon Farley, who'd fussed over Elaine, complimented the house and helped with the dishes the few times Mina invited Ben and his parents over for dinner.

'I will,' Ben said. 'How's Elaine?' he asked.

'She left the house,' Mina said, swirling her drink in circles in its glass. 'Apparently.'

'Really?' he said. 'That's great, right?'

She'd always liked how deep Ben's voice was.

'I guess so,' Mina agreed begrudgingly.

'But that's what you've wanted ever since I met you.' He sounded bewildered. He'd forgotten how complicated this was, or maybe he'd never really understood.

'Yeah, but she won't admit that she did, and she won't talk about it. I don't know how many times it's happened or where she goes. Kira's mum saw her, Kira called me, and here I am.' Mina took a sip of her drink.

'Right,' he said.

'Tell me about Paris,' she prompted, changing the subject.

'Okay,' he said. 'We – I – live out near Belleville. I work at a firm that specialises in intellectual property, specifically in the arts.'

'Amazing,' Mina said. 'And who's we?'

He smiled, but seemed tense. 'We is my girlfriend and I,' he said, with a look Mina couldn't put her finger on: bashful, maybe, guilty – but why? 'Her name is Aamira. She's a translator and an artist.'

'That's great,' Mina said blankly. She wasn't sure how she felt. 'How long have you been together?'

He pretended to count in his head as if he didn't already know.

'Seven years, give or take – I don't know exactly.' He knew. He watched Mina's face as she did the maths. She'd lived in London for seven years. They broke up when she'd moved. Seven years, seven years, seven years; it pinged around her brain like a pinball.

'That's great,' Mina said again, but she couldn't hide it, her skin tingled with it. She'd left and, in the process of leaving, had left him. She knew she had no right to be mad. And yet.

Mina heard someone singing a high note loudly and out of tune in the next room. 'Did you hear that?' Mina asked. She downed the last of her drink and, grateful for the interruption, she headed inside. This time, at least, she knew Ben would follow her.

At the main bar there were people clustered around tables near a low stage. A woman in a polka dot dress was up there singing '. . . Baby One More Time'. Mina clapped with delight. The only thing she loved more than watching karaoke was watching bad karaoke.

She slid into the leather booth near the stage and cheered as the woman landed about a mile off every note, each one as flat as a piece of paper. She started the last chorus too late and couldn't catch up, skipped a few lines. It was a mess. Mina loved it. She cackled.

Ben stood at one of the tables, flicking through a three-ring binder. 'Duet?' he mouthed. She shook her head and he kept flicking. He wrote his choice on a piece of paper and handed it to a man in a merlot-coloured velvet suit, bought the two of them fresh drinks and sat down next to her.

'Let's give it up for Joe and Tom, singing "Islands in the Stream",' the MC boomed into the microphone and everyone cheered, Joe and Tom's friends emitting lupine howls and banging their glasses and fists on the table. The taller, tanned one took Dolly's part and hit the high notes like a hammer on a nail. They harmonised like they'd been practising this at home and then kissed during the fade-out. The whole front bar cheered, Mina one of the loudest.

'Next up, we have Ben singing "Kokomo",' the MC announced.

Ben stood, took one last sip of his beer, and jogged up to the stage. On the screen, Mina could see an aquamarine sea, white sands, palm trees. The audience clapped and cheered for him as he listed the names of the islands, his voice deep enough, just right for it. Ben knew every word, he sang with his eyes closed, hit every note. He was a showman; Mina had forgotten that about him. Forgotten the hours she'd spent watching his band play in the front bars of pubs across Melbourne, cringing at how bad they were but admiring how little he seemed to care. The saxophone solo hit and he danced alone on stage, a swagger that was part Freddie Mercury, part Gob Bluth. Mina thought back to seven years ago, when Kira sat outside his house in the car, waiting for Mina to tell him she was leaving, to ask him one last time to go with her.

He'd been slouched bare-chested on the brown sofa he'd found three streets away on hard rubbish day and somehow carried home on his own. He looked defeated; he knew he'd lost.

'I can't stay,' she said. 'You know I can't.'

'You don't have to live in that house. Why don't you move in with Kira?' Ben stared down at the cold tea in his chipped Tigers mug. 'Move in here.'

'But she'll still be there, in that house. I don't want to be beholden to her for the rest of my life.'

'But she's your mum,' Ben said.

'Hardly.'

He walked her to the door and they hugged for a long time. 'It's not too late for you to come,' she whispered.

'It is,' he said, and he let her go. He let her go . . .

He finished singing and took a bow, the audience on their feet now. Mina didn't clap, she just watched him saunter off stage towards her.

'How'd I do?' he asked as he sat down next to her.

'You know, Kokomo's not even a real place,' she yelled over the MC as he invited the next singer up on stage. 'Well, it is, but it's an industrial city in Indiana, it's a long way from the tropical island paradise they'd have you believe.'

'Cool,' he said sarcastically, staring down into his warm beer.

'They had a tornado there that blew over a whole Starbucks,' Mina said.

'You're mad at me. About the timing. I can tell.'

'I'm not,' she said, but she was.

'You left me,' he said.

The woman on stage was sing-talking 'Ironic', grabbing her head like she had a bad headache.

'I didn't leave *you*,' Mina said. 'I just left. Jesus, why does everyone keep saying that?'

'Fine, you *left*, but in leaving you broke my heart.'

'You could've come with me. And how did you end up in Paris seven years ago instead of in London with me?'

'Because I got over it and I moved on,' he said. 'I'm happy now.'

'I've moved on too.' She would tell him about Jack if she had to. She would make up a story about how he loved her, worshipped her, was going to marry her.

'You still seem angry to me,' Ben said, apropos of nothing. 'You've had this chip on your shoulder for-fucking-ever.'

Mina felt like she'd been slugged in the guts.

'That's not fair,' she said quietly, wounded.

'You need to stop feeling so sorry for yourself,' he said. 'It's boring.'

'Let me out, I want to go home.' Mina shuffled closer to him but he didn't move. She stared at him, waiting, willing him to move, but he just sat there, not looking at her.

'Can you please let me out?'

Ben took a sip of his drink and kept his eyes on the stage. Mina swore under her breath and shuffled away from him. She shuffled around the corner, along the wall, around another corner, then the whole length of the bench on the opposite side.

She stopped across from him. *'Au revoir,'* she said. Then she stood and walked out of the pub.

MINA BOUGHT CHOCOLATE at the 7-Eleven, a whole slab of Dairy Milk, and sat on the tram watching herself eat it in the reflection of the darkened window. Fuck Ben, she thought, the humiliation burning in her cheeks. Fuck Melbourne, this Pac-Man city with its ghosts around every corner. Fuck Paris. Fuck artists and fuck all of France.

She felt her phone vibrate against her leg and pulled it out of her bag. It was probably Ben apologising. Or maybe it was France, texting to say it was sorry. She looked at the screen.

Jack. Three messages from Jack.

She put her phone facedown on her leg. Turned it over again to make sure she hadn't imagined it. She couldn't read them yet; she couldn't bear it. What could he possibly have to say now, when more than a week had passed since she'd got up and left him too? Why was she always turning her back on things?

She stared at her screen as the tram turned the corner and edged down Miller Street. She pulled the cord and the bell dinged, the tram ground to a stop. *Jack Adams (3)*. She ran through what they might say.

One: *I want you.* Two: *I miss you.* Three: *I love you.*

One: *I can't stop thinking about you.* Two: *I need you to come back.* Three: *I love you.*

One: *You disgust me.* Two: *I hope you never come back.* Three: *I hate you.*

One: *You're fat.* Two: *You're ugly.* Three: *You're stupid.*

She stepped off the tram. She was ready. The bedroom lights of suburban houses glowed against the dark starless sky. She unlocked her phone. The little white wheel was spinning in the centre of a black screen. The battery was dead.

Her stomach bottomed out and she started doing that half-walk, half-run of someone who's running late for something. It was past eleven when she burst through the door. All the lights were on, she could hear the TV down the hall.

In her bedroom Mina plugged her phone in. She sat on the bed and held it, waiting for it to come back to life. Her knees bounced.

'Come on,' she whispered. The screen flashed white and she entered her passcode. The messages:

🎉🎉🎉🎉🎉🎉🎉
CHECK YOUR EMAIL
🎉🎉🎉🎉🎉🎉🎉

She opened her Gmail. Nothing. She pulled and pulled and pulled at her work email until sixty-four new messages downloaded. She scanned down through meeting requests, updates on briefs. She pulled the screen again and again.

There was one from George with the subject heading: *Exciting team changes.* She opened it.

Hi guys,

Stop checking your emails on the weekend! At least, after you read this one . . .

I am pleased to announce that effective Monday morning, we have promoted Jack Adams to creative director, sharing the challenge of managing the agency's award-winning creative output with me.

Since starting at Peach just over a year ago, he's proven himself to be a true leader, executing exceptional work, helping us win new business opportunities and inspiring the team.

We've been grooming Jack for the role since he started and are excited to see where he'll take us.

Mina Gordon will continue in her role as associate creative director, working under Jack and myself.

Any questions, you know where I am.

GP

A key turned inside her. She read it again. Once more, just in case.

'Fuck,' she whispered under her breath. 'Fuck, fuck.' She let her phone go to sleep, and threw it hard onto the floor. She lay facedown on the bed. Rolled over, then back again. She lay with her eyes open, wide and dry, her chest tight. *Fuck*.

Ten

MINA WOKE LATE FROM A troubled sleep during which dreams came to her one after the other, like paper spat out of a photocopier. In one, she opened a drawer filled with balloons that floated out and turned into bats; in another Jack was squeezing one of her nipples, George the other: honking them like old fashioned bike horns. She thought about George's email. It was as if a knife was unpicking her stitches, reopening a wound. She picked her phone up off the floor; a jagged crack ran down the screen from top to bottom. She had three new messages from Jack. One from George. She didn't open them.

She looked around the room at the soft pinks, the dull light like white smoke, as heavy as a medicine ball. Her eyes found the wardrobe her dad built. He'd made her help him. She'd stood around feeling the boredom throb through every part of her body as she passed him nails and screws, watched him bang and hammer and sweat and curse, watching as the flat pieces of wood became something.

Mina used to find it embarrassing that everything in the house was handmade, cobbled together and slightly wonky, but now she realised what it must have meant to him. At work, he assessed insurance claims, spending his days looking at things that had already come apart. What a relief it must've been to see things come together for a change, to have a hand in the making of a home, a family.

Mina got up and opened the wardrobe door. Inside, stacked neatly: her assignments, every edition of the university paper in which she had a story; her school reports; certificates from writing competitions. She found an old pair of shorts and a PJ Harvey t-shirt with a hole in each armpit, bought at a summer music festival a lifetime ago. Taking off her outfit from the night before, she changed into the shorts and t-shirt and looked at herself in the full-length mirror. The shorts still fit, just. Her hips were wider than they used to be, her thighs a bit thicker. It seemed some things had changed after all.

There was a knock at the front door. She answered it.

A grocery delivery. Six big bags of shopping. She took them from the delivery driver, his thick dry fingers brushing hers as the bags changed hands.

'Oh, hello, Pete,' Elaine said from behind her.

Mina turned to put the bags down in the hall and caught Elaine giving him a little wave.

'Morning, Elaine,' the driver said. 'Just the usual for you today.'

'Thank you!' she said with an openness and friendliness that was reserved for strangers, it seemed.

The driver passed Mina a little stylus and she signed the screen of his tablet. Behind her, Elaine started carrying the bags to the kitchen.

'Hey, Pete, can I ask you a question?' Mina followed him outside.

'Okay.' He looked at her warily, the lines around his eyes crinkling as they narrowed.

'How long have you been delivering groceries to my mum?'

Pete passed through the threshold of the front gate, Mina followed.

'Couple of years, I guess? Hard to say exactly.' He glanced towards his truck, as if he was keen to leave, but Mina persisted.

'Have you ever seen her go outside in that time? Ever seen on her on the street, or' – she paused, couldn't think of anywhere else Elaine might need to go – 'in the supermarket?'

'No, I don't think so,' Pete said awkwardly. 'Sorry, I've gotta get on. I've got another four deliveries to do.'

'Of course.' Mina said. 'Thanks.'

She waited while he climbed into his truck. As he pulled away, she spotted a man running along the other side of the road. She watched him for a while, not ready to go back inside. His muscles bulged from out of his singlet top, and his skin glistened with sweat. As he got closer, Mina realised she knew that perfect nose, that strong jaw. He noticed her too, jogged across the road and stopped in front of her.

'Welcome home,' Brendan gasped, trying to catch his breath.

'Same to you.'

'You heard about that, huh?' Sweat dripped down his temples onto his cheeks, down to his jaw. His hair, still so thick, was stuck to his forehead in strands.

'Just something about your wife being a bitch,' Mina said, and Brendan laughed.

'Jesus Christ, my mother . . .' He shook his head.

'Valerie Cheng is a one-woman phone tree,' Mina said, and Brendan laughed again.

'Speaking of mothers,' he said. He raised an eyebrow, cocked his head towards the door. 'What's going on there?'

'I'm still trying to get to the bottom of that.' Mina looked down at her outfit, suddenly self-conscious; she wrapped her arms around herself. She hoped Brendan wouldn't notice all the ways she'd changed.

'Life, huh?' he said, as if it was the deepest truth anyone had ever uttered.

'Tell me about it.' She pointed towards the house. 'Well, I'd better . . .'

'Oh, yeah. Me too.' He pointed to his own house. 'Hey, if you're around for a while, we should go for a drink. You know, catch up on the last few years.'

'That'd be nice,' Mina said and her cheeks were off again, the flush spreading to her ears and prickling the skin on her chest. 'Okay, bye,' she said and squeezed through a too-small gap she'd made in the front gate.

'See ya round,' he said and jogged across the road to the Chengs'.

From the front door she watched him do twenty fast push-ups in the driveway. Then he jumped up and jogged to the front porch, looked across the road and waved when he saw her watching. She waved back and ducked inside, out of view. He made her feel sixteen again. She took a deep breath, thought about his skin, his hair, those arms.

When Mina entered the kitchen she found that Elaine had lined the six shopping bags up along the kitchen bench and was methodically unpacking them. Mina peered inside a few of them: some fresh vegetables, things in bulk that could be frozen.

'Pete seems nice,' Mina said as she started unpacking one of the bags: a jar of peanut butter, a box of teabags.

'Leave it,' Elaine said.

Mina pulled out a box of tissues, a jar of instant coffee.

'There's a system,' Elaine said tersely.

Mina held her hands up. 'I was just trying to help.'

'I don't need your help. I can cope perfectly well on my own. I have been coping perfectly well on my own.'

Mina felt the barbs pulling and kneading at her skin. 'Well, you know what? So have I.'

Elaine shut the cupboard door and rested her palm against it. She closed her eyes, took a deep breath. Mina took a breath herself, charged into the silence.

'It's been twelve years – *twelve years, Mum* – and then I get a phone call telling me that you've left the house.'

Elaine opened her eyes, focused them on the bag of mixed lettuce she'd unpacked. It was almost as if she hoped that if she didn't look at Mina, didn't acknowledge her, her daughter would magically disappear.

'One conversation,' Mina pleaded. 'I've come all this way. One conversation is all I want.'

Elaine pulled a cucumber from the shopping bag; Mina could see that her hands were shaking.

'What do I have to do? Just tell me what you want me to do.'

'I can't talk about this now,' Elaine said, so quietly it was almost a whisper. 'I can't.'

'So when? Tell me when! Because I'll wait. I've been waiting twelve fucking years, what's another few?'

'I don't want you to wait,' Elaine said coolly. 'I never asked you to wait.'

Mina turned her back; she didn't want Elaine to see her cry. She walked to her bedroom, slipped on her sneakers, took her phone, her keys, and walked out of the house, out of the gate and into the street. Jack had betrayed her and her mother had abandoned her. The anger bubbled over inside her. She'd made it a block before the first tears came. Once they started, she couldn't stop them, couldn't control them. Big trails of snot dripped from her nose. She wiped them on the hem of her t-shirt but they came again, again. She needed to see someone. Someone who could make her feel better. She texted Kira:

Are you around? Mum and I just had a fight, everything's gone to shit. I don't think I can be alone right now.

Kira's reply came instantly:

No! On set. I'm sorry. Anyone else around? Shelly? I'll call you as soon as I'm done.

Mina thought about Shelly's perfect home, her perfect family, her perfect wine collection. Shelly was a mother, Shelly had been a close friend once upon a time. Maybe she'd have some advice.

At least she'd have wine. What's the worst that could happen? Mina caught her breath and started walking.

THERE WERE CARS parked bumper to bumper on the street outside Shelly's. The gate was unlocked, the front door slightly ajar. Mina heard the drone of voices coming from deep inside the house.

She let herself in. From the open front door, she called a quiet 'hello?' but no one responded. It sounded like a party but Mina couldn't be sure. She crept down the hall. I'll just say hi, she thought, and then I'll leave. Or maybe she should just leave without saying hi. Yes, she should leave. But then where would she go? She couldn't bear to be alone. She couldn't go home. The company, whoever it was, would be a good distraction. She inched down the hall. She heard that Mr Scruff song she hated playing through very good speakers. Just say hi, have a quick drink, and then she'd go.

From the edge of the kitchen, she could see adults milling around outside. They were wearing slacks and shirts, an assortment of bright florals. There was the chaos of what seemed to be a hundred small children running and screaming, sitting and crying, fawning over Phillip, squealing as he licked their faces. Apart from Justin, who stood holding a beer and a pair of giant barbecue tongs, Mina didn't recognise a single person. They all looked old and rich, with their hair and make-up done. Every one of these people owned an iron and actually used it, Mina realised.

'Mina?'

She turned and saw Shelly standing behind her dressed in white capri pants with a long floral top stretched over her big round stomach. She was one of them.

'Hi,' Mina said nervously. 'I'm sorry, I just –' She saw Shelly look her up and down. 'I know.'

'What are you doing here?' Shelly walked past her to the kitchen. Mina hung back like a dog with an electric shock collar on. 'And what are you wearing?'

'I needed to see you,' Mina said.

'Okay.' Shelly looked put out.

'I didn't tell you the other day, but Mum's been leaving the house.' Mina heard the wobble in her voice.

'Mina, that's great.' Shelly smiled, seemed genuinely pleased.

'It is on paper. But the thing is, I don't know why.' Mina could hear the words spilling out of her but she couldn't stop them. 'She's not talking about it and we just had a huge fight and I – I don't know. I just didn't want to be alone. I'm sorry, I'll go.' After how much she talked up her job and Jack the other day, she couldn't bear to mention that too. How together Shelly's life was made hers seem like an even bigger mess.

'No, it's okay.' Shelly spoke to her in a soothing voice, as if she was one of the twins. 'Really, it's okay.'

'I'll go if you want me to,' Mina said, her voice breaking again. 'I just – I'll find somewhere else to go.'

'What about Kira?'

'Working,' Mina said.

'Ah.' Shelly softened a little. 'This is all the senior management from Justin's firm. There are a lot of people to impress.'

'I'll stay in here,' Mina promised. 'I won't talk to anyone.' She crossed her arms, as if that would hide how bad she looked, how bad she felt.

'You don't have to do that,' Shelly said. 'But at least wash your face. You look' – she paused – 'crusty.'

Shelly carried a jug of yellow liquid bobbing with fruit and mint outside. She walked over to the men and topped up a few drinks. She stood next to Justin, laughed at a joke, then leant in and whispered in his ear. He looked over at Mina. One of the men in pastel pink shirts followed Justin's gaze and looked Mina up and down. He raised an eyebrow at Justin, who looked at Shelly – not angry, just nervous. They had a silent argument that concluded with Shelly shrugging and Justin turning his back on her to lift each burger off the grill and flip it over with his giant tongs. Mina noticed the little belly that'd rounded out in front of him, just like his father's.

Mina stepped across the threshold and into the kitchen. From the fridge, she chose a beer, opened it and took it with her to the bathroom. She sat on the toilet and looked at herself in the mirror. Her hair looked slept-on, skew-whiff, and a white crust of dried snot had formed a ring around each of her nostrils. She peered into her bloodshot eyes. She looked terrible. She washed her hands, splashed water on her face, she wet her hair and combed it back into place with her fingers. Remembering what Valerie had done the day she arrived, Mina pinched at the apples of her cheeks, then lathered up a wad of toilet paper with hand soap and mopped at her armpits, across her chest, her stomach. She used the monogrammed hand towel to dry herself, then folded it neatly and put it back on the brass ring. She moisturised her arms, legs and face with hand cream that smelt of mandarin and polished wood. In the warm yellow light of Shelly's third bathroom, she looked not transformed, but almost acceptable. She finished the beer and rammed it into the tiny bin beneath the sink. Jiggling her arms and legs, she shook Elaine out of her mind, Jack out of her body; she was okay, this would be okay. One more drink and then she'd go. She took four deep breaths and opened the bathroom door.

Back in the kitchen, Mina opened the fridge and took another beer that she would pretend was her first. She drank three big sips then skulked at the edge of the deck, trying to stay out of the way. If she didn't talk to anyone, she couldn't say anything stupid. She looked at her phone; all those unread messages and emails sat like landmines.

She watched the party move through its motions. Mason and Jason lay on their backs on the deck. Shelly dropped to her knees next to them, her shoes kicked off to the side. She held her hands in the air and threatened to tickle their bellies, and they squealed with a mix of joy and fear. Nearby, the men around the barbecue were laughing as they watched the sausages sizzle.

Mina's stomach growled. She inched towards the table of hors d'oeuvres. There were little vol-au-vents, homemade sausage rolls, lots of tiny things on mini bits of bread, a giant prawn cocktail – all laid out like a spread from a nineties women's magazine. She took a bit of everything, returned to her post and ate them quickly. She didn't want to be here but she couldn't go home either. She couldn't.

Mina watched the trees blow in the gentle wind, she watched the children play. Phillip sniffed the ground near the barbecue then tried to jump up at the grill. Justin shooed him away and he ran around the garden, past the playing children and their doting mothers, straight to Mina.

'Hello, Phillip,' she said and patted his mop of brown curls. 'You are quite cute, I guess,' she told him as he urgently sniffed her hands and her knees. He licked at her shoes, licked her leg. He nuzzled his head forcefully between her legs, sniffing and licking. She took a step back but he followed. She pushed down on his head, gently at first but then forcefully to get him away from her. He jumped at her, threw her off balance. She grabbed onto the glass door to steady herself. Phillip jumped again, his paws on her thighs. His curly body humped at her, thrusting back and forth. She felt something wet brush against her leg and she screamed, trying to push him off with her one free hand. He pushed back but she had nowhere to go. She could hear people laughing, big meaty man laughs, the shrieks and giggles of women.

'Get off me,' she screamed.

He continued to rut against her leg. She tried to kick him free but her knee made contact with the dog's ribs and he fell sideways, his body cracking on the wooden step. There were a few gasps, and Mina looked up in time to see one of the women covering the eyes of her child. Phillip whimpered, stood, and limped off around the side of the house, his tail between his legs.

'Jesus, Mina.' Justin followed Phillip, carrying his giant barbecue tongs with an oven-gloved hand. 'Phillip, here, boy,' he called.

Mina slipped back inside the glass door and the party slowly came back to life, eyes turning away from her, women turning their backs, whispering. Mina could feel Shelly's eyes burning into her. She needed to leave.

'Well, that was the most interesting thing that's happened all day,' a voice behind her said. Mina turned to see a man of fifty-something sidling up beside her. He was wearing a white Ralph Lauren polo shirt, khaki slacks. The amber glass of his beer bottle sweated beneath his sausage fingers.

'I think Phillip likes me,' Mina said, and he chuckled. They stood side by side and looked out over the party together. Justin re-joined his semi-circle of men by the barbecue. One of the men patted him on the back and they laughed. Justin rolled his eyes.

'Who the hell calls a dog Phillip, anyway?' the man asked.

'Right?' Mina laughed and turned to look at him. What was left of his hair sat just above his ears, circled around the back of his head. Mostly grey with flecks of blonde still hanging on. He had the big, straight teeth of a rich Liberal voter.

'I'm Charles,' he said and held out his hand.

She shook it firmly. 'Mina.'

'Mina,' he repeated. 'That's an interesting name.' He sucked in his thin top lip and let it out with a wet pop.

'I was actually just about to leave.' Mina took one last sip of her beer.

'Please don't leave me here with these people,' he said, his tone mock pleading, but she had a feeling he wasn't joking. Mina turned to take him in properly, the stocky legs, the cygnet ring on his pinkie finger. 'I'm the one they're trying to impress, you see.'

'Oh, you're the boss I wasn't meant to talk to,' Mina said. 'Whoops.'

He laughed and looked her up and down.

'So are you impressed?' she asked. 'Is anyone other than Phillip getting a raise?'

'Ha!' He cackled and slapped his hand on his leg.

Justin heard the laugh and looked around for his boss. He saw him talking to Mina and his eyes widened, blinked with a clean, white panic. Mina met his gaze and moved a little closer to Charles.

'A raise!' He was still laughing. 'I tell you what, you'll get one if you come and work for me.'

Mina screwed up her face. She wondered if he even hired any women, if he too would promote all these men over her. 'I'm okay, thanks,' she said. She could feel his eyes on her, Justin's eyes on her.

'So, Nina,' he said. 'You're not married to one of these chumps' – he pointed at her ringless finger – 'so what are you doing here?'

'That's a good question,' she said. 'I should go.'

'No, please stay,' he begged her. 'Tell me, where are you from?'

'I'm from Melbourne originally but I live in London now. Shelly and I went to uni together.'

'Ah, old London Town,' Charles said in a bad impression of a posh English accent. He laughed too loudly, looked at her, licked his lips. 'That's an expensive place to live. What's a girl like you earn over there?'

'A girl like me earns just shy of eighty thousand pounds,' she said and turned dramatically, walked to the kitchen and helped herself to another beer. At the fridge, she wondered how much more she'd be earning if she'd got that promotion. She wondered if Jack had been earning more than her all along. She opened the beer then returned to Charles's side.

'You're yanking my chain,' he said.

'I wouldn't ever want to, thank you,' she said.

'I'm impressed. So, what's your plan?' He shifted into work mode, into man mode.

'Plan?'

'Your five-year plan, your retirement plan. Investments, property, super.'

'I don't really think about "the future".' Mina made exaggerated quote marks with her fingers.

Charles looked at her with something resembling pity. 'Single girls like you need a plan,' he said. 'With that kind of dosh, you could buy an investment property here. Or come back here, settle down, be comfort—'

There was a sudden thud against the window like a small ball had been kicked at them, a rubber bullet fired. Mina looked down and saw a little bird lying stunned on the deck, its golden-brown chest rising and falling quickly, tiny hooked beak open and huffing in air.

'Oh my God.' Mina handed Charles her beer and stepped to the other side of the glass. She bent down to it. 'Poor little guy,' she said. Its teeny eyes were closed. She stroked its little wing. She wanted to pick it up, fix it, but she didn't know how to without hurting it or scaring it more. She put one hand flat on the ground next to it, prepared the other to shimmy the bird's body onto it, as a whirr of caramel jumped towards her and knocked her off her feet. Phillip crouched down and scooped the bird in his big pink mouth, swallowing it whole before bounding off towards the barbecue. Mina sat for a few seconds in shock, stood up, brushed herself off. She went back inside, took back her beer from Charles and downed the whole thing.

'I take that back,' she said. 'My plan for the future is to not end up like this.' Mina pointed to the garden, only realising too late there was someone else in the room. She turned to see Shelly behind her. 'Shell,' she said.

'I'm sorry if she's bothering you, Charles,' Shelly said, but Charles was staring off into the garden, pretending he wasn't part of this.

'Quite the opposite,' he said, 'but I'm all out of drink.' He held up a half-full bottle. 'Pleasure meeting you, Nina,' he said, and walked outside.

'I think you should go,' Shelly said in a low whisper, thick with hurt.

'I'm sorry – I didn't mean *this* this.' Mina wasn't sure she believed what she was saying. Why had she come? Why had she stayed?

'I don't hear from you for almost a year, you don't even tell me you're home, and then you *need* to see me?'

'I wouldn't have come if I'd known you were entertaining. It's just – I missed you. I missed how much fun we used to have,' Mina said, stretching the truth, too embarrassed to admit she was desperate and alone.

'That was ten years ago,' Shelly said. 'We're not at uni anymore. I have responsibilities.'

'And I don't?' Mina demanded.

'Of course you do, but if you're really responsible for someone, you don't just leave them for seven years,' Shelly said, her voice about to crack.

'I didn't leave you,' Mina groaned. 'I just left. I'm allowed to leave!'

'Not me – your Mum,' Shelly said, one hand holding her bump as though the weight of the conversation was bearing down on her.

Mina felt her stomach wrench.

'You're right,' she said, shaking her head. 'I'm a terrible person. But what was I supposed to do? Stay here for the rest of my life and look after her? Marry my uni boyfriend, have a couple of kids?'

'And what's so bad about that?'

Mina winced as she watched Shelly's body change shape, her spine stiffen.

'I didn't mean . . .' Mina didn't know what she meant.

'I know you think you're better than me. You and Kira, both of you.'

'What? No, I don't think that, I've never thought that,' Mina protested. 'I just –' She stopped. She knew she shouldn't finish that thought, but she couldn't help herself. 'I just thought you wanted more than this.'

'More than what?'

'Shell, you were going to make a difference, make art, inspire people. You were going to *be* something.'

Shelly recoiled as though Mina had plunged a knife straight through her heart.

'I *am* something! I'm a mother, I'm a wife – what's more important than that?' Shelly was whisper-yelling at her now. Mina had never heard Shelly yell at anyone before. 'What about you?' she demanded. 'What about this great screenplay you were going to write, this big life you were going to lead?'

'I write scripts for a living,' Mina said defensively.

'You write ads. You sell stuff to people that they don't want or need. It's not art.'

'My job is more than that,' Mina whispered.

'Is it? What are you *really* doing, Mina?'

Mina couldn't answer her; she didn't know.

'I know that things have been shitty for you since your dad died.' Shelly sounded exasperated, exhausted. 'I know that Melbourne's not London. I know you think I'm *just* a mum, but my life is full. All of this, Justin and the boys – this is paradise to me.'

Mina swallowed. 'I know it is, and I'm so happy for you,' she said. She looked out towards the garden, too embarrassed to meet Shelly's eye, and met twelve pairs of eyes instead.

'Please just go,' Shelly whispered, then she walked back to the party, back to Justin. She put her arm around him. He brushed the hair out of her eye and kissed her cheek, spoke to her softly, sweetly.

Mina's body burnt; shame pulsed just under her skin. She walked down the hall and out the front door, pulling it closed behind her. She leant back and banged her head against it gently, then walked slowly home.

Eleven

'HELLO AGAIN,' BRENDAN CALLED OUT to her as she was about to cross the street. He walked down and met her at the bottom of the driveway. 'We need to stop meeting like this. People will start to talk.' He laughed at his own joke, put his hands in the pockets of his jeans. He was wearing one of those long t-shirts favoured by men south of the river; its scooped neck showed off his smooth chest.

Mina smiled stiffly. She couldn't summon even a sympathy laugh.

'Wow, tough crowd,' he said, shifting his weight from one foot to the other.

'Sorry, I've had a monumentally awful day.' Mina's eyes welled with tears.

'And it's barely two o'clock. I have something that might help.' Brendan pulled a joint from his shirt pocket. Mina made an involuntary *ooh* sound.

'I just got it. Wanna? Mum and Dad are out.'

Mina followed him up the driveway and through the side gate to the Chengs' back garden, its beds budding with the green-spiked stems of spring bulbs about to bloom.

Brendan sat down on the back step, the concrete porch behind him, and fished a lighter out of his pocket. He lit the joint, inhaled deeply once, twice.

Mina felt her phone vibrate again. She looked at the screen: a new message from Jack, one from George. Would it never end? She groaned, put her phone to sleep.

'Everything okay?' Brendan asked as he exhaled a cloud of smoke towards her and handed her the joint.

'It is now.' She sat down next to him and put the joint to her lips. She let the smoke fill her whole body; let it sand down the sharp edges of that day, that week, this life.

They passed it back and forth in silence except for the crackle of burning paper and weed. Mina put her hands behind her, her legs out in front of her.

'That's definitely helping,' she said and let her head drop back. Everything felt broken. Elaine, Jack, now Shelly. Everything smashed to pieces like a dropped vase. But the weed made her feel as if she was on the other side of the road from it all; like she couldn't reach the pieces to stick them back together even if she wanted to.

'This is a fun outfit,' Brendan said, eyeing her too-tight shorts and t-shirt.

'Like I said, terrible day.'

Brendan plucked the joint from her fingers, took the last drag, then stubbed it out in a pot of pansies, buried it deep down under the soil.

'Glad I could help take your mind off things,' he said.

They both watched a dusty cobweb as it swayed lightly in the breeze.

'Do you ever look at other people and wonder how they've got their shit so together?'

'Every day,' Brendan said. He lay back on the concrete. 'I got fired. Don't tell anyone, though. They think I quit.'

'Whoa.' Mina lay down beside him. 'What happened?'

'Long story,' he said evasively. 'What about you? Don't you have a life in London, a boyfriend who misses you?'

'Ha!' Mina said too loudly.

'You know' – he rubbed his face in his hands – 'I always thought Kira would be the one who'd have to move home first. Even Lottie.'

'You did always seem like you had everything figured out,' Mina agreed.

'So did you,' he said.

She looked at him and raised an eyebrow. 'And look at us now.' Mina started laughing, and once she'd started, couldn't stop. Brendan laughed too. They lay there for several minutes, racked with it, gasping for air, until, at last, it subsided. Mina wiped a tear from her cheek.

'Why doesn't anyone ever tell you how hard it is to be an adult?' Brendan asked. He turned on his side to face her, his head propped up on his hand.

'You know that pretty much every book, movie and song that's ever been written is about how hard it is to be an adult, right?'

He frowned. 'I had literally never even thought of that,' he said. 'Even *The Lion King*?'

'Oh my God, Kira was right: you *are* an idiot,' she said, laughing again.

'Hey,' he said in mock offence and reached out as if to hit her, instead letting his hand fall onto her stomach. He moved closer to her, his face looming over hers, huge like the sun.

He bent down towards her and she let his lips touch hers, let his tongue press up against her closed mouth, until panic rose up in her, compelled her to move. She squirmed out from under him.

'Sorry, I need to go home,' she said.

He lay back down on the concrete, looked up at the underside of the porch's corrugated-iron roof.

'Thanks for the distraction.' She stood and brushed herself down.

'No worries,' Brendan said, not looking at her.

'See you round.' And she walked away.

MINA LAY DOWN on her bed. She felt sufficiently stoned, buffered, wrapped up in cotton wool and ready to face whatever awaited her on her phone. She read Jack's messages first.

🎈🎈🎈🎈🎈🎈🎈🎈🎈🎈🎈
Did you see your email?
🎈🎈🎈🎈🎈🎈🎈🎈🎈🎈🎈

Then George's:

Mina, can you give me a call as soon as you get this? Doesn't matter what time.

Opening her work email, she saw that eleven people had responded, congratulating Jack on his new position. *Well desrevedd, mate,* Ian in strategy wrote. Mina imagined his fat fingers hitting all the wrong letters on his keyboard. Lizzie replied, just to her.

WTF???? I'm sorry! I hope you're okay down there. Xxx

She deleted them all. She deleted all of Jack's texts, too, and George's.

She closed her eyes. All the bad things that were happening floated around in the darkness. They looked like Microsoft Word Art, in brightly coloured gradients, arched and squashed at different angles. She thought about Brendan's mouth on her mouth.

She opened a new note on her phone and typed a list of everything that needed fixing. She heard her dad's voice in her ear. 'Nothing's lost forever if you have a plan for how to find it.' She wrote in caps: *THINGS TO FIX,* then:

Mum
Peach
Jack
Shelly

Rising, she walked determinedly down through the house; she felt high enough to tackle number one on the list, to get to the bottom of it once and for all.

Elaine's bedroom door was open, the bathroom door was open, the kitchen and living room were dark. The house felt even emptier when it was empty, Mina thought, her brain crawling as slowly as a traffic jam. The house was empty. It was empty.

She stood over the kitchen sink and splashed water on her face. Was there a way to get un-high? she wondered. Like drinking coffee to sober up? She laughed to herself, an almost-cry.

Where could her mother have gone? Mina checked all the rooms again just in case. But it was happening. It was really happening.

She scrambled around in her room for her keys, her phone, and jogged across the road. She felt like she was moving in slow motion, like there was a low mist rolling across the northern suburbs of Melbourne.

She knocked as hard as she could on the Chengs' front door.

'You back for more already?' Brendan asked when he opened the door.

'She's gone,' Mina said, out of breath but she didn't know why. 'Mum's . . . gone out.'

'Shit,' he said in slow motion panic. 'Where'd she go?' He peered across the street to the house as if he might spot her.

'I don't know,' she said, she whimpered. 'Can you help me look for her?'

'Umm . . .' He seemed to be searching for an excuse.

'Please,' Mina said, her voice cracking. She started to cry, big wet tears.

'Okay,' he said. 'Let me get my keys.' He hurried down the back of the house. Mina paced around the living room, stood by the open door. She noticed that the wedding photo of Brendan and Kylie had been moved to the back of the hall table, covered by a photo of Loretta during her goth phase: thick black eyeliner, a blunt fringe, those big cheeks. Mina stroked it lovingly. Sweet Lottie.

She heard Brendan's footsteps coming back up the hall.

'Did you try calling her?' Brendan locked the front door behind him and they walked down the driveway.

'She doesn't have a mobile phone,' Mina said. 'She's not exactly very mobile.'

Brendan snorted a little laugh and Mina laughed too. 'Fuck,' she said. 'I'm too high for this.' She rested her body against Brendan's big black car.

'Come on,' Brendan said. 'We'll drive around the neighbourhood, see if we can find her.'

'Cemetery,' Mina said, the thought coming to her like a lightning bolt. 'Maybe she's gone to see Dad.' She opened the car door and slid into the passenger seat, buckled her seatbelt; the pressure of it across her chest made her feel better for a second, safe.

From the driver's seat, Brendan reached over and took her hand, inspected her knuckles. One of them had split open when she'd knocked too hard on the front door. Blood had spread slowly through the creases and wrinkles of her skin. It looked like a John Olsen painting, a photo of a Martian landscape. Mina lifted her knuckle to her mouth, sucked the dried blood fresh again.

'I like the sound it makes when it starts,' Brendan said. 'Listen.' And he turned the key in the ignition, closed his eyes as the almost silent engine purred in the driveway.

'Come on.'

'I think I'm too high to drive,' he said and rested his head on his hands against the steering wheel.

'You're not,' she said and took his arm by the sleeve, shaking it. 'Come on!' She was whining now; she barely recognised her own voice. 'Please? It's just up the road – you can do it.'

'Okay.' He put the car in reverse and backed it slowly down the driveway.

'God, everything is fucked,' Mina said. 'I've fucked it all up.'

'Hey,' he said gently. 'This is not your fault. We'll find her.' He put the car in drive and set off too slowly.

She wiped her eyes with back of her hand.

'Thanks,' she said. She felt like a kid, sheepish after a tantrum. Brendan turned left, the car moving at a crawl.

'You're driving like a stoned person – go faster,' Mina said, and Brendan upped his speed by about five kilometres an hour. They approached the roundabout.

'Straight through,' Mina said, and she looked right down Miller Street. 'Wait!' But it was too late: Brendan was driving north. 'I think that's her.' She turned to look over her shoulder and saw a woman the right size, the right shape to be Elaine. Mina realised she hadn't seen her mother in proper daylight in twelve years, hadn't seen her outside the house since the day of the funeral.

'Turn around,' Mina said. 'It's her.'

Brendan performed a slow and messy turn into the path of an oncoming tram. It angrily dinged its bell at them as he turned the wheel, again as he reversed, twice as he moved forward and back and forward again until he got out of the way. He waved at the driver to apologise and the tram shuddered off around the corner. Brendan drove back through the roundabout and slowed again.

'She's with someone,' Brendan said as Elaine turned back towards the house.

'Drive slowly,' Mina ordered.

'Is that . . . ?' Brendan asked, then in a whisper answered his own question: 'That's my dad.'

Mina squinted. He was right. They sat in the car and watched Elaine and Arthur walk away from them. Not too close to each other but still, together. Outside, together.

'Am I really, really high or is this actually happening?'

'It's really happening,' Mina said. 'You don't think . . .' She watched them cross the street and disappear through the Gordons' front gate.

'No, no, no,' Brendan said, shaking his head like a wet dog. 'I don't.' He was angry. He turned into the street and inched the car towards their houses.

'Should we go in there and, you know' – Mina screwed her face up at the prospect – 'confront them?'

'I can't go in there,' Brendan said.

'What if they're . . . ?' she moved her shoulders uneasily, an awkward dance.

'Don't,' he said, his hand in the air to silence her. 'There's no way.'

'I can't go in there either,' Mina said. 'Not like this.'

'Hang at my house until Dad gets home. Then you can make a break for it and we'll pretend none of this ever happened.'

'Very grown up,' Mina said, reluctantly agreeing to the plan.

Brendan parked in the street in front of the Chengs' and the two of them ran up the driveway, through the gate, along the side of the house, in through the back door and down the stairs.

'You're still hanging out down here?' Mina asked as the fluoro light in the basement buzzed and flickered on. The old blue sofa was still against one wall. There was a big TV, that was new, but the Pearl Jam poster he'd put up in the mid-nineties was still there, with a greasy Blu-Tack stain in each corner. It smelt like old weed and something else; something human.

Mina hadn't been down there in years; in high school, she'd spend whole weekends in the basement with Kira when Brendan was away at swim meets. One weekend they stole Arthur's beers from the basement fridge and got drunk; another time they read every letter to *Dolly* Doctor from the twelve magazines they could find, then stole Valerie's hand mirror to take turns looking between their legs. 'Mum's been bugging me to take a look down there for years,' Kira said, hands over her eyes on the other side of the room as Mina examined the layers of skin, the flaps and folds. Entranced by the softness of it, the way everything folded in on itself, the body just layers of things on top of each other.

'It makes me feel young,' Brendan said as he took two beers from the little bar fridge and sat right in the middle of the sofa.

'God, I feel so weird,' Mina said as she shook her body, suddenly aware of every part of it, of the nakedness of skin. She felt the basement air against her arms and legs, her back, her face like she was wading into warm water.

'You are weird,' he said. 'I always liked that about you. Kira's weird little friend.' He took a sip from his beer, watched her body move.

'Thanks.' She raised her eyebrows at him. 'I always thought you hated me.'

'You were just always around,' Brendan said.

'It was so much more fun over here,' she said. 'Can you blame me?' She plonked herself down next to him on the sofa.

'No.' He handed her a beer. She twisted it open and took a long sip.

'You had it so easy at high school,' she said, not looking at him. 'You were smart and good at sport, good-looking and popular. You were just the best at everything.'

'You try being the only son of Chinese parents. I didn't have a choice but to be the best at everything,' he said. 'And what do you mean *were?*'

'Okay, you're still good at sport,' she said and saw his eyes on her, felt the heat of them. 'God, what a day.' Mina exhaled loudly.

'You must be stressed. Come here and I'll give you a massage.' He tapped the bit of sofa between his legs.

Mina put her beer on the side table, felt herself get up and sit down on the floor between Brendan's legs. She felt like she was covered in Vaseline, wrapped in cling wrap. She could smell his jeans. She looked up; in the reflection of the giant TV she looked like a grown woman being birthed. Brendan pulled her hair out of its ponytail, put her hairband around his wrist. His hands dug deep into her hair as he pressed his fingers against her scalp.

She watched herself in the reflection of the TV as he gathered big clumps of her hair between his fingers. She looked like a scarecrow, a water fountain. He started rubbing her scalp in a circular motion. Mina found it neither pleasant nor unpleasant. She silently begged her body to react to him, to wake up, to feel something, anything.

He moved his hands down to the base of her skull and kneaded her muscles, her bones. He used his thumbs and forefinger to work at the knots, to poke first, then to stroke. He kissed the top of her head and she could tell in the reflection of the TV that it was less tender than it was convenient.

'Mmmm,' he said, rubbing his face into the top of her head. 'You like that.' A statement not a question.

She sat still as he moved his hands down from her shoulders and under the collar of her t-shirt. He stroked the tops of her shoulders; his thumbs rubbed up and down the straps of her bra and needled into the skin over her shoulder blades. Then he leant forward and slipped his hands all the way down her chest and inside her bra, a hand cupping each breast, rubbing them up and down. She couldn't fight the feeling of absolute nothingness inside her. Love as a vacuum, a blank slate. She imagined his hands were Jack's hands, were Ben's hands, and nothing moved, nothing twitched. She looked at the curled edge of the poster, imagined they were a *Yield*-era Eddie Vedder's hands. She couldn't tell if she wanted this or just didn't not want it enough. He took a nipple between each thumb and forefinger and pinched like a crab.

'Turn around,' he said and pulled his hands from out of her top. 'On your knees.' She moved forward onto her knees and shuffled around to face him. She was glad she could no longer see her own reflection in the TV. She didn't need a live action replay of this; living it was plenty.

She looked down and saw he'd pulled his penis out of the fly of his jeans already. It was a medium-sized, fat penis. It was not tall and smooth and perfectly straight like Jack's. There was a slept-in smell in the room as though they'd just woken up. She wanted to wake up.

'Put it in your mouth,' he said, as if what was expected of her wasn't clear. 'I want you to suck it.'

She lifted herself up; her body made an L shape. It was not L for longing or lust, she thought as she put the penis in her mouth. She wrapped one hand around it and stroked it from bottom to top and back again. His balls were slumped out like empty plastic bags.

'Oooh yeah,' he said in the way she'd heard men say in porn. 'Suck it,' he said. It did not taste the way Ben or the others had tasted. She moved her head up and down it and he fizzed on her tongue. She let her hand do most of the work until she felt her head being pushed firmly down. He pushed and pushed until the end of him hit the back of her throat. She gagged, and spit dripped from her mouth onto his jeans. He held her there for too long, eventually releasing her so she could push herself up. She gasped for air.

'Yeah, you like that,' he said and he was inside her again. She moved quickly, she wanted it to be over. All she could think about was what was necessary to make it over. He grunted and gargled like he was being choked and she knew it would be soon. She moved her hand quickly, quicker.

'I'm gonna come,' he moaned.

She looked up; his eyes were wide. With one last stroke of her hand she pulled back and let him splatter on his jeans, on the hem of his t-shirt. He dropped his head forward, he was panting.

'Fuck,' he said in a low, deep rumble of a voice. She wiped her mouth with the back of her hand then reached for her beer and drank it all. She sat back, her legs folded under her. She could see he was holding his phone, the video on the screen still active. It took her a second to understand what was on it. A woman lay naked on a table. She was surrounded by men. Some of them were inside her, some of them were pawing at her. There was so much pink, splayed and splayed, on show for all to see. The woman writhed, arching her back, her body possessed, her legs spread and welcoming, her arms reaching. Hands reached and grabbed and slapped and pulled and took and took. Brendan didn't look away from the screen, he just kept watching. Mina looked at his penis: all flopped over. L for limp, L for lifeless. The air in the room was thick with the smell of him; even through the beer he was all she could taste.

'Watch this bit,' he said and he pointed at the screen. 'This is a good bit.'

She looked up just as two of the men entered the woman at the same time. She couldn't tell who was in which part of her. She stood up.

'I'm going to the bathroom,' she said and moved towards the stairs.

'Can you bring me back some toilet paper?' he asked, beer in hand, not taking his eyes off the screen, off the flesh, the entering and exiting, the taking and taking.

Mina walked up the stairs, down the hall, through the living room and straight out the front door. The late-afternoon sun, the fresh air, was sobering. She stood still on the front porch to catch her breath, to let her brain catch up. She looked over the street in time to see Arthur exit the crooked gate and walk towards her. He waved when he saw her there, as if nothing was untoward. Did he know about all that flesh, the grabbing and slapping, did he know the growing list of things she'd fucked up, all that pink, everything turned upside down?

When they met at the bottom of the driveway he gave her a quick, loose hug. 'Your mum told me you were back,' he said. 'How are you?'

'I'm fine, thank you,' she said. 'I was just hanging out with Brendan.' She pointed back to the house.

'Sad business, that,' he said, shaking his head. 'Kylie was really good for him.'

'Were you just with Mum?' Mina asked, watching for his reaction, trying to uncover something, anything.

'Just a quick check-up,' he said and gnashed his teeth dramatically.

'I didn't know dentists did house calls.'

'Only the renegade ones,' he said. 'You should come over for dinner before you head back to London.' He smiled and started heading for the house before she could answer. 'See you soon,' he called, and then he walked up the driveway and into the house.

MINA SAT IN her room with the door closed. Her tiny prison cell. Flashes of the day ran through her head. A highlights package of misery: Shelly, Elaine and Arthur, Brendan, the feeling of it hitting the back of her throat, his hand on her head, the good bit.

She opened her laptop and found the website. She scrolled through the videos and, three pages in, saw one that was close enough. It was a different woman but she moved the same way, writhing like a body being exorcised as they grabbed and pawed and jabbed at her. Two more men approached the woman, her body cast in their shadows. Bodies as darkness, bodies in the shade. Mina closed the window, closed her laptop. She knew then that this wasn't love. That it wasn't something Jack could give her, it wasn't something she wanted from Brendan. Love shouldn't be darkness or shade; love didn't take and take and take. She wondered when things might start to give a little. Who might start to give a little.

She stared at the list on her phone then typed *Me* at the bottom of it. She opened her work email and wrote a new message:

George,

I am writing to inform you of my official resignation as ACD at Peach. In accordance with my notice period, my resignation will be effective on 31 October. This notice period will be taken as personal and annual leave, meaning I will not be returning to the office.

Please note that this is a direct result of recent team changes.

Yours sincerely,
Jasmina

She reread it, pressed send. She deleted 'Job' and 'Jack' from her list.

She opened WhatsApp and typed a message to Shelly:

I'm sorry about today. I'm sorry about not being a good friend over the last few years. I hope you'll let me make it up to you.

Mina stood under the shower. She closed her eyes and let the hot water run over her, wetting her hair. She washed Brendan off her body, Jack too. She put her pyjamas on, wrapped her hair in a towel. She followed the noise of the TV down the hall to the living room, where Elaine sat on the sofa, the screen dancing in front of her. Mina had never thought she'd find it so comforting to know exactly where to find her.

Elaine was watching a game show Mina had never seen before. Mina sank onto the sofa.

'*Vitalogy* was a successful album for which American band?' the host asked.

'Pearl Jam,' Mina said. She lay down with her head in Elaine's lap, the big curl of the towel resting on the sofa's arm. She felt her mother's body loosen beneath her and her hand drop to rest on Mina's shoulder.

Elaine

Twelve

THE GREEN-STRIPED WALLPAPER, THE BLOOD-RED wood, it made Elaine feel glamorous. She sat at the bar, atop a high leather stool, her legs too short to reach the floor, the low heels of her shoes clanking against the metal bar as she swung her feet nervously.

If he comes, it means something, she thought. It means love or at least the promise of it. Please come, she begged silently. Please come. Please come. Please come. Please come.

She stared at the row of taps and read the names of beers she'd never heard of, some she'd seen ads for. The tall, bald bartender pulled a pint for a man standing at the end of the bar; it looked black, thick like gutter water with an off-milk froth. Behind the bar were rows of spirits in bottles. She recognised two of them: the brandy her mum drank a small glass of every Saturday night, two on Christmas Day; the whisky her dad brought out at the end of the dinner when she and Bill had announced their engagement. A glass for him and a glass for Bill.

The barman approached her. Elaine noticed that his eyes were the same green as the wallpaper, the same green as the carpet.

She wondered if they were always that colour or if they'd changed gradually since he started working there. She didn't know if this was even a thing a body could do. She was only just learning the magic her body was capable of. At this point, it felt like anything was possible.

'What'll it be, love?' he asked, an English accent buried deep in there somewhere.

She felt her face flush. 'A small glass of Carlton Draught,' she said, so tentatively it was almost a whisper. It was the beer on a billboard she'd seen from the tram. She knew the suburb; she and Bill had eaten in an Italian restaurant there once.

'A pot of Carlton it is.' The bartender pulled a glass from under the bar, cocked it on an angle and poured the beer.

She looked around the bar. It was a festival of men in there. Men laughing, talking, their voices like far-off traffic. They were familiar men – bankers, insurance men, all too much like Bill. She knew she'd picked the wrong kind of place.

'It's close to your work,' she'd told him. 'Just come for ten minutes.' Just come, she'd begged him. Please come. Please come.

In the twenty-four hours between her asking and her dangling her feet nervously from the high stool, Elaine had rewritten her whole future, a frenzied imagining of a new life. She saw beauty where previously there'd been little – the way the sun shone through the blinds in the morning, fractured light fanned in beams; the colours of the rainbow lorikeets that sang and danced in the gums. Everything seemed more magical to her, more colourful, more real, more true, more alive.

'That'll be a dollar fifty,' the barman said and Elaine found the change in her purse, her hand shaking ever so slightly as she passed it over.

She looked at the amber liquid. It fizzed and bubbled, the sweating glass crowned by a small white head. She took a sip and it tasted bitter but not bad. She took another and she liked it more. She waited. Every time the door opened, her heart would split wider and wider, a volcanic fissure, a rift valley. She'd crane her neck hoping it was him, but each time saw another man in a suit. Not him. Not yet. Soon, though. Soon. The longer she waited, the more time she had to inflate what his coming or not coming would mean. Her heart growing like rising dough.

Please come. Please come.

Her beer was warm, mostly just froth by the time he slipped through the door. He wore a blue jacket, jeans; he'd not yet changed into his work uniform. Her whole body stiffened at the sight of him, his black hair, big eyes. She didn't think she'd ever seen someone so beautiful, so perfect. And he was here for her. He saw her and walked to her with his head down. He seemed to be shrinking himself so as not to be seen, but she saw him. She couldn't believe he'd come.

'Thank you for coming,' Elaine said through a smile as he climbed onto the stool next to her. She couldn't stop her mouth from turning up at the sides, couldn't hold herself back. He came. He came.

'I haven't got long,' Arthur said.

'We don't need long,' Elaine said, and he looked at her finally, right in the eye, and her stomach flipped and danced a whole routine, she was a showgirl doing the cancan, Fred and Ginger in *Swing Time*. He looked past her and around the room. He was stiff and quiet.

'I'm not sure this is a good idea,' he said and lifted a finger to get the bartender's attention. 'Whisky, neat,' he said, and the man set to work, not saying a word. Arthur looked around at the other patrons; she could tell he felt out of place.

She wondered if any of them knew Bill, if she'd see someone she'd met once at a barbecue or a dinner party, made small talk with around a table of nibbles, whose wife she'd helped clean up the way the wives always did. She didn't care if anyone saw her. She didn't care because he came. He was here.

He handed over a five-dollar bill, took his change. A wordless transaction. A measure of whisky, a short fat glass. He took a large gulp of it.

'But you came anyway.' Elaine let herself believe in it, sink into it.

'I did,' he said. 'But my shift's about to start. I have to go.' He finished his drink, slid off the stool.

'I'll walk with you,' Elaine said and followed him out the door onto Spring Street.

There was an afternoon hum. People crowded the streets, peeling off towards trams, trains, pubs. A few tourists stood on the steps of Parliament House and posed for photos, a seagull turned and swooped high in the bright blue sky. Elaine loved the buzz of the city, the ding of the trams, the busy shops. Being there with him made the place seem even more alive, compelled her to notice all of it. He led her west towards Chinatown, down a small street lined with the backs of big office blocks. They walked through the draught of air-conditioning units, machines whirring behind big grates and grilles. Kitchen hands and chefs stood smoking in alleys, grease smeared down their off-white whites. A delivery truck honked its horn.

He forged ahead of her; he wasn't tall but he walked fast, ducking and weaving through the crowd. Elaine broke into a slow run to keep up with him. She shouldered her way through a tight group of men in suits and ties.

'Where's the fire?' one called, and she knew that it smouldered and smoked inside her.

She caught up to him and, with a tug of his hand, pulled him into the laneway between two restaurants. It was lined either side with bags full of rubbish. The skeleton of a fish lay against the wall, sitting upright as if waiting for someone. Its flesh scraped free, its skin gone.

'Why did you come?'

'Because I'm only human,' he said. 'Because sometimes I can't help but wonder if things could end differently.'

'Like a choose-your-own adventure.' Elaine smiled.

Arthur's eyes flicked up to hers.

'What if . . .' She had her back against the wall and he stood close to her but they didn't touch. People walked up and down the streets at either end of the laneway, a rush and colour of life.

He held her gaze for one, two, three seconds, stepped closer to her so the fronts of their bodies almost touched. 'We could just start a whole new chapter?' he said as he took a step away from her.

'A different story altogether.' She followed, took a step towards him. She had to know if his heart beat as hers: if his heart was open to this.

He stepped back again.

'I don't know what you think this is.' He glanced down at her wedding ring, at his own. 'But I have to get back to work.'

'Meet me here tomorrow before your shift,' she begged him.

He looked at her and sighed deeply. 'I don't know.' It was neither a confirmation nor a denial. She'd take it. She'd take whatever tiny part of him he was willing to give.

She watched him walk back down the alley and, once he'd turned the corner, she followed. She wanted to remember the way his arms swung, the tilt of his neck, assign every strand of his hair to memory, the collar of his jacket, the fleshy part of his palms below his thumbs, every eyelash, each step, all of it. He darted left down the alleyway and into the back of the restaurant where she'd first seen him.

FRIDAY NIGHT WEDDING *anniversary dinner instructions*, read the note Bill had left for her that morning. Thorough as ever. *The glass building. The ninth floor. Ask for me at the main reception desk. Susanne (short black hair) will help you.*

She took the lift up to Bill's floor. She wanted to wait for him on the street, to watch the after-work crowd walk past in their business suits, the women in high heels clicking on the footpath as they made their way home for the weekend. She wanted to watch the tourists gaze up at the big buildings in awe, marvelling at the things humans make. But he'd insisted. She wasn't sure if he wanted to show the office off to her or show her off to the office. She would play the game for him if it made him happy (a feeling he seemed to recognise with ease).

On the ninth floor, the lift opened to a big reception desk, a huge bouquet of flowers on each end. Susanne welcomed her with a beaming smile. She was younger and prettier than Elaine had expected.

'Bill told me you were coming,' she said. 'He talks about you all the time. It's nice to finally meet you.'

'Yes, you too,' Elaine said, even though she'd only heard of Susanne that morning. She wondered what else – or who – Bill was hiding. She wanted to meet all the secretaries, all the women there. She wasn't jealous; she liked to imagine him interacting with them, hoped there were secrets between them, jokes they shared. She wanted him to have facets, different sides, stories she didn't know and would never find out.

Susanne picked up the phone, dialled Bill's direct line.

'Mrs Gordon is here.' She waited, giggled, hung up. 'He'll be with you soon.'

Elaine let her eyes wander around the reception area. There was a fish tank along one wall, lit by an eerie blue light. Inside it, weeds swayed slowly in the bubbling water. Tropical fish floated in slow motion, barely swimming. They looked miserable.

'There she is,' Bill said, and Elaine turned and smiled at him. She'd always liked him in a suit. He kissed her cheek and stood next to her in front of the tank.

'Don't you think they look sad?' Elaine said. She put a finger up to the glass.

'Fish have short memories,' he said. 'By the time they realise they're miserable they've forgotten again.' He slipped an arm around her shoulders. 'Let me give you a tour of the office.'

After she'd shaken hands, kissed the cheeks of the men she'd met before, whose houses she'd nosied around when she was meant to be inside getting another bowl of dip or a forgotten salad from the fridge, Bill guided her south through the busy streets.

'There's a place I want you to try,' he said. 'We go there for lunch sometimes. I think you'll like it.'

The Lotus Flower was bustling. In one corner, a group of friends talked loudly, a man in a denim jacket waving his chopsticks in the air as he spoke. There was a young family seated at a round table, a few couples just like them.

Bill ordered them each a drink and they clinked their glasses together.

'Happy anniversary, Lainey,' he said.

'Two years.' She smiled, disbelieving. She was happy. She was sure she was.

'Married for two years and I'm still the happiest man alive,' he said and passed her a menu.

Elaine flicked through the laminated pages. 'There are too many options.' She tried to imagine what some of the dishes would taste like based on their names.

'Do you want me to order for both of us?' Bill asked.

She snapped her menu shut and smiled at him. He made eye contact with the waitress and ordered with confidence. She'd never known anyone who approached things the way Bill did: headfirst. She admired it. She did.

'I'm going to the ladies'.'

Elaine walked down the long hall. There were photos in frames, red lantern decorations. The entrance to the kitchen was to her left. There were smells wafting from it she didn't recognise. She peeked in. It was full of men in white shirts, white pants, barking orders, laughing. Food was tossed up high from big round pans, busy and greasy, hot; a wall of orange and purple flame burst up around one of the pans and she gasped. A man at a long metal bench caught her eye. He was movie-star handsome. He held a huge cleaver and thwacked it down onto the carcass of a roasted duck. She watched his arm come down, his face deep in concentration. Clean hacks right through its greasy skin, its wet meat, its little bones. He looked up at her and something in her body split as though he'd cleaved her too, cut right through her skin, through the wet muscle flushed with blood. She felt it all the way down to her bones. He smiled at her and something bubbled up and over and into a boil. Her face flushed.

'Out of the kitchen, please, miss.' One of the waiters shooed her from the door and back into the hall.

She retreated, but not before taking one last look at him. He looked too, his arm raised above his head ready to strike.

She hurried down the hall to the bathroom, locked the door behind her. She felt a heartbeat between her legs, the blood rushing around her body. She splashed water on her face. What was happening to her? She needed to snap out of it, needed to act as if nothing had happened. She didn't know how she could go back out there knowing what she knew, knowing suddenly, unquestionably, that she wanted to be taken apart piece by piece, dismantled and put together anew. She straightened her skirt, took a deep breath. She tried to empty her head of this new sound that buzzed and chattered, the first words of a conversation between her bones, her fingers, the folds of her skin, all the parts of her that made her feel inside out sometimes.

A spread of food had arrived at the table in her absence: pork in a bright pink sauce; crumbed and fried chicken in a sticky yellow sauce; a big plate of fried rice jewelled with cubes of ham and peas, carrots and those tiny pink prawns.

'Finally,' Bill said, his napkin tucked into the collar of his work shirt, his tie taken off before he left the office and laid neatly across the papers in his brown leather briefcase, his top button undone. Elaine undone. 'I thought I was going to have to eat it all myself.' Bill reached over and squeezed her hand as she sat, two little pumps, then picked up a spoon and served her some rice.

'It's so hot in here,' she said. 'I'm feeling a little flushed.' She fanned herself with her napkin. 'I'm just going to pop outside and get some air.' Her chair scraped against the floor as she pushed it back. 'Start without me,' she said. 'I'll just be a minute.'

She weaved her way out past the family, the young children giggling as they spun their lazy Susan, out through the door of the Lotus Flower and into the warm evening. She ducked into the alley beside the restaurant and stood with her back against the bricks. She breathed in the evening air, thick with the city, the smell of food and bins, heavy somehow and warm. So warm. She closed her eyes on the street, the sounds of voices, cars passing, honking every so often. Life circling and buzzing.

'Are you okay?'

The voice made her jump. She opened her eyes and she saw it was him, his white apron smeared with sauce, a cigarette in his hand.

'I'm okay,' she said, and she smiled.

His Adam's apple bumped around in his throat as he swallowed. 'Just as long as the food's not making you crook.'

His voice was deep; deeper than Bill's. He finished his cigarette. She saw a wedding ring on his finger catch the light as he tossed the butt, still smoking, onto the ground. He moved his body as if to go but she didn't want him to.

'Is this your family's restaurant?' she asked quickly, too quietly, the words a jumble in her head.

He turned back and moved closer to her, stood closer to her, she wondered if he could see her heart beating, pushing the blood around and around, to her skin and back.

'No, just a job while I finish studying,' he said, his eyes on her face, on her shoulders.

'What are you studying?'

'Dentistry,' he said.

'Wow, so you'll be a doctor?' Elaine was impressed by him, by his smooth skin, by his high cheekbones.

'Close enough.' He wet his lips. 'My break's over. I need to get back in there. But it was nice to meet you . . .' He paused.

'Elaine,' she said and she put her hand out.

He shook firmly, his hand lingering on hers or hers on his.

'Arthur,' he said and let go of her hand, looked at her for one more second, then two, before turning and walking back into the restaurant.

Bill was already onto seconds when she got back to the table, his plate a sticky mix of rice and sauce, a few pieces of chicken off to the side, bits of bone or tendon, discarded body parts.

'You feeling alright?' he asked through a mouthful of rice. There was a grain of it stuck in his beard.

'Fine.' She pulled her plate towards her, put her napkin on her lap and smiled at her husband. 'I think I just overheated,' she said and tucked into the plate of cold food.

On the walk back to the station, Bill took her hand, his fingers intertwined with hers in knots like rope. They sat backwards on the train out of the city and Elaine watched the tall buildings get smaller. Two- and three-storey apartment blocks crowded the sides of the tracks, then houses, then bungalows all the way to the end of the line. The pink of dusk turned to the black of night, lights twisting and turning through the glass.

Thirteen

MORNINGS, NOT ALL BUT OFTEN, Elaine would wake early and listen to Bill sleep. He'd sigh and snuffle, sounds she was sure would turn into snores as his hair greyed, as he aged. In the almost-light of dawn, she'd feel a low ache in her stomach, creeping, then lingering. She'd try to single out and identify the feelings, their root cause. Is this happiness? she'd ask herself, wondering if perhaps happiness was just the absence of any real discernible sadness, happiness was a feeling without shape, without edges. Impossible to define. Maybe you just know it when you feel it? But how?

One weekend, six months after they'd met, not long after he'd told her he loved her (late at night in a darkened bedroom; she'd said it back though she didn't know, how did you know? *How did anyone know anything for sure?*), they drove south a little, east along the coast, then inland, the road lined with tall, thin gums. Beyond the trees, small hills, lush green with the winter rain. She was nervous about taking him there. About what he'd think of her after he'd met her parents, if he'd wonder if she was like them, if the two of them would turn out like that too. She worried about what they'd think of him: if they'd disapprove or, worse, not care either way.

'It's so green out here,' Bill said as she directed him down small country roads. 'I don't think I've ever seen this colour green before.'

They slowed and turned left, drove up through the big gate, the stones from the long driveway skidding and thumping and clunking under the car, either side of them the fields dotted with sheep.

'Lainey, are those lambs?' Bill asked. She was not sure she'd ever heard him so excited.

'I'd say they're about two months old,' Elaine said.

'Do you think I'll get to pat one?'

'If you can get one to stay still.' She looked over at him. He was grinning. She smiled too.

He pulled up at the end of the driveway by the huge hedge that formed a right angle around two sides of the cold stone house. Bill killed the engine; it ticked as it cooled.

'I'm so nervous.' She held her hand up to show him it was shaking.

'I'll be on my best behaviour,' he said. He took her hand, brought it up to his mouth. His beard scratched her skin as he kissed it.

'It's not you I'm worried about.' She touched his cheek. 'I apologise in advance.'

They walked around the hedge where a small, stern woman was waiting for them on the verandah, her arms crossed. Elaine greeted her mother with a kiss on the cheek, Bill shook her hand. Inside the dark house, Elaine gave him a tour, dragging him away from the baby photos that sat in dusty frames on dusty shelves to show him the kitchen, the small bathroom they'd all share. In the hall, they divided the contents of the overnight bag: her pyjamas chucked on the bed in her room, his tucked under the pillow in the guest room. Later, when her father came inside for dinner, he hugged Elaine quickly, leaving space between their bodies. He shook Bill's hand and the two men stood awkwardly, talking about insurance for an hour while Elaine and her mother moved silently around each other in the kitchen.

After dinner, Elaine and Bill insisted on cleaning up, a break from conversation that felt like mashing uncooked potato; a timeout while they thought of something, anything, to talk about.

'Is it just me or is it cold as ice in here?' Bill asked. He gave an exaggerated shiver, his arms across his body.

'I warned you,' she whispered. 'Imagine my childhood.' Elaine stacked the last of the dry dishes back into the cupboards.

'How'd you turn out like this?'

'I'm not sure I'm so different from them.' She fought the urge to leave the damp tea towel scrunched up on the bench, to chuck it on the floor, to set fire to it and throw it out the window. Instead, she folded it neatly and put it to dry across the oven's long silver handle. She'd spent twenty years trying to understand the ebb and flow of Beverly's moods, what set her off, what placated her. It wasn't worth ruffling any feathers now. She felt Bill behind her; his hands found her hips.

'You're a wonder,' he whispered and kissed her neck, her shoulder.

She turned to face him. She liked having him there as a buffer, an antidote. I am happy, *I am happy*, she said to herself. She knew a person could convince themselves of almost anything. She kissed him to seal the deal.

ELAINE LAY IN bed and listened to Mina move around in the next room. Having another heartbeat in the house had thrown her off kilter, changed the rhythm of her day. It was as if they were both trying to perform a dance to which neither of them knew the steps.

The house looked different with Mina in it, worse somehow. Elaine noticed the threadbare rug, the dust on the bookshelf, the ring her coffee cup made on her bedside table, as though she was seeing them for the first time. She felt embarrassed about the last seven years. That there were almost no new things, just old things, like sunken ships, still lying where they fell apart. Why did she have to come back? It would've been better for Mina if she'd just stayed away forever, called sometimes. Elaine knew she couldn't fix this.

'I guess you know why I'm here,' Mina had said when she sat down opposite her at the table, fresh off the plane.

'Why don't you tell me?' Elaine suggested, trying to hold everything together, trying not to crack.

'Mum . . .'

Elaine looked at her daughter's face. She hadn't changed much in seven years. She looked tired, her hair was shorter – Elaine wondered when she'd cut it, why – her eyes (still grey, still big) more disappointed now than sad. Elaine had run through some excuses, tried them out in conversations in her head ready for when Mina called, but none of them were convincing, none of them would get past her daughter.

She had built this house on lies; she had to do everything she could to keep it standing.

Elaine thought about hugging Mina, wondered if that would cancel out the questions, stop them before they started. Maybe wipe the slate clean. Elaine only knew that she wanted what was best for her daughter, whatever that was (she was sure it was for Mina to leave, to stay away, to not be burdened by this). She felt tears welling in her somewhere. They sat there for a minute in silence, their hands still touching.

'Are you –' Mina started to ask but Elaine stood.

If she couldn't tell her the truth, the least she could do was feed her.

'You must be hungry,' she said.

In between searching for new cake recipes to try and reserving books on the library website for Valerie to collect, she would search for Mina's name once a week, save links about advertising campaigns she worked on, the 'Creative Women to Watch' article she featured in. Elaine liked to keep an eye on her without Mina knowing she was watching. Without Mina worrying. Still, Elaine didn't realise just how much she'd missed her daughter until she stood there in the kitchen with her, watching her eat her toast, watching the way she tucked her brown hair behind her ear, chewed on her lip when she was nervous, flared her nostrils when she was desperately searching for what to say next.

'Thank you,' Mina said. 'I might have a shower and a lie-down if that's okay.' She handed her plate to Elaine, filled a glass with water and disappeared to the other end of the house.

When Elaine had seen the car slow on the street as she walked back from the pharmacy, Valerie waving at her from the driver's seat, she'd wondered how long it would take for Mina to call. But Mina didn't call. She got on a plane. She flew twenty-four hours, came all the way in on that freeway the radio said was always clogged up with traffic for no reason. She turned her key in the lock, her nervous voice at the front door, a warm hand reaching across the table. Just one of those actions alone would have made Elaine feel bad but all of them compounded, a sequence of events that, once started, couldn't be stopped, hammered the guilt harder down onto Elaine's shoulders.

Elaine waited until Mina had shut her bedroom door before she turned on the TV. She flicked through the channels. The last hour of the morning shows were usually reserved for B-grade celebrities, human interest stories and weather. She watched one of them anyway. Sometimes she'd look the hosts up online afterwards. She liked knowing their secrets. She liked the pictures of them in normal clothes, without their make-up. She often wondered how they kept it so together on-screen when at home everything was falling apart.

After the weather, she flicked through the channels. She had more channels than she knew what to do with since she'd bought this new TV online, had it delivered then let it sit in a box in the corner until Arthur and Valerie could come over to install it. It dwarfed the old TV, and its screen was so flat and thin. She couldn't believe how thin things were getting. Everything portable and light, everything small enough to fit in your pocket. Everyone able to know where everyone else was at all times.

SHE WANTED TO see Arthur; no, she needed to see him. It ate away at her for the two days after she'd met him. A niggling thought, a growing warmth.

The following Monday, Elaine waited for Bill to leave. She called in sick to work (a muffled cough, a croaky throat). She took the train to the city. On the walk from the station she talked herself into it, practiced what she might say: *Hello again.* How she might say it: whispered so softly it was barely audible, mysteriously aloof, confidently, as though she was meant to be there, as though they both were. But as she walked under the big gates to Chinatown, stood across the road from the Lotus Flower, she couldn't even bring herself to go in. She was too nervous, too something. She didn't need to define the feeling. (*This is love.* She knew it was.) In the restaurant across the road, Elaine asked for a table by the window, one with a view of the Lotus Flower, a view of the alley beside it. She wasn't hungry, so she moved her fried rice around the plate with a fork. She dropped it when she saw him, metal clanging against china. He was standing in the alley with another man in a chef's uniform. As they smoked cigarettes, she willed him to look at her, to know she was there, to recognise her and be glad. To be happy. She wanted him to have thought about her all weekend the way she had him. She wanted to look into his eyes again. She remembered the way he'd looked at her in the kitchen, cleaver cocked above his head.

The next day (a chesty cough, a fever now) she forced herself to go into the Lotus Flower. She sat alone at a table for two with a white tablecloth, wooden chopsticks she had no idea how to use in two perfect straight lines in front of her. She asked about the duck she'd seen Arthur preparing and the waitress flicked through the menu in Elaine's hands.

'Duck pancake,' she said. 'It's delicious.'

Elaine ordered one serve – a quarter of the duck, hacked away from the rest of it by a strong arm – and a glass of water. She sat and waited, waited for the courage to walk past the kitchen, waited for her blood to stop pulsing so hard and fast. She'd walk past quickly first, just to get a glimpse of him. Then outside in the alley, he'd shake her hand again, his fingers so sticky the two of them would be stuck together forever.

When her food came, she put the pancakes together in the order the waitress explained. The meal was a combination of flavours she'd never tasted before: sweet and sour, rich. Her mouth tingled. Her whole body tingled.

She left her handbag draped over her chair and walked slowly, nervously back towards the kitchen. She felt calm and ready. She stood at its entrance; it was busy with the rush of lunch, orders being barked, pans sizzling. She peered in quickly. There were seven men all dressed in white. She tried to find him in the chaos, lurking just at the edge of the door so as not to be seen, not yet.

'Bathroom's down the hall.' It was her waitress. She pushed gently past Elaine and stood between her and the kitchen.

'Sorry, I got lost!' Elaine said, pretending to be embarrassed.

In the bathroom, she looked at herself in the mirror. She looked nice in white, she thought. She undid the top button of her shirt and let it flap open a little, showing the pale skin of her chest. She let her hand rest there for a moment, to touch her skin, the skin uncovered by the shirt, the skin under the shirt. She had a feeling that she'd never had before, one she struggled to put her finger on at first: a steeling, a strengthening, but not of muscle: of resolve. She felt powerful. She walked back out of the bathroom, through the two doors, down the hall. At the entrance to the kitchen she caught the attention of a young kitchen hand, no older than sixteen. She beckoned him over. 'Is Arthur working today?' she asked.

'He's doing two till close today, I think,' the kid said. 'Want me to pass on a message?'

'No, thank you,' Elaine said, and the kid shrugged and went back to his station. Elaine looked at her watch; it was almost one.

Out in the warm afternoon, as if by gravitational pull, as if her body had memorised the route she'd studied on the map, she found herself walking north.

The dental school was housed in a drab grey cube. She sat opposite it and waited and watched. A woman walked past her with a tiny dog, their bottoms wiggling the exact same way. She wondered whose behaviour mirrored whose, or if they'd evolved that way together. Was it possible for two people to grow together? She had seen couples become more alike the more time they spent together, but could two people change and grow into something else entirely?

She wondered if Arthur had mannerisms, if he used his hands when he spoke, if he furrowed his brow when he worried, if he had a tick, something he'd do compulsively when nervous. Since she'd first seen him, she had thought about Arthur so often, with such intensity, that it felt as though he was in her. That he was under her skin, living and breathing, walking around inside her. She wondered if people had children because they loved each other so intensely that they wanted their bodies to live and breathe as one. Love: the word hung in the air around her like smoke from a cigarette, like breath you could see on a cold day.

'Excuse me, can you please tell me how to get to –' She paused. 'Oh, hello, it's you.' She smiled at Arthur, her hand resting gently on his arm. 'We met last week,' she said, putting her hand to her chest, ready to reintroduce herself.

'Yes, I remember, nice to see you again,' he said and smiled at her. He remembered her. He was happy to see her. He had wanted to see her again, she was sure of it. Had he thought of her as she had him – in bed at night surrounded by the heavy breath of sleep, on the train, in class? Had he looked at his notes and seen he'd doodled her name? Had he wondered how he'd see her again, how he'd find her?

She'd jumped up when she'd seen him leave the building, head down against the wind that blew through Melbourne's gridded, girded streets. She crossed the road and almost ran after him, trying not to attract attention so she could make her bumping into him seem as natural as possible.

'Arthur, right?' she said as if it had just come to her.

'That's right,' he said. 'Elaine, how funny to bump into you.'

'I was just hoping a stranger could help me find my way and then it's you,' she said. 'Not a stranger at all.'

'Practically a friend,' he said with a smile that hinted at something – but what? Elaine needed to know. 'Where do you need to go?'

'Back to Flinders Street, but I always get confused about which direction I'm going.'

'I'm heading down that way – you can walk with me, if you like.'

'Are you sure?' Elaine said, and she churned and churned, her insides a soft serve machine. 'I don't want to be an inconvenience.'

'Not at all,' he said and he set off, his hands in his pockets.

'You had class today?' Elaine asked. She had a lot of questions (what does the skin on your neck feel like, on your chest, what are the noises your body makes, how do you smell, how do you taste?).

'Yes, we learnt about the thrilling world of fillings,' he said and chuckled to himself. 'Do you work near here?'

'No, I had a meeting up near the hospital,' she lied. She was desperate for him to know she was there for him but too scared to tell him. 'I work at a library.' Elaine had to break into a trot to keep pace with his long stride.

'What's that like?' he asked.

A tram dinged loudly as it trundled south towards the city.

'It's nice to help people find books they'll like. It makes me feel like I'm a travel agent, but instead of other countries I help people visit other lives.'

'Always a return trip, I suppose?'

'Unfortunately,' Elaine said and their eyes met. She smiled. 'What would you do?' Elaine asked. 'Where would you go if you could just go and live another life?'

'What makes you think I'd go anywhere?'

'You're only human,' Elaine said, and Arthur raised an eyebrow at her. He felt known by her, she knew he did.

'How about to Nantucket in the 1850s?'

'If you don't mind smelling of whale guts and all your teeth falling out from scurvy,' Elaine said and their elbows brushed as they walked on. She felt like a flock of birds was taking off inside her.

'Good point. What about Pompeii?' Arthur suggested. 'Seemed like they were having a grand old time of it, until . . .'

'Lava can be a bit of a killjoy,' Elaine said and they both laughed. The air buzzed between them.

'Okay, so what about you? My guess is, middle England, early 1800s.'

'Austen? Too chaste,' Elaine said. 'We'd be expected to marry after a conversation like this.' She looked at him when she said it; he looked back, smiled. 'I'm more of a Lawrence girl.'

'You're making me blush.' Arthur laughed, tugging at the collar of his t-shirt.

The light changed and they crossed into the city proper, walking beside each other in easy silence.

'You're very well read,' Elaine said.

'You're surprised a lowly cook likes to read?'

'I didn't mean that,' she said. 'I'm just impressed.'

'Everyone needs an escape.' Arthur held her gaze for a few seconds (to Elaine it felt like hours).

As they got closer to the intersection of Chinatown, where Arthur would go and work until close, chopping and splitting, breaking things down and down, Elaine summoned all the courage she had.

'What time do you start tomorrow?' she asked when they stopped.

'Two,' he replied.

'I have to get home, but tomorrow you should meet me for a drink before your shift,' she said. 'In the bar at the Windsor? I'll be there at one-fifteen. Come.' And she put her hand lightly on his arm and she stood close and she was sure that he looked at her skin.

'I'll try,' Arthur said, and Elaine couldn't believe her brazenness, she couldn't believe her luck.

Fourteen

SHE COULDN'T KEEP STILL ON the train to Flinders Street. She checked her watch, fixed her hair, undid a button on her shirt, did it back up, undid it again. She tried to catch her reflection in the window but the sun was too bright, the sky was too blue, too big. There was too much of everything.

It had only been a day since he came to the bar. She'd felt every second of every minute, every hour since, as though she were walking up an escalator that would never end. That evening, she and Bill had walked down to the water, ten short minutes past suburban houses, trees leaning slightly away from the sea, growing with the breeze, unable to push back or go another way. They ate fish and chips on the pier, sitting on a bench facing the sea as gulls circled widely, then closer, landing on the wooden planks beneath their feet. They opened their mouths and begged for scraps with hoots and squawks. Bill chucked them chips and laughed as they fought over them. Elaine could feel the air from their wings as they bustled and hollered. Elaine could feel everything.

After a restless sleep, after Bill had left for the office, kissing Elaine's cheek with marmalade-stuck lips, she'd showered, moisturised her arms, her legs, smeared the thick white cream across her stomach and rubbed it in. She dried her hair, pinned it back in a French twist the way her mother had taught her. She let a few loose strands fall down beside her face. She tried on three different outfits, standing in front of the mirror and looking at herself as he would. With every movement, the nervousness lathered and lathered inside her.

The train pulled into Flinders Street and Elaine walked up the stairs and out into the street. She had memorised this walk now, from the station, up busy Swanston Street, through the tall gate to the spot where she'd said she'd be. She looked at her watch. She was fifteen minutes early. Fifteen excruciating minutes in which to play out the scenario of what happens if he comes, of what happens if he doesn't. Fifteen minutes of bargaining, of making promises she wasn't sure she could keep.

At one thirty she stood up straight, she smoothed down her skirt. She undid the top button of her shirt, did it up, unbuttoned it again. With every new person that walked by, her heart bent and stretched, somersaulted, a gymnast on the floor, a figure skater flying through a double axel. Every thirty seconds she looked down at her watch, she looked up, down at her watch again. After ten minutes she loosened her spine, she turned and looked at the bins, stacked with white bags of rubbish, she looked down at herself, at her patterned skirt that sat just above the knee, at her sandals, her freshly painted toenails, at her hands, nails pink to match her toes, the same pink as one of the flowers that repeated itself again and again on the pattern of her skirt. Her cheeks burnt pink too.

What was she doing here in an alley by some bins? She looked at her wedding ring, a thin gold band; she turned it around her finger, she pulled it up over her knuckle. She looked at her hand without it on: the skin where it had sat every second of every day for two years was paler, just slightly, her skin indented. What was marriage but a reminder pressed into skin? Her hand felt naked without the ring, her hand felt free without it. She slipped it back on, looked up to see Arthur standing at the end of the alley watching her.

'You're actually here,' he said, shaking his head in disbelief.

'I told you I would be.'

She walked a bit closer to him but stopped. She wanted him to meet her halfway, wanted to see if he would. He took a few steps closer, stopped.

'I wasn't sure you'd come.' She felt like she was in a game of tug of war, one in which she'd happily let go of the rope and let Arthur win.

'Neither was I,' Arthur said.

'Did you think about it all night?' she asked him. She couldn't move.

'I made a mental list of the reasons why I shouldn't come,' Arthur said.

'And all the reasons why you should?' She stayed where she was. She knew that he would come. 'And "should" won?'

'Dead heat.' He smiled shyly, to himself, not to her.

'Well, that's quite a conundrum.'

'Isn't it?' He took a small step closer. 'But what I don't understand,' he started. Stopped. Their whole interaction a stutter, a murmur, a flutter. 'What do we do now I'm here?'

Elaine smiled. 'We talk,' she said.

'We talk,' he repeated. 'About what?'

'Everything,' Elaine said. 'I want to know everything.'

IT'D BEEN JUST hours since she'd seen him, since they'd talked in the alley. It'd been less than a week since they'd first met, but Elaine's life felt irreversibly changed.

She killed time wandering through the perfume hall of one of the department stores, spraying scents from little glass bottles onto pieces of cardboard. She found one she liked and sprayed it on her wrists, dabbed it on the nape of her neck, on the point of her chest where her shirt fell open. She had never owned perfume before; she wondered if she could start now, if Bill would even notice and, if he did notice, if he'd know what it meant.

She ran her hand along the shelves in the State Library, touched the spines of the old books. She'd always found comfort in the neatly organised shelves, in the system and order of a library. Light streamed in through the big domed ceiling. Elaine sat on one of the wooden chairs at the wooden desks beside students reading thick textbooks, the near-silence punctured by coughs and sniffs. Humans are unable to keep their bodies quiet, Elaine thought, barely able to hear herself think over the noise of her own.

She found the old cinema she and Bill had gone to once. She paid five dollars for the double feature and sat in the dark room while new worlds unfurled before her like flowers budding then blooming.

Finally, the sky darkened, shops shuttered, the Lotus Flower's doors closed. Arthur was one of the last to leave. Elaine watched him from the alley opposite the restaurant. She could make out his figure in the light of the streetlamps, of passing cars, of neon-lit shopfronts. She walked far enough behind him that if he turned, he wouldn't notice her at first. She liked the way he walked, big strides down Swanston Street.

She bought a train ticket at the window, moved through into the concourse. Whenever she lost sight of him for a few seconds, her heart seized. Then she'd spot his jet-black hair, a glimpse of his blue jacket and relax again. The train pulled in and she let the passengers alight, a trickle of them walking out of the train and up the stairs. People on their way out, people on their way home. She stepped into the carriage behind Arthur's. Through the glass door she could see the back of his head bent over the newspaper on his lap, bobbing in and out of sleep.

She didn't take her eyes off the back of his head. She had to be ready to jump off the train when he did, to stay far enough back from him so he didn't see her. The driver announced the station and Arthur stood, steadied himself, walked to the door. When she was sure he wouldn't be able to see her, she did too. She watched him walk along the platform and into the darkness. Elaine followed him for fifteen minutes; she timed it on her watch. She made note of everything, all the street names, so she could look them up later, so she could find her way back. Across St Georges Road and into the back streets, into lightless suburbia. She watched Arthur turn and walk up a driveway: the house two storeys, brown brick with white pillars. He dug around in his pocket for his keys and let himself in the front door. She looked at the street number, ninety-nine. She stood outside and watched – for movement, for signs of life – but the house stayed still, stayed quiet and dark. Elaine wanted to stay too; she wanted to curl up in a ball right there on the footpath and follow him to school the next day. She turned to walk back to the station and noticed the house opposite: a little white cottage, not long built, on the fence a sign: For Sale.

She found her way back to the station. She scanned down the lines of the timetable for the next train to the city. She checked her watch. She'd missed it by ten minutes, the last train of the night. Elaine stood stock-still on the platform. Stupid, she thought. I'm so stupid. She felt the darkness of the suburbs creeping towards her. She tried to stay calm, to think through her options. It was past eleven. Bill would be beside himself with worry. And for what? For what? She sat down on the bench. What did she expect to happen here? That she and Arthur would *be* together? She didn't even know what that meant, only what it looked like in her head, what it felt like to her there on the bench; there, at night in the dark, in every moment she was awake. She wouldn't know how to explain it if she was asked. What was the difference between love and desire, desire and infatuation? She didn't know. How does anyone ever know?

She looked in her purse. She didn't have enough money for a taxi. I could sleep on this bench, she thought. I could just live here at this station, stay here forever. I could knock on the door of Arthur's house, try to explain. Try to pretend it was another coincidence. She couldn't believe she was so stupid. And for what? she asked herself again. What void was she trying to fill? She looked up and saw an orange glow. She shuffled down the bench to get a better look. A payphone. A beacon.

'Elaine?' Bill picked up on the second ring, his voice frantic on the other end.

'Yes, it's me,' she said.

'Where are you? Are you alright? I've been so worried,' he said.

'I'm fine!' she assured him. She didn't want him to hear the worry in her voice. 'I was just in the city and I got on the wrong train.' She gave a light laugh.

'Where are you?' he asked.

'I'm in Thornbury.'

'Thornbury?' She could almost hear him shaking his head. 'How the hell, Lainey?'

'I was tired,' she said, 'and I nodded off. Next thing you know: Thornbury.'

She sat on the train platform under the bright station lights. She tried to imagine the surprise and worry of Bill's evening. What had he thought when he got home and she wasn't there? Maybe he'd assumed she was still at the library, maybe he thought she'd popped to the shops and would be back any minute. How had his mind changed as he waited, where did his thoughts go? Perhaps he'd imagined a plot twist, a different trajectory to their story. Or maybe he'd just assumed she'd come back to him, the way he assumed everything would go according to plan. Every step thought out, no surprises.

When Bill finally arrived, he ran onto the platform calling her name, then held her close to him. He was still in his suit. She sat silently next to him as they drove east first and then south. She was thankful to be in the car with him, she was. She was thankful for him. He was good for her. But with every kilometre they drove she couldn't shake the feeling that she was just getting further and further away from Arthur. Further and further away from something she didn't understand yet but that she knew she couldn't shake. She watched the lights of oncoming cars in the reflection of her husband's glasses, twinkling like stars in the dark.

ELAINE DANCED AROUND Bill in the kitchen, fussing over him, playing the good wife, trying to make amends, trying to cover it up. She made him coffee as he read the newspaper, as he did every morning. She kissed him on the cheek as she delivered it. He put the paper down and looked up at her.

'You really scared me last night,' he said.

'I know,' she cooed at him. 'I'm sorry. I scared myself.'

His toast popped up and she buttered it, lathered it with the marmalade he liked, placed it next to him as he folded up the paper and put it in his briefcase.

'I'd never been to Thornbury before,' she said as she walked him towards the door. 'It was quite nice.'

'It's rough up there,' he said.

'It might be the only place we can afford to buy right now,' she said. 'It might be nice to have something that's just ours.'

'You find me something you're worthy of up there and we can talk about it,' he said and kissed her on the lips quickly and then again, his mouth open on her mouth. She kissed him back, she put her hand on his cheek, he pulled her close. All Elaine wanted was to be full up, to be close.

SHE STARED OUT the train window. This time, in daylight, she could see Merri Creek from the bridge as it passed beneath them, weeping willows dragging their long branches in the brown water.

She watched the different types of people coming and going from the train. She heard different languages. She didn't recognise any of them but she liked how they sounded. She liked how different the north side was from the south, from the bay. An old woman hobbled onto the train with her shopping trolley. She smiled at Elaine, and Elaine felt more at home than she ever had in Frankston, than she ever had on the farm.

She got off at the same stop as the night before and retraced her steps: across the main road, along and up and up. She had always been good at directions, but she knew she was going to struggle to find her way back from this.

The street looked different during the day; the houses a bit more rundown, gardens untended, wild. She peered over the white fence. A small path led to the front door, a pencil pine small but growing in the front garden. A bay window in the front room, the weatherboards white, the trim sage green. The house couldn't have been more than a couple of years old. It felt good to her, right. She wrote down the phone number on the sign in the little notebook she carried in her handbag.

'Are you in the market?'

She turned to see a woman behind her. She was short, beautiful, long black hair snaking in a perfect braid down her back.

'We're thinking about it.' Elaine noticed a bump under the woman's dress, a pregnant stomach just popped. 'Do you live in the area?' Elaine was sure she already knew the answer but prayed to be wrong, prayed to the God she'd ignored all throughout her Catholic schooling.

'I live there.' The woman pointed at the house across the street, the two-storey brick house she'd seen Arthur go into the night before.

'I'm Elaine,' she said. This was the woman Arthur slept beside at night, this was the woman he'd married. She put her hand out to shake the hand that touched Arthur.

'Valerie,' the other woman said. 'The people who live here now aren't very nice,' she whispered. 'But you seem nice. You should move in.'

'Maybe we will.' Elaine laughed, then asked: 'When are you due?'

'August,' Valerie said. 'I hope it's a boy. Arthur wants a girl.'

'Arthur?' Elaine asked innocently.

'My husband – he's a good man,' Valerie said, then with a mischievous smile: 'So stupid sometimes, though.'

'Oh God, aren't they all?' Elaine said, and the two women laughed like old friends.

ON THE TRAIN home, Elaine thought about her encounter with Valerie, about how much she'd liked her, how she'd felt comfortable with her immediately. She started remodelling the new life she'd imagined for herself as if it was still-wet clay – malleable, nothing fired, nothing set in stone. What if this new life had enough room in it for everyone, if each thing she loved could be stacked up, all the parts one on top of each other until she was finally whole?

Back in Frankston, she walked as quickly as she could from the station to their street. It was still warm; it would stay warm well into the evening. And after dinner, she'd agree to a walk along the water where Bill liked to stroll down through the saltbushes and watch the dogs run on the sand, watch the sky change from blue to dark blue to black.

She fumbled for her keys in her bag, dropped them twice on the brick path that curved ever so slightly around to the left, imperfectly piercing the lawn. She unlocked the door, dropped her bag on the table next to the phone and riffled through it. She pulled her notebook out of her bag, dialled the number.

'Hello, I'd like to buy a house you have on the market,' she said confidently.

She gave them the address, and they asked if she'd been to an inspection. She realised she didn't even know that was a thing she was supposed to do. She'd never even dreamt of buying a house, never knew what was possible. She wrote down the time of the open inspection, thanked the real estate agent profusely, pencilled the time on the calendar that was stuck to the fridge with a magnet in the shape of a fairy penguin, bought as a memento during their honeymoon on Phillip Island. She bopped the penguin on the nose with the eraser end of the pencil and paced around the house, waiting for Bill to come home. Waiting to tell him the news.

ON SATURDAY MORNING they drove north, bypassing the city, through suburbs Elaine had never been to. They listened to the radio. Bill tapped his fingers on the steering wheel, whistled along. He seemed excited too, ready for something to happen, ready for change.

They got there early – Bill always insisted on being early – and parked out the front of the house. Bill eyed off the neighbours' houses one by one, quietly assessing their value. Elaine stole glances at the house across the street. What if he walked out his front door and into the street? What if he looked out the window? There was nowhere for Elaine to hide.

A car pulled up behind them, and a man in a suit started unloading 'Open for Inspection' signs. Bill watched him in the rear-view mirror for a few seconds, then climbed out, shook his hand and within a minute they were joking about something. Elaine checked her make-up in the mirror, just in case, then joined them.

'This is my wife, Elaine. She's the one that found the house. Has her heart set on it, don't you, Lainey?'

Elaine shook hands with the agent; his hand was limp and clammy.

'I've just got a good feeling about it,' she said as he handed her a piece of paper with a floor plan on it.

'Might as well give you a head start,' he said and led them in through the front gate. 'This area's going to increase in value steadily over the next decade or so. You're smart to get in early.' He winked at Elaine and turned the key in the front door. She got a glimpse down the dark hall, one long wall, polished floorboards. She couldn't put her finger on why, what it was about this house, this street, Arthur: she just knew she was home.

'It's a perfect home for newlyweds,' the real estate agent said. 'Plenty of room to bring up a little one.'

'Or two,' Bill whispered in her ear.

They stood in the middle of the garden, just a square patch of dirt, and Elaine showed Bill how their future could look. Vegetables down here, sunflowers taller than the fence, a whole world she created just for him, just for her. For them. A make-believe that made her so giddy at times she would forget what was real and what wasn't.

IT'S A GOOD stepping stone,' Bill said as they drove home from signing the papers, both their names on the contract. 'A smart first investment.'

'And it's going to be our home,' Elaine said. She'd learnt a long time ago not to be hurt by the practicality with which Bill approached everything.

'Yes, that too. It'll make a beautiful home.' Bill reached over and put his hand on her knee, leaving it there until he needed to change gear.

They moved in two months later. Six boxes of books, kitchen boxes full of oblong things, Bill's suits on coathangers laid carefully on the back seat of the car, a small suitcase filled with Elaine's dresses and skirts. Bill insisted on helping the removalists, carrying things to the van in the wrong order, mostly getting in the way.

On their first night in the new house, they had dinner on the floor as the low skies of autumn brought the wind, brought the rain. They'd get a proper table soon, one just the right size to fit the space at the end of the hall, eventually a new sofa, curtains. All the things that, on paper, you needed to make a house a home. But that night, there on the floor, as Bill turned the metal key of the cage that surrounded the champagne cork, freed it with his thumb with a pop, Elaine felt the embers of a fire crackle inside her.

They lay in their new bed facing each other in the dark, Bill's hands finding their way to her bare skin. Elaine felt like a body stuck between two things.

'I thought I lost you for a while there,' Bill said in the dark.

'I'm here,' she said, and she climbed on top of him, her face hovering above him while they moved against each other. 'I'm here.'

The next morning she watched Bill leave for work, hovering near the bay window that looked over the street. She saw movement from over the road, Arthur in the driveway taking Valerie somewhere. Valerie waved, Bill waved, Arthur nodded as he opened the car door for his wife and she squeezed herself into the front seat. Bill jogged over to them, swapping his briefcase to his left hand, Elaine watched them talk, shake hands. She felt a particular thrill, a strange sense of triumph, watching them interact with each other. She felt as if she'd miraculously pulled off an impossible plan, as if everything was coming together, as if this was a good and normal thing to do. The right thing to do. I am happy, she thought.

Bill pointed to the house and Arthur looked. Before he got in the car he looked again, staring through the curtains as though he knew she was there and he was watching her too.

'YOU'VE GOT A good view of our house from here,' Valerie said as she peered through the bay window. 'Good for spying.' And she chuckled to herself, holding her stomach like a cartoon of a jolly old man.

She'd stopped in with a welcome gift and Elaine insisted on giving her the tour, intent on making friends, getting closer.

'That's a good baby-making bed,' Valerie said and ran her hand over the smooth wooden frame. 'Artie studies and works so much, we barely had time to make this one.' She stroked her stomach in circles. 'Ooh, feel.' She grabbed Elaine's hand and put it on her stomach. Elaine felt it flutter, felt it move, a tiny person, half him, half Valerie.

The restaurant closed for four days over Easter and Elaine's heart jittered and quivered at the prospect of seeing more of Arthur, at the chance of him seeing her too. Every morning she dressed in a nice dress, she put make-up on, she put her hair up, took it down. Standing before the mirror she looked at herself in profile and from front on, she sucked in her stomach, willed her breasts to be bigger, fuller, wished for her skin to be as beautiful and firm as Valerie's. She envied those willowy arms, that lovely thick hair.

It was just over a week later, on Easter Sunday, when it finally happened. The phone rang and Bill answered, he laughed down the line, Elaine heard the singsong of a woman's voice. He offered to bring something, said they'd see them at half-past twelve.

'Who was that?' Elaine asked, hovering around him as he hung up the phone.

'Valerie,' he said. 'From across the road.' They were invited to lunch.

Elaine joked about finally meeting the elusive Arthur. She said his name as though it had inverted commas around it. Said it as though she didn't believe he was real.

On the doorstep, she tried to imagine what he'd say, what he'd do, how happy he'd be to see her. Would he let on that he knew her? *What a coincidence*, they'd both say. *Fancy that!* Her hands shook. She held one in the other to steady them, to stop herself from crumbling.

Bill rang the doorbell.

Valerie let them in, asked them to take off their shoes before leading them through the front room full of photos, a tiled floor, down a small dark hall. In the kitchen was a big round table set with chopsticks and bowls of sauces. Arthur moved between the chopping board and the stove, his back to them at first while he mixed and tasted. Elaine's heart wrestled itself inside her chest.

'Artie,' Valerie said, 'our guests are here.'

He turned around, throwing a tea towel over his shoulder.

'Nice to see you again, Bill.'

The two men clutched each other's hands firmly in a shake. As they pulled away, Bill held up a sticky hand.

'Sorry, sauce.' Arthur laughed, passing him the tea towel. He turned his attention to Elaine then. 'And you must be Elaine.' He put his hand out to shake hers too, and when her hand touched his she knew this had all been worth it, knew it wasn't in vain. 'Val's told me a lot about you.' He squeezed her hand so tight that for just one second she thought it might pop.

'Yes, me too,' she said meekly. She could feel the heat rising up her chest, creeping up her neck, licking like flames at her throat. 'About you.' She smiled and Arthur smiled, Valerie smiled. Bill watched his wife from the corner of his eye.

'What's for lunch?' Bill asked. 'It smells delicious.'

'Chinese food,' Arthur said.

'When he's not studying to become a very rich dentist, Artie cooks at the Lotus Flower in Chinatown,' Valerie said as she sat, one hand rubbing her back.

'We've eaten there!' Bill said, astonished. 'It's good, that lemon chicken dish you do.' He looked at Elaine. 'That was where we had our anniversary dinner, remember?'

'I remember,' Elaine said, her stomach curling like paper set alight. Did Bill know? Did all of them know? 'How funny!'

She tried to catch Arthur's eye but he'd turned his back to stir a pot on the stove, turned his back to hide how he felt.

'Well, this is nothing like that horse shit food,' Valerie said as she poured small cups of jasmine tea. 'Sit, sit.' She passed a cup to Bill, one to Elaine. 'This is real Chinese food.'

Elaine sipped her tea, hot and bitter. She looked over to where Arthur was opening the fridge and caught his eyes on her. She felt a darkness in them; she wanted to bask in his shadow.

Elaine stayed quiet during the meal. Arthur didn't direct any questions at her, just at Bill, who explained insurance to them like it was the most fascinating thing in the world: more fascinating than the tendon that twitched in Arthur's neck whenever Elaine looked at him, her eyes passing from one man to another while she listened to them talk.

So much had happened lately, Elaine couldn't remember exactly how long it had been since she last saw him, since it had just been the two of them. She'd been busy making a life for them, creating a world in which they were close. She watched him as he explained the food, the Chinese broccoli, how it was hard to get so they'd started growing it themselves. She knew that if she could just get him alone he'd remember how it was. Like lightning sparking in a forest, it was inevitable, it was nature.

'Can I use the bathroom, please?' Elaine asked. She looked at Valerie, in Arthur's direction but not quite at him.

'No, it's just for family,' Valerie said, a stern look on her face.

'Oh, I'm sorry.' Elaine bit her lip; Bill gave her a sideways glance.

'Just kidding.' Valerie laughed. 'The downstairs toilet is broken – use the bathroom upstairs.' She gestured then groaned. 'I'm too fat to move. Artie, you show her.' She was too pregnant for him to argue. He stood and put his napkin on his chair. Elaine followed him, her heart beating so loud she was sure everyone could hear.

At the top of the stairs he stopped so suddenly that she crashed into the back of him. He turned. 'What are you doing here?' His voice a furious whisper.

'I didn't know you lived here until it was too late,' she whispered back softly. She wanted to put her hand on his chest to soothe him, to remind him, but she stood there helplessly, hands by her side.

'I don't believe you.' He took two steps away from her. She didn't follow at first; she just stood and willed him to look at her. He moved to the door of the bathroom and pointed. 'In there.' The bathroom was tiled in beige.

'I didn't know, I swear.' She stood in front of him again. There was barely any air between them, barely anything at all. 'Maybe it's fate,' she said and he let his eyes meet hers.

'I don't believe in fate.' Arthur took a deep breath. 'I'm not sure I believe in coincidences either,' he whispered. 'What do you want from me?'

'I thought because the universe has brought us together' – Elaine saw Arthur's jaw clench as she spoke – 'that perhaps we're meant to be friends. You, me and Valerie, Bill.'

'Valerie can never know about –' He stopped.

'There's nothing to know,' Elaine said quietly. 'We're just two neighbours who met today.'

'She can never know.'

'Never. I promise,' Elaine said. 'So how about it? Friends?' She held her right hand out, willing him to take it, to touch her, to believe her. He looked down at it, a beat, two, then shook, his eyes meeting hers as their palms touched, their fingers touched, as they stood there together, bonded forever.

She listened to his footsteps down the carpeted stairs. She walked away from the bathroom towards the front of the house. The door to the master bedroom was open, in it a queen-sized bed, perfectly made. She ran her hand across their bedspread and the whole bed wobbled. She poked it, pressed it, sat down on it. The mattress was filled with water, the waves vacillating as she moved up and down.

Against the wall, a dresser with photos of parents, of their wedding: Valerie in a red dress, Arthur in a suit, both of them smiling. It made Elaine smile too. She had never really known what it was to want; now she did, it was like a pipe had burst. She couldn't stop it even if she tried. She pulled open a drawer and peered inside, closed it silently. She wanted to touch everything. She felt awake in this house. Everything so close, Arthur so close. She was home. She really was home.

Fifteen

THERE WERE NEW SMELLS IN the house after Mina arrived from London. Elaine wished she knew what kind of detergent she used to wash her clothes, where in the house her washing machine was, what her kitchen looked like. Elaine washed her hair with Mina's shampoo and conditioner, big bottles decanted into little bottles without labels. One had an S written on it in red marker pen. She went to sleep with wet hair and her bedroom smelt of her daughter, of her daughter's life. Mina's toothbrush was hot pink and white, some of the bristles stuck out at odd angles. She could tell this meant Mina was not good at taking care of herself. She added it to the short list of things she knew about her daughter. This woman. This stranger.

When she was sure Mina was out, she went into her room and looked at the strange array of clothes she'd brought with her: nothing that matched, nothing warm, two pairs of sneakers. Elaine assumed she'd packed in a hurry, throwing things into a bag. Was she frantic with worry? Was she at home when she got the call?

How did she get to the airport? Elaine wondered if someone had driven her. Was that a thing people did for each other in London?

Elaine's days had more focus with Mina there; she had a hook upon which to hang things. She became dedicated to finding ways to stay out of the way; to seem to sleep in when Mina woke early, to be out of the bathroom when Mina needed it, to watch TV at a volume that made conversation difficult, to appear busy and light, to dodge questions, avoid detection.

She knew Mina wanted answers but Elaine wasn't sure where to start or if she even knew how far back the story began. Rivers begin with a single drop of water (sometimes they can grow and grow, burst their banks, destroy everything).

When Mina was home and Elaine couldn't avoid her, she wouldn't ask questions, but she'd listen carefully to stories about where she'd been, about who she was, all the while mentally filling in the blanks of the daughter she used to know. There were flashbacks to old names, another life. There was Kira, of course, and Shelly and Ben. Elaine was surprised to hear Mina mention Ben.

HE SHOWED UP in dirty tracksuit pants, old sneakers. He was a mess. Mina had been gone a few weeks already, Elaine wading through the new silence, new freedom of her life.

'I hope you don't mind?' he said and started crying at the front door.

Elaine had made tea while he pulled himself together in the bathroom.

'I can't believe she's really gone,' he said into his mug, his shoulders hunched.

'She's not dead,' Elaine said. 'She's just in London.'

'I know, I know. But why did she leave me?'

'She didn't leave you – she left me.' Elaine said what she'd known for weeks, what she'd suspected for years would happen.

'I just thought that if she loved me enough, she'd stay.' He lay his head down on the table dramatically. 'I should've known she'd go. I regret everything.'

'You should never regret love,' Elaine said to him. 'Even if it turns your life upside down, even if it breaks your heart. It's all we have.'

Ben sat up. 'You must've really loved Mina's dad,' he said and wiped his nose on his sleeve. Elaine wished she could tell him the truth: that there *was* a kind of love between her and Bill, of course there was, but there was something else, there'd always something else: a past or a future, a longing. All she knew was that love, real love, was worth fighting for, pursuing, waiting for.

'Why didn't you go with her?' she asked.

'I have a lot of reasons to stay,' he sniffled.

'You have one pretty good reason to go.'

'Do you think I'm too late?' He started to cry again.

'There's only one person who can answer that.'

'I don't think she wants me to, not really.'

'Sometimes in love we don't know our own minds.' Elaine tapped her hand on his.

They hugged goodbye at the door and she watched him mope down the path to the gate. She doubted she'd ever see him again, doubted he'd go to London for Mina. Elaine knew there were two kinds of people: those who stay and those who leave.

That night, as she lay in bed in her quiet house, she tried to think about her daughter starting her day in London. Where was her office? How did she get to work? Was the Tube dangerous? But her mind returned to Arthur like a yo-yo, just as it always did. To Arthur's breath, Arthur's hands. He hadn't touched her in five years. Not since after Bill died; not since then.

Sixteen

ELAINE STOOD IN THE DOORWAY of Mina's room and watched her slip her feet into a pair of black velvet platforms. She crouched and guided each strap through the gold buckles, wobbling, steadying herself, wobbling again. When both were secure, she stood up straight. Elaine couldn't believe she had a twenty-year-old daughter. She looked so tall, so grown up.

'I don't think they made them that high when I was your age,' Elaine said. She wanted to put her arm out to give Mina something to hang on to. She worried about her ankles. She worried about her skinning her knees, snapping one of the bones in her wrist if she put a hand out to break her fall.

'Not on the farm anyway,' Mina said. She stood side on to the mirror, turned to look at herself from front on, from the other side, from behind.

'Does this look alright?' she asked and turned again, and again.

'You look beautiful,' Elaine said. 'But that skirt is very short.' Elaine worried about that, too.

'This is just the length du jour, Mum, get with the program.' Mina smoothed the fabric of her skirt. She seemed self-conscious. Elaine wished Mina could see herself as she did: her big eyes, her short nose – all her features were perfect because they were hers.

'Back in my day, a skirt that short would've been practically against the law. Especially in your nan's house.'

'Heaven forbid you ever do anything to break the rules,' Mina said, smearing foundation all over her face with a sponge, dabbing and smoothing it under her eyes, down past her jawline, a new skin. Elaine liked watching her transform, felt envious that she hadn't yet signed up to anything, that she could become anyone she wanted.

'Remind me where you're going tonight?' Elaine said as Mina pencilled black kohl across the top of her lids then pulled her eye down and traced the inside too, across her tear duct. One, then the other.

'Out,' Mina said and tightened her lips, smearing bright red lipstick across her bottom lip, then across her top. 'With Kira and maybe Shelly.' She smacked her lips and rubbed them together. Elaine pulled a tissue from the box on the dresser and handed it to her. Mina pressed her mouth against it and passed it back into Elaine's outstretched hand.

'And you'll be home when?'

'Later!' She smoothed her skirt again, leant towards her reflection in the mirror to examine her eye make-up. 'I'll call if I'm staying at someone's house. You don't need to worry.'

Mina shimmied past her. Elaine followed her as she clomped her way down the hall.

'Who's gonna win?' Mina asked as she plonked down on the arm of the sofa next to Bill.

'Couple of worrying ducks in the middle there but I think we've got it in the bag.' Bill didn't take his eyes off the screen.

'Yay,' Mina said sarcastically and Bill grabbed her, playfully threatening to knock her off her seat. Mina laughed and whacked his arm. 'I'm going now.'

'Take some money.' He bent forward and fished his wallet from his back pocket, pulled out a twenty-dollar note.

'Dad, I don't need your money.' She tried to wave it away.

'Just take it,' he said, rolling it up and forcing it into her balled-up fist.

'Fine.' She put her arm around his shoulders and kissed the top of his head. 'Thank you.'

'Be good,' he said and waved her off, eyes on the cricket.

'Always,' she said. 'Bye, Mum.' And she waved the twenty-dollar bill like a flag of surrender as she passed Elaine in the doorway.

Elaine waited until she heard the door slam and the hinge of the front gate squeak before she moved into Mina's spot on the arm of the sofa. Bill looked up from the screen and put one arm around her waist, pulling her down onto his lap before she toppled over onto her side, onto the sofa.

'Stop it,' she groaned and pulled herself up, righted her skirt down over her shins.

Bill laughed, his eyes focusing back on the screen. 'Lainey, do you ever wish we'd had another one?' he asked, and she felt her heart twist like a wrung-out cloth.

'We'd have had to move,' she said. The thought had crossed her mind, of course it had. The fullness she felt when she was pregnant with Mina, the distraction of having a baby and then a toddler, it sustained her, it calmed her. But as Mina got older, when she stopped needing Elaine's body to stay alive, when she went headstrong into kindergarten, then school, Elaine felt it all come back: the ache in her guts, the ants under her skin, the constant hoping, the endless wanting.

'You and Valerie still would've been friends if we'd moved a couple of streets away.' Bill glanced over at her, smiled and shook his head.

'I think the one we got is more than enough,' Elaine said.

'Yeah, me too,' he said and, without missing a beat, 'What's for dinner?'

'How about that pasta bake you like?' Elaine said.

'The creamy one?' Bill licked his lips and rubbed his hands together.

'You'll have to pop to the shop and get some milk, though.'

'Can it wait until the match is over?'

'Only if you don't mind eating at ten o'clock.'

'Fine!' He stood up. 'But if I miss a good wicket, I'll never forgive you.'

'Thank you,' Elaine called after him. 'And get some cheese and some bread. And chocolate!' she yelled just as the door slammed behind him.

She turned the volume down on the TV. In the kitchen she started grating the last of the cheese. She heard the front gate creak; what had he left behind? He was always leaving things behind. She walked to the front door, opened it with her lips already curled into a smile.

Arthur stood on the front step. He was holding a book sheepishly in both hands. 'I just wanted to drop this book off for you – thought you might like it.'

Elaine held the door open for him to pass and he put the book on the hall table, next to some keys, next to a Woolies catalogue, some other junk.

'Bill's gone out,' Elaine said, but she knew he knew. She knew he'd heard the car start, watched Bill go. She'd known something was happening, that something had changed. At Sunday lunch a few weeks ago, he'd passed her a plate and his fingers had lingered on hers just a second longer than they needed to. A few times when she'd been watching him leave for work through the front window – now Mina's room but still the best view in the house – he'd looked too, as if he knew she was still there, still watching, still waiting after all these years. There was something new (something old) in his eyes. She was sure of it.

'I know,' he said.

They stood, the rumble of the crowd growing as a cricket ball was whacked for six.

'He'll be back soon,' she said, turning to lead him down the hall.

'Okay.'

Elaine couldn't remember the last time the two of them had been alone. There were the scenarios she'd played out in her head: the one where he would knock; the one where he wouldn't, he'd just let himself in, unable to stop. Some she played out all the way to an end, finishing as she did, abating the force of the ache, the vibrations inside of her. Sometimes she thought about it so much, so hard, that the space between what had happened and hadn't happened grew too small to discern. But this time, this was real.

'I saw the girls all dressed up,' he said in the living room. He sat right on the edge of the sofa as if he might need to get up suddenly at any point.

'They're so grown up.' Elaine sat beside him, a little too close, but he didn't move.

'Kira's talking about moving into a share house soon, Lottie will start uni in a few weeks.'

'Soon it'll just be us,' Elaine said.

He looked at her then, sat back on the sofa, held her gaze.

'I think about that sometimes,' Arthur said. 'Wonder if –' He stopped talking, looked down. She wished he'd never stopped talking.

'If it could ever have been just us?' she said, and their eyes met again. He put his arm out along the back of the sofa, his hand almost touching her shoulder. 'We could've blown everything up,' Elaine said. She felt her heartbeat in her limbs, in her stomach, between her legs. It felt loud enough to shake the walls, make the whole house come tumbling down. She willed it, just for a second, she willed it all to fall.

She waited for him to speak. She waited, as she had always done. And here he was. Arthur had come. Older, but the same bones in the same skin, the same man she had watched become a father, run a successful practice, be a good husband, a good friend, the same man she had always loved with a ferocity she couldn't understand, with a depth that was inexplicable.

'Maybe it's better this way,' he said.

'Maybe we'll never know.'

'Maybe.'

Elaine felt herself laugh from sheer frustration, from resignation, from the realisation that life was nothing more than maybes.

He dropped his hand onto her shoulder, let his fingers rest on the top of her arm. Elaine put her hand on his. They sat like that for a few seconds, their skin touching, their fingers on each other's fingers, their lives intertwined.

'I should go.' He pulled his hand back.

'Maybe you should,' she said, and he stood quickly, looked down at her. He didn't smile, didn't speak, he just looked at her the way he had that first day in the kitchen, in the alley, across dinner tables, rooms, cars, streets. That look. The weight it held, the distance she let it carry her.

Arthur walked out of the living room, up the hall. Elaine stayed seated, didn't follow him at first, but once the door was closed she rushed to Mina's room and stood in the dark. She watched him cross the street and turn back to look at the house. He lifted his hand in a solemn, still wave and her stomach curled. He turned around and walked up the sloped driveway, up the two steps to the porch, and went in the front door.

She wandered slowly back through the house. In the kitchen, she chopped a few vegetables and then stood, backed up into a corner, wedged into the part where the benchtops met. She replayed the whole thing in her head again and again, committed it to memory, laying down take after take as though recording a TV show. Something about it bugged her. Something niggled. She felt unsatisfied as one does at the end of a book one loved. She wanted more; she always wanted more. She wanted to rewrite the story. Change the ending. She stood in the darkening room and thought about how she could bury every maybe in cement, firm it up, tie it down.

THE SOUND OF the phone ringing made her jump. She had no idea how long she'd been standing there but the room was dark. In the few steps to the phone, she imagined everyone it could be. She thought it might be Arthur. Maybe Mina to say she was staying at Shelly's. Maybe the car had broken down and Bill was calling to let her know. But the voice on the phone was a woman.

'Yes, I'm his wife,' she said.

'Mrs Gordon, I'm calling from the Royal Melbourne Hospital,' the woman said, and she still thought Arthur. Had he fallen? She thought Mina. Bill always came third to her. Last.

'Your husband collapsed, Mrs Gordon. We need you to come to the hospital immediately.'

'Oh,' Elaine said. 'Okay.' And she hung up. She didn't think to ask if he was alright, still breathing, alive. She scooped the chopped vegetables into a bowl, the cheese too, and put them in the fridge. She found a pair of shoes. She fingered the copy of *The Line of Beauty* Arthur had left on the hall table, ran her thumb over the pages, collected her keys and walked across the street.

'GO PARK,' VALERIE said to Arthur as they pulled up at emergency. She'd barked orders at him as they drove south, their journey at the mercy of trams that stopped and started like a heart. What if she knows? Elaine's body tightened at the thought of it, of Valerie watching the way she and Arthur moved around each other, feeling the shock of the sparks when they touched. Mina too. If they all talked about it behind their backs, waiting for the opportunity to accost them, to reveal a wall of evidence and suspicions, all strings leading to Elaine.

Elaine's door opened and she felt her body being propelled from the car towards the sliding glass doors of the emergency room. It was Valerie's hand on her back helping her through. It was Valerie who marched up to the front desk.

'Bill Gordon,' Valerie said. 'William Gordon.' She increased the volume of her voice, its sharpness. 'William Gordon.' She slapped her hand down on the desk. The woman typed loudly, hollow clicks of the keyboard. A charm bracelet tinkled on her wrist, the hat against the shoe, a dog. Monopoly pieces.

'And are you family?' the woman asked. She had an accent, something from one of the cold European countries, one that had known tragedy.

'Yes, she's his wife. Elaine. Elaine Gordon. Come on!' she said, holding Elaine's elbow with one hand as if that was all it would take to stop her from falling apart, a finger over a hole to stop it all pouring out. The woman read something on the screen that softened her face, her voice.

'Wait over there.' She pointed at some plastic chairs. 'Someone will be with you soon.'

Elaine watched her make a phone call. She spoke softly as if telling a secret, she nodded a few times, hung up the phone. She looked at Elaine for a few seconds before turning back to her screen.

Arthur came in from the car park and sat on a hard plastic chair next to Valerie. She whispered to him; Elaine couldn't hear what she said, only the tone of it, deliberate, a person trying to stay calm in a crisis. She watched the soundless television in the corner of the room, a ticker tape of news: the aftermath of the tsunami, Prince Charles to marry Camilla. Love that waited, love that endured.

All around her, people were coming and going, legs were jittering, eyes drooped and closed with worry, with exhaustion. She saw a woman in a navy jacket and matching skirt approach the woman behind the desk. The receptionist nodded towards Elaine and the woman looked over at them, turned back, reached over and took a pen from beside the computer. As she walked towards them, Elaine heard her black loafers squeaking on the polished floor.

'Elaine Gordon?' she asked. Her voice was high and quiet, her hair pulled back in a too-tight ponytail that made her look constantly surprised.

Elaine nodded.

'I'm Lisa Abbott, I work here at the hospital,' she said. 'If you'd like to come with me?'

'Where's Bill?' Valerie chimed in. 'We want to see Bill Gordon.' She said his name slowly, pronouncing every letter

'Are you family?' the woman asked Valerie.

'Yes, we're family.' She prodded Elaine. 'Tell her.'

'Yes,' Elaine said.

'Okay, please follow me.' Lisa led them down a hall, her shoes squeaking with every step. She stopped at the door of a small room: a rectangular, windowless office with three vinyl chairs. Elaine sat down first, Valerie next. Arthur stood behind them.

'Elaine,' Lisa said, 'your husband collapsed in the supermarket and was unresponsive to CPR administered at the scene.'

Valerie gasped and put her hand over her mouth.

'The ambulance brought him here and he was pronounced dead at' – she looked down and read from her notes – 'seven forty-six this evening.' She closed the folder. 'I'm very sorry.'

Elaine looked at her mouth when she talked, at the gaps between her tiny teeth, a smear of pink lipstick across the front of them. Elaine felt Valerie's arms around her. She knew she was supposed to do something, to react, but she didn't know what or how. She couldn't do anything; she barely even remembered how to breathe. She sat very still while the information crept down through her body, warming it like whisky. When it hit her stomach, she retched, vomiting pieces of the dinner she'd snacked on down her front, onto Valerie's arm. Lisa leant back in her chair, picked up the phone. 'Can I get someone to two twenty-three to clean up?' she said quietly.

Arthur held his sleeve up to his nose; Elaine saw that his face was wet. She looked at Valerie, who just kept saying, 'There, there, it's okay,' and patting Elaine's shoulder through her tears.

An orderly knocked at the door and Lisa waved him in. He cleaned the floor around Elaine's feet, wiped some vomit off the leg of the chair. Lisa left and came back with a pair of scrubs for Elaine to change into, a plastic bag for her to put her clothes in.

Valerie shoved everyone outside and closed the door. She helped Elaine step out of her skirt, out of her top. She slid the pink scrubs over her arms, steadied her while she stepped in one leg at a time.

'I'm going to call Kira, get Mina down here,' Valerie said.

'Mina.' Elaine repeated the name as if she'd forgotten her daughter existed. She wobbled against Valerie's tiny frame, collapsed onto her, the scrubs around her ankles.

'Artie,' Valerie called. 'Artie.'

He appeared at the door and Valerie transferred Elaine's body onto him, leant down and pulled the scrubs up around her waist.

'Look after her a minute,' she said, and she picked up her handbag and ducked out of the room. Elaine pressed her body against his; she felt weightless against him for the second time that night.

'This is our fault,' she heard herself whisper into his neck. 'We did this. We did this.'

He held her close to him, he planted a hand firmly on the back of her head and stood quietly while she wept.

'MUM,' MINA RUSHED in the room and threw her arms around Elaine, who had stopped crying and was sitting, staring at the wilted peace lily in the corner. 'What happened?' She looked down at her. 'Why are you dressed like that? Are you okay?'

'I'm fine – it's your dad,' Elaine said, but she couldn't say the rest, she couldn't get the words out. The sobs started again, rolling in like waves.

'What?' Mina said.

The room was quiet for a beat, two, three.

Mina stepped back from Elaine. 'What about Dad?'

'Your dad's gone,' Valerie said from the door, her arm around Kira's shoulders. Like Mina, Kira was wearing a short skirt, a low-cut top; Valerie had tracked them down at a party somehow. 'He died. At the supermarket, he fell and he died.'

'What?' Mina was incredulous, in shock, her voice raised. 'Died of what? You can't just fall over and die in the supermarket.'

Elaine looked up at Valerie; she realised she'd forgotten to ask.

A tear ran down each of Mina's cheeks, then another and another. 'You can't just die in the supermarket.'

Lisa appeared at the door behind Valerie. She squeezed past them. The lipstick on her lips was pinker than before, reapplied, her front teeth wiped clean. She was holding a plastic bag of Bill's things – a watch, a wallet.

'You must be Jasmina,' Lisa said. She repeated her textbook apologies, her voice still calm, still small and high. She reminded Elaine of a sparrow.

'I don't understand.' Mina sat next to Elaine.

'He collapsed in the supermarket, an ambulance was called, someone attempted CPR at the scene. This is all we know until we perform a post-mortem. I'm sorry I can't give you any more information.'

'But in the supermarket?' Mina kept saying.

Elaine imagined the scene: Bill sprawled out in the dairy aisle, someone bent over him, their arms pumping, pressing down on his chest over and over. She pictured a woman in her forties wearing a tracksuit. Or someone younger, Kira's height but Mina's shape. She could've been going to a party too, young and going to a party, old and going to a party, brunette, a redhead. Elaine wondered if her arms ached from the exertion. If her hands were sore from pushing down on Bill's chest, if every time she moved for the next few days she'd remember. Bodies remember, Elaine thought, and hers shivered, hers sweated, hers longed.

She looked up and saw Valerie and Arthur hugging Kira as she cried. Her family had always felt like a fraction of the Chengs, even more so now they'd been divided by a third, one side of a triangle lopped off, unsteady.

'How do we know it's definitely him?' Mina asked, with a hint of hope in her voice.

Elaine looked up at Lisa, looked at Valerie.

'He had his driver's licence on him.' Lisa must have been asked this question a hundred times before. 'But we will need next of kin to formally identify him.' She looked down at Elaine.

Elaine heard a noise leave her mouth, a whale song, a mourning cry. She knew that if she saw him, even though he couldn't know anything anymore, couldn't have thoughts, couldn't see or hear, if she saw him, he would know what she'd done. He'd know everything.

He could never know, she thought. It would kill him. She struggled to breathe in, struggled to get the breath out again.

'It won't be for a couple of days,' Lisa said, as if that made it better.

'It's okay, Mum, I can do it.' Mina stood.

Elaine reached up and held her hand, shook her head, trying to tell her not to.

'It's okay, Mum,' Mina said. 'I'll take care of it.'

Seventeen

THERE WERE SO MANY FORMS. Arthur and Valerie pored over them, asking questions so Elaine didn't have to. She signed where Valerie pointed, let Valerie hold her by the elbow and lead her back out through the maze of hospital corridors to the waiting room where Kira and Mina sat silently holding hands. Arthur brought the car around to the automatic doors and sat in the driver's seat while Valerie arranged the passengers. They drove home, up through the dark, empty streets, everyone quiet. It felt like the city was deserted, like everyone was gone, not just Bill.

'This will help you sleep.' Valerie sat beside her on Brendan's single bed and held out a glass of water and a pill. Elaine took it without question. When she slept she dreamt of the farm, of big wide skies, the smell of sheep, a childhood with a distant fence. It came to her in bursts: the shearing shed, early-morning walks to the big tall tree, long dead but still standing. Her mother closed up tight like a fist when she was around, when her dad was around. Plates put on the table with a bang, doors slammed, words hissed rather than said. One memory came back: a sound so foreign she followed it, so new she needed to know what it was. Through the hedge, she saw her mother talking to the farm overseer. Just talking, not standing too close, not touching, but talking and laughing, their bodies shrouded in what Elaine knew instantly, even through the spindled fingers of the conifer, even at fifteen, to be love. Love that unfurled and softened. Love worth sneaking around for. Love worth waiting for.

Elaine tossed and turned, time curling and fading like the edges of the Pamela Anderson poster she saw whenever she opened her eyes, still Blu-Tacked to the outside of Brendan's wardrobe door. In her waking hours, she felt as though someone had rolled back her skin, scooped out her guts and sewn her back together. The needing, the wanting, the hollowness raged inside her. She longed for closeness, she longed for a hand on hers; whose, she wasn't sure. She willed herself to sleep. In sleep there was darkness in which it was impossible to discern one shape from another, one feeling from another.

WHEN ELAINE WOKE, it took her a few seconds to realise that she was in her own bed, that Bill was gone. Her shoulders stiffened at the sound of her daughter moving around the house. She slid back down into the bed, into the sheets, damp with her sweat, due to be changed, but by whom? Elaine didn't think she had it in her to hold her arms up long enough to let the inside-out cover fall down over her head, to find the corners, to stand there like a kid at Halloween. She couldn't ask Mina, wouldn't. And Valerie, dear Valerie, had already done so much.

There were still hints of Bill in that bed she wasn't quite ready to wash away. Once, twice, three times a day, Elaine found herself lying on her stomach, facedown on the fitted sheet that kept breaking free at the corners, encroaching ever closer to her like a storm cloud, a stream of lava. She'd slide her hand under his pillow. Her hot fingers would find the shorts he sleeps in – slept in, slept in, soon she'd get used to thinking about everything to do with Bill in the past tense – still folded neatly. She'd rest her hand on top of them, sometimes burrow inside a leg. The coolness under there let her think for a minute, let her start to pick at the string, to loosen and untangle the knot inside her.

For most of her life, Elaine had felt like an escaped helium balloon in a shopping centre, bumping up against things, trying to climb higher and higher, its escape, hers, thwarted by a high ceiling against which she'd bang and bang then slowly deflate. She thought back to her childhood on the farm with two parents who weren't shy about how little they tolerated each other, the seven years of Catholic boarding school she spent with nuns whose three true loves were the Father, the Son and the deprivation of joy. Elaine could hardly be blamed for looking for love, searching for it in any shape or form. And then she met Bill, a man who had always grounded her. His logic, his pragmatism, his calmness. He'd pull her back down to earth, hold on tight.

Mina's footsteps stopped outside her door. Elaine pulled the sheet over her head as the door opened. Mina moved something on the bedside table, put something down. There'd been so few noises in the house these last few days that Elaine recognised them all. She heard Mina retreat, take a few steps towards the door, pause as if to say something, as if she was about to rip the sheet off Elaine's body, scream at her to move, to get up, to deal with this. But she didn't. She closed the bedroom door behind her, the front door too. Elaine heard the squeak of the gate, wood hitting wood as it shut.

She pulled the sheet down, sat up and looked at the bedside table. Mina had moved a plate of cold stiff toast to make room for a jar of white daisies, a few of them missing petals as though someone had started a game of He Loves Me Not but abandoned it halfway through, too scared to find out the answer.

There was a card, too. There'd been so many cards: purple with butterflies, cream with lilies, pink with lilies, some doves. Who decided that lilies, butterflies and doves were appropriate symbols for everything they'd lost? Elaine tried to conjure an image that could portray what this felt like: the splatter of a nebula in a faraway sky, a sinkhole, a landslide. Something big, something uncontainable.

The card on the bedside table was different. Elaine picked it up. It was hand-painted, and the scene glowed golden like the low sun in autumn. The dead trunk of a tree, its bare branches like the arms of a skeleton, cast a long shadow on the cooked grass. The little dots of sheep everywhere, the big green hedge, the edge of the house just visible. It was a view of the farm from one of the dirt roads out the back of Nilma. Elaine could almost smell it, it felt so real, so close. She knew who it was from before she even opened the card. He was still there after all this time, still waiting. She put the card next to the daisies. She slid her legs out from under the sheet, put her feet on the floor, stood and walked down the hall to the phone. She dialled Jeff's number.

Eighteen

THE FUNERAL CAME TOO SOON. Elaine couldn't believe it'd been eight days since Arthur had come, eight days since Bill had gone. She would've liked another month, a year even, to pull herself together. She had never felt tiredness like this before, even in that first year after Mina was born when she was up and down four, five times a night. This was different: this had no purpose, no end in sight.

She didn't know how she was going to face everyone at the funeral, or if people would come at all. She remembered her mum when her dad died. She'd organised everything, made lists, made calls, made sandwiches, scones even. Where had she found the strength to measure out the flour, to set a timer, to be precise about anything, then scoop jam into little bowls, whip cream? Elaine felt sad she hadn't inherited Beverly's fortitude, but at the same time she was glad to be without her mother's temper, her inability to control it.

Her legs stuck to the seat of the car on the short drive to the funeral home, to the red-brick chapel she'd passed a hundred times, a thousand even, but never really noticed, never thought would become a flag in the ground, a new monument in her life. There were so many people inside. Everyone dressed in black despite the weather, despite that heavy heat that made them sweat through their clothes within seconds. They all shifted uncomfortably in their seats. A few people fanned themselves with the booklets they'd been given. Elaine realised she was holding one but had no idea who'd put it in her hands. There was a photo of Bill on the front. One from a long weekend the three of them had spent down the peninsula more than a decade ago; before the grey crept into his beard, appeared over his ears, like a dusting of snow across the top of his head. She remembered Mina running into the water, eight or nine years old, all elbows and knees, not baulking at the cold, not shying away from the size of the waves. She had never been scared of anything. Elaine sat on the beach and watched Bill follow her into the blue. The two of them racing out past the break, Mina putting her arms around his shoulders while they treaded water, shrieking with laughter as she dunked him under then raced back to shore.

Elaine looked at her daughter there in the chapel, her body rigid, eyes straight ahead. They sat next to each other but they didn't touch. She wondered how much of Beverly was in Mina. She wished she understood the things we inherit, the things we pass on. She wished those were things you could choose, a list you could tick or cross.

A woman in a navy dress spoke for a while about Bill the insurance man, Bill the husband, Bill the father, Bill the friend. Mina got up next. She was so poised as she spoke, Elaine hardly able to make out her daughter's words above the noise in her own head, but she was aware of people around her responding, heard people laughing, saw them crying. Mina sat down and let out a sigh of relief. Kira, sitting on Mina's other side, took her hands and held them until the song Mina had chosen started playing. It was that one from *Graceland* – not Bill's favourite but a tune he'd frequently find himself whistling around the house, then Elaine would find herself singing days later until eventually Mina would yell at them for getting it stuck in her head too. A song passed between them wordlessly, as if by osmosis. By the time the silly tin whistle started, the casket was gone, Bill was gone. He was gone.

'YOU SIT HERE and we'll get you something to eat,' Valerie said, lowering Elaine down on the sofa. She was glad to be in the air conditioning, glad to have a moment in which she wasn't surrounded by people. Everyone wanted to speak to her but no one had anything to say. Just the same platitudes, as though they'd all read the same book about what you're supposed to say when someone dies.

'Valerie,' Elaine said.

Valerie stopped and looked at her.

'Thank you. For all of this.' Elaine shook her head, trying to fight back the tears.

'Shhh, stop that. You'd do the same.' Valerie put her hand on Elaine's cheek, smoothed back her hair. 'Family, remember.' The two women hugged, just for a second, and Elaine let a tear escape and soak into the shoulder of Valerie's black silk shirt.

'People will be here soon. I need to get ready. You stay put.' Valerie hurried off towards the kitchen. Elaine heard cupboards opening and closing, drawers being slammed. She stood, a little unsteady on her feet. She realised she hadn't eaten all day. She walked around the room and looked at the books in the bookshelf. All Arthur's taste, all her taste. She looked up at the family portrait above the mantelpiece, all five of them dressed in their matching outfits. The girls in red velvet dresses, the boys in matching waistcoats. Bill always made fun of it. He could barely keep a straight face when Valerie invited them over for the grand reveal. He and Mina stifling their giggles, egging each other on. Elaine thought it was beautiful, a testament to the way Valerie kept everything and everyone together.

'God, I hate that thing.'

She turned. Arthur stood holding two glasses of whisky, neat.

'Thought you might need one of these today.' He held a glass out to her. She took a few steps closer to him, took one from his hand. He clinked his glass to hers. Said, 'To Bill.'

'To Bill,' she echoed. She swallowed the whisky down in two sips, liked how it felt as it oozed through her, into her empty stomach.

'About the other night,' she started, but she didn't know how to continue, didn't know what she wanted to say, what she was allowed to say.

'I know,' he said. He didn't look at her, couldn't. 'What I mean is – I guess I don't know.'

Elaine didn't smile, didn't speak. She waited for him.

'I guess it blew itself up.' Arthur looked at his empty glass.

'I didn't mean what I said at the hospital about this being our fault,' she said.

'I know.' His hand twitched like he wanted to move it, put it somewhere. It stayed by his side. 'We just need to get through this and then' – he paused – 'well, then I don't know what. But we just need to get through this.'

'I don't know how,' Elaine said, her voice quivering, the tears coming now, up and over, strong and fast.

He pulled her into his arms. She let herself be held, then lifted her arms too and held him back. She felt each breath he took, in and out, the ones that shuddered a little with his tears.

'Oh, you two,' Valerie said from across the room. 'Oh goodness.' She ran over to them and put her arms around them both. 'It's okay, it's okay.' And they stood like that for thirty seconds, maybe more, and Elaine felt a part of something, she felt a hole filling in, she felt like a line drawing finally being coloured in, all the way to the edges, then over and over.

THE SAME PEOPLE who'd been at the chapel milled around in the Chengs' living room, offering Elaine more anecdotes, more platitudes as they nibbled on sandwiches Valerie and Arthur had made, cut into quarters and piled onto trays. Elaine ate two quarters of a ham and cheese sandwich, she drank another whisky slipped to her by Arthur when no one was looking. She watched Mina walk from group to group, twenty years old and she already knew how to behave on a day like this, at a time like this.

Elaine knew there were things about Bill that would be gone forever. The way he'd tug on the bit of beard under his chin when he was trying to solve a problem; his big toes that looked more like thumbs and the way he'd laughed every time she'd made fun of them for more than two decades. But looking at Mina, she realised that so much more of him was in her: the way she talked with her hands, the bony parts of her shoulder blades that jutted up on either side of the straps of her dress. It was all Bill. She was all Bill.

Elaine felt her weight on the sofa shift as someone sat down right beside her. She pulled her eyes away from her daughter and let them take in the white moustache, the white hair that was cut short around a bald dome of head, dotted with sun spots from decades spent outside. She hadn't seen him in ten years, since her mum died, since they sold the farm.

Jeff put an arm around Elaine's shoulders in an awkward, sideways hug.

'You're here,' Elaine said, then she nestled into him, let him hold her against his chest while she sobbed. He hadn't worked on the farm in fifteen years but he still smelt like he'd put in a hard day's work.

'I'm so sorry about all this,' he whispered.

'Me too,' she whispered back. 'Thanks for coming.' She pulled back, sat up straight, wiped her eyes, her nose, with the back of her hand. 'I've been thinking a lot about Mum this last week,' she said.

He smiled. 'I think about her all the time. I miss her every day.'

'I don't. I mean, I do, but,' she smiled, too, 'do you know I only ever saw her laugh once in my whole life?'

'She was always laughing,' Jeff said, shifting in his seat.

'I heard a noise behind the hedge and I snuck around and I saw her talking to you. I'd never seen her like that before. So' – Elaine searched for the right word – 'happy.'

'We had a good time together, your mum and I.'

'I wish she'd left with you,' Elaine said. 'She'd have been a better mother if she wasn't so miserable.'

'I suggested it – multiple times,' he said. 'She said she couldn't.'

'But you waited all those years for her and you never knew how it would turn out.'

'That was the choice I made. I decided that no matter what happened, she was worth it.' Elaine looked at Jeff as he paused, tears gathering in his eyes. 'Some things are just worth the wait.'

Elaine felt her feet plant firmly on the ground, send out roots.

'And you're still here.'

'I promised your mum I would be here if you needed me.' He took her hand in his, both their palms clammy. 'Now I need to get on.' He patted her hand twice, a sign that it was time to let go. 'You can call me, anytime.'

'I know.' Elaine took a deep breath. 'Thanks, again, for coming.'

'Of course,' he said, kissed the top of her head, put a hand either side of his legs and pushed himself up. And as Elaine watched him walk across the living room to the front door, she dug in, she promised she'd stay no matter what. She knew now that some things were worth the wait.

Nineteen

ELAINE STOOD BY THE WINDOW and watched them leave for the hospital, Valerie bent over with both arms against the bonnet of the car while she breathed through a contraction. Arthur rubbed her back, helped her into the front seat, ran around to the driver's seat, backed slowly out of the driveway.

Two days later, she watched them bring him home: a tiny swaddled perfect thing, Valerie holding him to her chest as she walked slowly to the front door.

Elaine couldn't wait. She went over the next day and shuffled forward on the sofa while Valerie stood from the armchair and bent down to deliver tiny baby Brendan into her arms. His head fit perfectly into the crook of her arm. His little face twitched, his tiny lips opened and closed like a goldfish. He grizzled a tiny baby grizzle. Elaine had never seen anything as perfect as those tiny fingernails, those little ears, his legs like a frog's.

'He's amazing,' Elaine said. She looked up at Valerie, who beamed. At Arthur, his forehead creased with worry. As Elaine held Brendan, her body throbbed with something, with longing, but for something else, for something new.

Over the next few days, weeks, months, Elaine found herself still drawn to the house across the street, but now she was drawn to Brendan's soft black hair, his tiny little nostrils that flared as he cried.

'What does it feel like?' Elaine asked Valerie, who was holding Brendan wrapped in a blanket in her arms as he fed.

'It hurts like hell,' Valerie whispered. 'Like little knives slicing my nipples.' She looked down at the boy and she smiled through the pain, in spite of it.

'I mean motherhood,' Elaine said. 'Tell me what it feels like.'

'Like I have won a prize,' Valerie said. 'Like I have been granted a wish I would never even have known to ask for.' Valerie stroked the top of Brendan's head with her thumb. 'I don't want to sound like one of *those people*' – Valerie used a finger to press up the end of her nose like a pig's – 'but I didn't know I could feel so whole.'

Elaine watched them together and wondered if the hole inside her could be filled this way, the earth kicked in, packed down, smoothed over. She thought about the tide crashing in over the side of a rock pool. She wanted to be filled to the brim, heavy enough to sink to the bottom, life clicking over under the surface like an old clock as the water comes and goes.

Elaine hadn't known she was at the top of a slippery slope until she held baby Brendan, until she saw Valerie holding him, feeding him, loving him. At first, she hadn't realised Bill was right there with her, but as the months passed she watched her husband coo over the boy, cheer loudly when Brendan rolled himself over for the first time, when he took his first step, his second, every step for the next two weeks. She watched as he spent hours trying to teach Brendan to say 'footy' before he'd even uttered a sound that came close to Mum and Dad.

Bill and Elaine stayed behind after Brendan's first birthday party. Bill insisted it was to help clean up but he and Arthur spent the rest of the afternoon running around with Brendan in their arms, making aeroplane noises, car noises, truck noises, a mess. At bedtime, the two men took Brendan upstairs 'to give Valerie a break'. Through the baby monitor, Elaine heard them talking sweetly to Brendan, their deep voices down low. They sang nursery rhymes to him as he drifted off to sleep, all the words mixed up and the melodies a mile out of tune. Elaine's heart soared, not just for Bill but for Arthur, Valerie and Brendan too. Valerie caught her eye, wiggled her eyebrows up and down. Elaine smiled. Bill would be a good father, she knew it. And she thought that maybe she could be a good mother.

Bill practically skipped across the road after the party. It was only eight, so they pottered around the house, moving things from one place to another, finding things to do that didn't need to be done. Elaine made a pot of jasmine tea with leaves Valerie had given them, Bill flicked through the channels, stopped on a cop show. He sat down close to her on the sofa, their thighs touching, their arms touching, neither of them watching the television, not really. She'd only seen Bill nervous once before, his leg jiggling in the car on the way to the town hall. She in a cream silk dress, he in a brown suit, the jacket ever so slightly too small. She'd reached over to him and squeezed his knee, he'd calmed, smiled at her.

On the screen, there was a shoot-out, one of the cops ducked behind a car as bullets hit metal, bounced and ricocheted. On the sofa, Bill couldn't get settled, couldn't keep still.

'I don't know about you but I'm knackered,' Bill said. 'Bedtime?'

Elaine stood and walked to the TV, turned it off as one of the bad guys took a bullet in the shoulder, fell down screaming. She abandoned her tea, still hot, not even poured from its pot, and followed Bill to the bathroom. They brushed their teeth. Elaine felt giddy. She wondered if they'd talk about it first or if they'd just let it happen, let whatever was going to happen, happen.

She went to the bedroom while Bill flossed, washed his face with a hot face cloth, the same routine every morning, every night. She dug through the deep, wide drawers of the antique dresser her parents gave them as a wedding present, found the nightie she'd bought on a trip into the city before they'd moved, one of the trips into the city to meet Arthur. Those trips had brought them here; maybe it had all been for this. Maybe. She'd got the train in, met him in the street, wandered through the shops, killing time before his shift finished. What had she thought would happen? What had she wanted? Perhaps she was right at that first lunch they'd had together at Easter. It was just friendship. It was meant to be the four of them, five of them. Six. A family.

She undressed quickly, let the silk slip over her body. It was cold at first but warmed with her skin. She imagined Bill's face when he saw her in it. How his eyes would widen. She willed her mind to stay put, to linger on Bill, but it was like a puppy that had slipped its leash and run. She switched off the overhead light, slipped underneath the covers. And there, she let herself imagine what Arthur would think, too; what he'd do.

'Lainey,' Bill whispered when he got into bed.

She rolled over to face him; she could still make out his face in the almost-black. She put her hand on his side where his t-shirt had ridden up, one of the few hairless parts of his torso.

'Seeing Brendan growing up . . .' he said. His voice wobbled a little. 'You know – it's made me . . .'

'Me too,' Elaine said, and she shuffled over, pulled herself closer to him. 'I think I want one too.'

THAT NIGHT, THEY started trying. At first, in the trying, Elaine felt closer to Bill. She felt resolute. Like her night-times, sometimes her mornings, sometimes her Saturday afternoons, her Sunday evenings, were numbers in an equation, and when the calculation was just right, it would all make sense, would all add up to something. After two months, she started paying close attention to the calendar on the fridge. After six months, she circled days in red. She would wait till it was her turn to close the library, and then she would borrow stacks of books full of medical advice and old wives' tales. She was willing to try anything. After nine months, the trying was contained only to the days when success was scientifically possible. On the others, the non-circled days, Elaine would roll over at bedtime and pretend to fall asleep quickly; breathing the way she imagined one would, deep and steady.

Trying.

Elaine started to detest the word, hate the inference that if they just put the effort in, if they wanted it more, it would happen.

She'd lie there afterwards, her legs elevated, and she'd try to want it more than she'd wanted it last time. The trying to want worked better than the trying, and soon the want was so big she was worried there was more of it than there was of her, that it was possible for her to disappear inside it, for it to swallow her whole. She felt like a kid trapped down a well, the walls too slippery, too high for her to climb out on her own.

'We've been trying for a baby,' Bill announced as he stood up to carve the chicken one Sunday lunch.

Valerie squealed with delight and jumped up, kissed them both on the cheek. Almost-two-year-old Brendan stared slack-jawed at the noise.

She and Bill had mostly stopped talking about it by then. There'd been many unwelcome periods, many failures. Elaine would always know they were coming before they came. She'd snap at Bill, get angry at the smallest things, then seven days later she'd wake in the morning, sit on the toilet, wipe and see blood. The rejection came like clockwork. Her body denying her the thing she hadn't known she wanted so badly until she saw someone else with it, until she was sure she knew she couldn't have it.

'What does Valerie have to say about it?' Bill had asked Elaine when he found her sitting on the edge of the bath. 'I bet she has some good advice, some herbs to try. She's got a solution to everything.'

'We haven't talked about it,' Elaine said. She put her head in her hands. 'I don't want her to think I'm a failure.'

'Lainey' – Bill knelt down in front of her – 'you're not a failure. It's only been a few months. And you don't know how long it took them to conceive either. It could've been years.' He put his hands around her calves, kissed her knees. 'I just think you really need a friend.' He stood up and lifted her into his arms. She let him hug her, kiss her ear and her hair. She didn't understand how he could be so confident. He just seemed to know, when all she ever did was want for the things she didn't, couldn't, have.

'It's the best thing you'll ever do,' Arthur said as Bill slid the knife along the chicken's ribs. He lifted his beer to Bill. Bill drank too.

'Thanks, mate,' he said.

'Oh, I hope you have a girl. Then she can marry my boy and we'll terrorise them for the rest of their lives,' Valerie said, clapping her hands. 'In-laws from hell,' she cackled.

Bill dragged the knife along the chicken's spine, pulling the meat up and away. It steamed, hot and moist.

'We've been trying for ages,' Elaine said to Valerie later, as she handed her a plate rinsed clean of suds. Valerie took it from her and leant with her back against the kitchen bench as she dried it with a tea towel Janine from Bill's office had brought back from a trip to the Great Barrier Reef, an illustration of tropical fish, brightly coloured coral. A green turtle coasting across the top of the scene. 'How long did it take you?' Elaine asked, even though she was scared of the answer.

'We were lucky,' Valerie said quickly. 'But everyone's different. You'll get there, I have a good feeling.'

Elaine turned to her. Hot soapy water dripped off her hands onto the floor. 'Maybe I need to see a doctor,' she said. 'There's probably something wrong with me.'

Valerie threw the tea towel down on the bench and pulled her friend close to her. 'There's nothing wrong with you. Why do we women always assume it's us?' She pulled back, kept her hands on Elaine's shoulders. 'It's almost always the men and their little swimmers.' She moved her index finger around like a wriggler in a glass of water.

Elaine laughed.

'If you're still having trouble in six months, then we'll go to the doctor, okay?'

'Okay,' Elaine said, and she did feel better, Bill was right.

'Plus, if you wait a little longer, maybe we can do it at the same time? We could waddle around the neighbourhood together.' Valerie picked up the tea towel and flicked Elaine with it, both of them laughing, joyful at the thought of being pregnant together.

'WE'RE HAVING A girl too,' Valerie shrieked when Elaine opened the door. Elaine was two months further along, the morning sickness lingering well past lunchtime and her first trimester. They hugged at the door, their stomachs touching, their daughters so close. She followed Valerie slowly down the hall to the living room.

She rested her head on the arm of the sofa to stop the room from spinning. Brendan was sprinting around the house making racing car noises, mumbling and giggling to himself.

'They'll be good girls to each other,' Valerie said, her hands resting on her stomach.

'Best friends,' Elaine said. 'Like us.' She smiled at Valerie.

'Family.'

Elaine squeezed Valerie's hand. She felt the tears welling in her eyes as the nausea swished inside her, as her baby grew and grew.

Elaine had thought she'd know when it finally happened (just like Valerie said it would, just like Bill knew it would), she'd thought she'd feel it bedding down inside her, but it wasn't until the angry day of her cycle passed without incident that she got hopeful. She looked at the calendar, counted, counted again. Every time she went into the bathroom, she'd check for blood, but there was no blood. She didn't tell Bill at first, didn't want to get his hopes up, but then one morning she walked into the kitchen and saw him staring at the calendar.

'Lainey,' he'd said, tears in his eyes.

'I don't know for sure,' she said, but she was already crying. It was too early; too early to imagine what the future could look like. But it was too late. He kissed Elaine on the mouth, on the cheek, on the neck as he pulled her into his arms. Bill, her Bill. Father of her child. A good man. She was lucky, she knew she was lucky. This is good, this is good; she repeated it like a mantra. I am happy, she thought, and this time she meant it, she was sure she did. She knew this baby would act as a lever with which to lift things up and away, a wedge to keep them there. Elaine wondered if Bill could see that too.

As the life stirred and fluttered inside her, Elaine tried to change the life outside of her too. She wanted to give this baby a fresh start, herself a fresh start, give Bill a chance. They rearranged the rooms, shifted their bed from the front bedroom to the smaller one; to the bedroom with a view of the monstera that grew wild down the side of the house. The baby would have the front room, the baby would have the view of Arthur coming and going, of the striped lights of cars crawling down the suburban streets at night, of her best friend walking down the driveway, ready for school. Elaine would put her first. She'd fill her with love, give her everything she could ever need or want. She'd forget Arthur. She could dissolve the glue that bound them. She could change. She knew she could.

MINA CAME HOME just before Elaine's favourite quiz show started. The pipes shuddered and moaned as the shower coughed and spluttered to life. Elaine listened to the sounds of her daughter in the house, sounds as familiar to her as her own heartbeat. She thought about how it felt when Mina was an unknown being, growing and filling the part inside of her where Arthur had previously lived. When she was pregnant, when her body was working in mysterious ways, every day a lesson in the unknown, Elaine was imagining a future that belonged not to her and Arthur but to her and her daughter. The love that she craved was already inside her, their lives intertwined, permanently linked. She had felt healed, unstuck. Free.

The red titles flashed across the screen, the host swanned around. The walls of the studio flooded the stage with bright primary colours. The contestants introduced themselves, the questions started. Elaine took the TV off mute just as Mina walked in, her wet hair twisted and wrapped in a towel. She sat down next to Elaine, swung her legs up onto the sofa and lay her head down on Elaine's lap. Elaine rested her hand on the top of Mina's arm, stroked it with her thumb. She felt Mina's pain as her own, all of Mina's anger and longing, her love, bubbling and swirling through their shared blood.

It had been so long since they'd been like this together. Elaine had always assumed that a child's body would fit back together with her mother's like Russian dolls. Even when Mina left, as Elaine watched her wheel her suitcase out of the gate and across the road to where Kira stood next to the car ready to drive her to the airport, Elaine hoped their bodies would remember each other.

'I can't say no to this job,' Mina had whispered as they hugged. 'It'll just be for a little while.'

'I understand,' Elaine said. 'Call me when you arrive, let me know you're okay.'

'I will. And maybe when I find a place you can come and visit,' Mina said. Elaine couldn't tell if she was being sarcastic or hopeful. Either way, it hurt.

They'd hugged again, and as Elaine watched the car drive away she felt relief and she felt the guilt of the last few years fly away with her daughter. She had set Mina free. She had made way and now all there was left to do was wait.

The host shook hands with the contestants while the credits rolled. Mina reached for the remote control and muted the TV.

'I saw you on the street with Arthur today,' Mina said.

On the screen the six-thirty news showed images of a hurricane battering the Caribbean en route to Miami. Grey clouds and rain squalled across the screen, a car turned on its side, its passenger unable to walk against the force of the wind. Palm trees bent and blew at right angles, high grey seas swirling and swirling.

Twenty

ELAINE TOOK THE REMOTE FROM Mina's hand and turned the TV off. She felt her organs expand inside her chest, against her diaphragm: a low-pressure system building and building inside her.

'Sit up,' Elaine said.

Mina sat up and turned to face her, sitting cross-legged on the sofa. She untwisted the towel and let her wet hair fall onto her shoulders.

'You've got your dad's worried eyes,' Elaine said. 'He used to look at me the same way.'

'What was he so worried about?' Mina asked, draping the towel over the back of the sofa. She ran her hands through her hair, teasing the wet tendrils apart with her fingers.

'Me,' Elaine said and laughed a breathy, nervous laugh. 'I was so young when we got together. The same age as you when you met Ben.' Elaine didn't know where to look for the words that would make this make sense. 'I always joked that your dad was born exactly how he was always going to be,' she said. 'He was stubborn and uncompromising. He loved me like that too.'

'And you?' Mina asked.

'I loved him because he gave me you,' Elaine said.

Mina sucked in her big bottom lip. That was Bill's too. All of her belonged to Bill.

Elaine shuffled through the thoughts in her head, lined them up like Scrabble tiles on a rack, trying to find the best words. But how do you map the path you let love push you down?

'We waited a long time for you.'

When Elaine was pregnant, she imagined the two of them would talk like this all the time, that they'd live in their own little world, speaking a language only they understood. But now her daughter looked at her like she was speaking in tongues.

'I thought it might never happen, that there was something wrong with me.' She braced herself for a joke from Mina, but she was quiet. Elaine had thought for so many years about how she would tell this story, but it wasn't until she sat down to do it that she realised how far back it started, that the roots of it were buried so far underground, were all connected, each other's life source. All Elaine had ever wanted was to love and be loved: how had it come to this?

'When you were born, I suddenly felt like my life's purpose was to keep you alive and watch you grow, to love you. And God, I loved you so much.' She corrected herself quickly but not before Mina winced. 'Love you. I love you,' Elaine said, but Mina didn't look at her, couldn't. 'The thing is, you just – you didn't need me.'

'Of course I needed you.' Mina furrowed her brow and Elaine saw years of worry there on her face, a topography of sadness etched and worn in skin. She wanted to reach over and smooth them out. She didn't. She kept her hands in her lap so Mina couldn't see them shaking.

'You only ever wanted your dad. If you fell over, you'd cry for him. You'd ask for his help with your homework. I'd give you books to read and you'd talk about them with him. It just felt –' These feelings had been swirling around in Elaine's head for thirty years; she'd never had to put them into words before. 'It felt like I was on the outside, just a witness to your life.'

'I never left you out on purpose,' Mina said. 'I'm sorry if it felt like I did.'

'No.' Elaine touched her now. 'That's not what I meant. This isn't your fault.' Mina's hand was hot; Elaine squeezed it. 'My God, I'm making a mess of this.'

'Just keep going.' Mina squeezed back. 'Please don't stop.'

Elaine thought back to Mina's childhood. All the times she'd watched her daughter walking hand in hand with Bill, the nights she'd wake up crying and call for him.

'I think I needed you too much,' Elaine said finally. 'I thought you'd always be part of me, you'd always be mine. But of course that's not how it works. I realised as soon as you were born that you are your own person. You were never going to be what I needed because you had to be you. And you are amazing. Look at you. I wouldn't change you for anything.'

She saw tears well in Mina's eyes.

'But the thing is,' Mina said, 'I did need you.' She let go of Elaine's hands to wipe the tears that had overflowed and were streaming down her cheeks. 'When Dad died, it felt like I lost you too. I did everything I could to get you back, but you were gone.' Mina looked up, looked into Elaine's eyes. 'Where did you go, Mum?'

ELAINE KNEW THE pattern of the light in the living room, in the kitchen: in summer, it crept and leaked like ink seeping into paper; in autumn, there were long golden splinters into the late afternoon. After winter, she'd open the sliding doors and let the house breathe, let it sigh the dust from its lungs. She'd hover at the door, at the precipice, and smell the suggestion of spring in the air, the wattle, the nearby blossom, cut grass, a neighbour whipper snippering. But she'd only go out there when she knew he'd gone out. She knew that from the garden you couldn't hear the clank of the ring latch as it turned and unleashed the arm, the creak of the gate as it opened and closed again, the bang of a sharp-knuckled, ball-fisted knock on the front door. She needed to stay where she could hear the gate, where she could hear the door.

The day after the funeral, she set her alarm and got up at seven. She made tea, made toast, took them to the dining table. She hadn't been in the living room since the night Bill died. Every surface was covered with flowers, dead or dying. Some in glasses, in vases, in baskets and jars. She had her breakfast on the sofa. (The last place she'd sat with Bill, the last place she'd sat with Arthur.) She felt a storm brewing inside her. What if he'd gone to the supermarket around the corner? What if she'd gone instead? Was he going to die anyway? Was his body as sure about that as he had been about everything else? There were too many what-ifs, too many maybes. She felt suddenly as though there were too many possible endings, too many twists and turns. She felt overwhelmed by the unpredictability of life, by how the future was unknowable. Maybe this meant there were no wrong choices, no right answers. The more she thought about it, the harder it became to catch her breath.

She stood. She wanted to move, to be busy. She took a bin bag from the kitchen drawer and emptied the jugs and vases of their dead and wilted, brown-stemmed, crunchy-leafed flowers. Some still had the little sachets of flower food attached to the stems with sticky tape. She threw those out too. She tipped the slimy brown water into the sink, soaked the smell out of the vases with warm soapy water, made a stack of cards to remember to send thankyou notes, left herself a reminder of whose phone calls she had to return.

The dishes and plates of food that had been crowding the fridge were now stacked up in a neat pile on the far end of the kitchen table. By the looks of her, Mina hadn't eaten much of them.

From the front of the house there was a squeak, a bang. She held her breath. A knock at the door. It felt as though her heart stopped beating for five seconds as she walked up the hall. She wanted it to be him but what would it mean if it was? And what would it mean if it wasn't?

She opened the door to Arthur, plastic shopping bags dangling off his arms.

'Hi,' Elaine said.

'Heavy load coming through.' Valerie barged past him, past Elaine, made her way down the hall to the kitchen. Elaine heard the bags being placed on the kitchen bench.

'Hi,' Arthur replied, sheepishly lifting his arms up a little in case she thought he was there for any other reason. He followed his wife to the kitchen.

'You didn't need to do this,' Elaine said as she helped them unpack the shopping bags. 'At least let me give you some money.'

'You save your money for a rainy day,' Valerie said.

'Thank you,' Elaine said. She put a packet of Ritz in the cupboard, took a tube of toothpaste and a bar of soap into the bathroom. There was nothing Valerie hadn't thought of, hadn't taken care of. There was nothing for Elaine to do but sit and wait, sit and wonder, sit and hope.

EVERY KNOCK AT the door made her heart skip a beat. Usually it was Valerie alone, come for a cup of tea, a chat – often, for the first year, with pamphlets about different kinds of counselling or therapy she'd heard about. Once she came with Kira and they sat at the kitchen table with Mina. They took turns telling Elaine how much they missed Sunday lunch with her, missed shopping trips and birthday parties, family holidays.

'We miss him too, Mum,' Mina said, her eyes filling with tears. 'But life has to go on.'

Elaine sat quietly. Their eyes on her expectantly. She knew what they were trying to do but all she could think about, all she wanted to know was why Arthur hadn't come. If this was what Arthur wanted, wouldn't he have been there?

Another time Valerie brought a library book about hypnotherapy.

'It might make you more ready,' Valerie said. 'To, you know, get on with things.'

Elaine flipped through it quietly while Valerie extolled its virtues.

'Or, if it all goes wrong, it might make you think you're a chicken.'

Elaine looked up at her and smiled. 'I'll have a read.' She closed the book and put it back on the pile Valerie had delivered. 'Thank you.'

'All part of the service,' Valerie said, and she didn't mention the book again, even when it was returned to her a week later, wedged in between *The Road* (Arthur's pick) and *Eat, Pray, Love* (Valerie's).

Every time anyone brought it up, Elaine imagined sitting down to *talk to someone.* That's what everyone called it. That's what everyone was always suggesting she do. How would she even begin to explain this? Where would she start? With her childhood? In all the books she read and films she watched, it always started with the mother. How would she explain her mother and Jeff? And then what would come next? Bill, Arthur, Mina. The story, when she lined it up act by act, was equal parts mystery and fantasy. A plot she could talk about for years without ever fully understanding. But somehow she knew that if she just kept waiting, everything would reveal itself. She knew that if she waited, he'd come. And that when he did, it would be worth it. All of it would be worth it.

She was in her bedroom when it happened again, two years after the last time. She was separating Mina's laundry from hers. Blouses and skirts, ripped jeans and black t-shirts. It was a Tuesday. She knew that because she'd go back sometimes and read that first message, read them all from the beginning.

She heard a clank, a creak, a knock.

Please come, please come, please come, she said to herself as she walked down the hall, checked her appearance in the mirror and opened the door to Arthur. Arthur alone. Arthur holding a white box by its plastic handle. It was a cold morning and she could see his breath. She stepped aside so he could come in and he walked down the hall.

Elaine closed the door, took a deep breath, followed.

In the living room, he'd placed the box on the table.

'I got you this,' he said. He opened the box in a way that felt ceremonial, the big lid bending back to reveal a little white rectangle surrounded by padding, cords wrapped up in cardboard and plastic. He lifted it out with one hand and put it in front of her, opened it. He peeled the protective shield from the shiny black screen, from the little white keys.

'We bought one each for the kids and Valerie thought you could use one too. To help you stay connected.'

'Arthur, that's too much.' She sat down next to him and saw the reflection of the two of them in the shiny black screen. Next to each other, together.

He plugged it in, turned it on. The screen came to life. She made a note to find out how much it had cost and write them a cheque, force it into Valerie's hand. If she wouldn't accept it, she'd ask Mina to take it over, to leave it on the kitchen table or slip it into Valerie's handbag when she was out of the room.

Sometimes she'd find the cheques torn up in the kitchen bin, other times they'd be shoved through the letterbox. Occasionally, she'd see on her bank statements that Valerie had deposited the cheques, accepted the money. Elaine felt glad to be unburdened by it. Money from the sale of the farm, Bill's life insurance money, all of it had come into her life as a direct result of someone leaving it.

'I've organised a faster internet connection for you too,' Arthur said. 'A man's coming tomorrow to install it.'

'Thank you,' she said, and he stopped unravelling the long cord that would run from the modem to the wall. 'Thank you,' she said again.

'It's a pleasure,' he said without smiling, without showing pleasure. She wondered if this was as agonising for him as it was for her. 'Let's connect you now and I'll show you how to use the email, how to search for things.'

She made him tea while he tapped away at the keyboard. He unplugged the phone and ran a long cable from the plug to the kitchen table. She watched him work, sat beside him while he carefully explained to her how to connect to the internet, everything she could look at while she was there. He created a Hotmail account for her, wrote down all the passwords and login details. He opened a new message and typed in his email address, his name, the @ symbol, the name of the dental practice he owned. He wrote in the body.

Dear Arthur,

This is my email address. You can write to me here whenever you like.

Love,
Elaine

He typed *Love* without hesitation, pressed send. She smiled, heat rising through her body. She tried not to look at him.

'The internet guy will come tomorrow at ten. Any problems, you can just send me an email.' Their bodies were next to each other. She felt electricity zap in the space between them, magenta and cobalt like a plasma globe at the science museum.

She followed him as he took his mug into the kitchen, walked with him to the front door. 'Thank you so much,' she said.

'Let me know if you have any problems. The kids are probably better tech support than me, but I'll do what I can.'

'Thank you, and thank Valerie for me, please,' she said.

He opened the front door and stood there for a second, for two. She had so much to say but she didn't have the words. They'd come to her one day; that was worth waiting for too.

'Have you been out shopping without me?' Mina said when she came home the following afternoon and saw the box on the kitchen table, the new laptop beside it. She opened it, the screen came to life.

'Arthur set it up for me, for us.' Elaine stood next to her, beaming. 'We even have ADSL now.'

'Ooh la la,' Mina said. She used the trackpad to navigate with ease.

'You can use it whenever you like,' Elaine said. 'Even take it to uni if you ever need to.'

'Yay,' Mina said coolly, and Elaine felt like the strands of DNA that linked them were slowly unwinding. Was that a thing that could happen, she wondered, as two people drifted further and further away from each other?

After Mina had made herself something to eat and disappeared down the other end of the house, Elaine opened the laptop up again. She logged into her email, the password Mina's birthday. She had a new message. It was from Arthur, a reply to the one he'd sent himself earlier.

Victoria Hannan

Dear Elaine,

Thanks for your email.

I was wondering: have you read anything good lately?

A.

Twenty-one

THE RAIN WAS COMING DOWN in sheets. The type of rain that pooled in clogged gutters and cascaded in streams past windows.

She heard the gate, a knock at the door. His hair was dripping from the walk across the road. It had been ten years since the last time but he had come. He had come.

'Can I?' he asked and Elaine stepped back so he could pass her.

She closed the door behind him. He slipped off his shoes and walked down the hall. She followed him to the living room. Here he was again.

He said her name. 'Elaine.' She wanted him to say it again. To never stop saying it. 'I need to tell you something.'

He sat on the arm of the sofa, stood again. He moved around like he didn't know his own body. He wiped beads of rain from the sleeve of his woollen jumper. It was the green of the dark place in the middle of a forest.

'What is it?' Elaine stepped closer to him.

'I'm –' He turned and walked to the back door, looked at the rain-filled sky, over the tangle of garden, the unloved mess. 'I just found out I'm sick,' he said.

'Arthur.' She moved closer again, she touched his shoulder, he turned around.

'I'm sick.' He let out a whimper and started to cry, small restrained sobs at first. 'I'm really sick.' He stepped into her arms and let her hold him as he cried, he pushed his face against her shoulder, his tears wetting her shirt, wetting her, sinking into her skin, becoming one with her. She put her arms around him. She kissed the top of his head, her lips wet from the rain in his hair; she held him close to her chest while he sobbed. Inside, her body sang. A song of worship, an ancient hymn. He pulled his head back and wiped his nose with his sleeve. 'It's cancer. In my pancreas but it's got me good: it's spread everywhere.'

She held his reddened face in her hands, brought it up to hers.

'Oh, Arthur.' Elaine let out a little sob too. 'They must be able to do something?'

'They think it's too late,' he said and wheezed. 'They said I've got six months. All they can do is just manage it, manage the pain.' His throat sounded all choked up when he spoke. Elaine wondered if the cancer was in there too.

'Valerie,' Elaine said. 'Is Valerie okay?' She felt her heart stretch to breaking point inside her chest. Poor Valerie, she thought, her poor dear friend.

'They don't know.' He stepped back from her. 'I can't tell them.'

'Arthur,' Elaine said. 'You have to.'

'I will, I will,' he said. 'I need some time. And I need your help.' He looked at her.

She nodded; she'd do anything.
'You'll have to leave the house,' he said.

Mina

Mina

Twenty-two

'I DIDN'T GO ANYWHERE. I was here all along,' Elaine said, and Mina wanted to roll her eyes, wanted to throw a tantrum, to scream.

'You know what I mean,' she said, her voice solid as a rock.

Elaine sighed. 'I don't know how to explain it.'

'Okay, let me ask you a question then.' Mina didn't pause to let Elaine protest. She knew this was a thread she had to pull or the truth, or something resembling it, would never unravel, would never be revealed. 'What were you doing with Arthur today?'

Elaine took a sharp breath as if Mina had surprised her, as if Mina had pushed her hands out and shoved her in the chest, bowled her clean over.

'You won't like the answer,' Elaine said, her voice quiet.

'I don't care – I just need to know,' Mina said.

So Elaine began. Mina watched her mouth form the words, watched the wall come tumbling down.

'I met Arthur when I was twenty-three years old. On my – your dad's and my second wedding anniversary. He was cooking in a restaurant in Chinatown. I saw him in the kitchen and –' She paused, and Mina saw her mother's face flush.

'And?' Mina couldn't let her stop. Not now.

'I think I loved him straight away,' Elaine said. She glanced up quickly then looked back down to her hands. 'I know I did.'

'Oh my God,' Mina said. She felt like she was going to be sick. 'Oh my God,' she said again. Louder this time. 'As in *in love*?'

Elaine nodded.

'You were *in love with Arthur*? Arthur from over the road?' Mina couldn't believe the words that were coming out of her mouth.

'I still am.'

'Wow,' Mina whispered. 'So you've been having' – she hesitated – 'an affair with Arthur for all this time?' Mina stepped out of her skin for a second, a thought creeping into her head that shook her to the core. 'Oh my God, he's not my dad is he?' Mina thought about Brendan's hands inside her bra, Brendan inside her mouth. 'Please tell me he's not my dad.'

'Of course he isn't,' Elaine said quietly, and Mina started breathing again. She thought about Brendan hitting the back of her throat. 'It's not like that.'

'So tell me, what's it like?' There were feelings inside Mina she'd never felt before, there were colours and shapes she didn't recognise. She thought about what Ben had said. He was right: this was what she'd wanted. Her mum leaving the house. This was what she'd begged, pleaded, bargained, even prayed for. Just once in a moment of desperation. She'd always told herself that she didn't care why it happened, she just wanted it to happen. But now. This. 'Tell me what it's like,' she demanded.

There was a flicker of fear in Elaine's eyes. 'I just –' she started, stopped again. 'I loved your dad. I did. But I always felt like I needed more.'

'More what?'

'More of everything.'

Mina felt dizzy, cold and hot at the same time.

'Did Dad know?'

'There was nothing to know.'

'What do you mean?'

'Mina . . .' Elaine shifted in her seat, she swallowed loudly. She looked away, towards the TV, towards the darkening sky. Mina thought about what she'd give to hear every thought that was passing through Elaine's head, not just the ones she was choosing to voice.

'If you had an affair, *are having* an affair' – Mina shook her head in disbelief, in something – 'then just tell me.'

'It wasn't an affair. I just – I love him. As more than a friend, different from family. I just love him.'

'Does he know?'

'Yes.' Elaine pulled at the skin on the back of her hand. 'He's always known.'

'Jesus.' Mina tried to think back to scenes of her mum with her dad, her mum with Arthur. Were there hidden clues that she'd missed? She sat forwards and looked at Elaine. Her mother. This woman. This stranger. 'I don't believe you.'

'Why would I make it up?'

'It just doesn't make sense, Mum,' Mina said, suddenly needing to move, needing to walk, to let the blood flow through her body. She stood up and walked to the glass sliding door. She pressed her hands against the cool glass. The information sat on her like a layer of sunscreen: greasy, warming to her skin, too thick to rub in. Mina looked at the dark sky, the glow of the house over the fence. She looked back at Elaine.

'Okay, so if it is true, you love Arthur, so what?' Mina asked. 'What's that got to do with you staying inside for the last twelve years, for missing my graduation, for choosing not to have a life?' She didn't mean to yell but she was yelling, crying too; she didn't recognise the noises that were coming out of her.

'Please come and sit down?' Elaine rose, shepherded her back to the sofa.

Mina sat, picked up one of the green velvet cushions they'd had since she was a kid. She used to love running her fingers along it one way, then the other, watching the colour shift, the way it reflected the light. Now it was just threadbare; it smelt musty, old. It made her feel sad. All of it did.

Elaine sat back down. She was quiet for a minute; they both were.

'Do you feel guilty about it? About being in love with Arthur?' *Arthur.* When she said his name it felt as if she was speaking in italics, as if his name should be bold and underlined. **Arthur.** **Arthur.**

'I did feel guilt. I felt guilty and alone. I had no idea who I was with your dad, let alone without him.' Elaine swallowed. She paused. She licked her lips, swallowed again. 'I felt like I needed to anchor myself to something. So I chose the one thing, the one person, I was sure of. And I waited.'

'You waited,' Mina repeated. Her brain felt like it'd been cut into slices. She couldn't even see the picture on the box, let alone work out how to put the pieces of the puzzle together. 'For Arthur.'

'When I say it out loud,' Elaine said, 'I know it sounds crazy.'

'Yeah,' Mina confirmed. 'It does.'

She slumped back in the sofa. She wondered how her life had become one of those Netflix movies she'd only ever watch when hormonal or hungover. Who would Zac Efron play?

'I need a drink. Do we have anything to drink?' Mina got up and walked to the kitchen, opening and closing cupboard doors, moving aside tall stacks of tinned tomatoes and chickpeas, standing on her tiptoes, peering.

'Try under the sink,' Elaine said from the door, and Mina crouched down, moved aside the Spray n' Wipe, bulk rolls of bin bags and packets of sponges, some shoe-shining brushes and tins of polish. She reached all the way to the back corner of the cupboard where a damp spot had darkened the wood and pulled out an ancient three-quarters-full bottle of Johnnie Walker Red Label. 'Where on earth did this come from?'

'It was your dad's,' Elaine said as Mina pulled a glass down from the cupboard.

Poor Dad, Mina thought. She looked up at Elaine, raised an eyebrow and wobbled the glass at her.

'Why not,' Elaine said and took a step towards her.

'Neat okay?'

'Neat's fine,' Elaine said and Mina looked at her, impressed. She handed Elaine a glass. Mina drank it down in two sips. She watched Elaine as she necked hers, not even wincing at the burn. Mina poured herself another, Elaine another, and took the glass and the bottle back to the sofa. She ignored the impulse to drink it quickly, then pour another, and another. She somehow had the foresight to imagine how much worse this would all feel with a hangover.

Elaine sat down next to her, closer this time but not too close, not touching.

'Okay, so here's what I need to know,' Mina said, putting the bottle on the floor, taking a sip from her glass. 'Why not "anchor" yourself to me?'

'You already had so much to deal with,' Elaine said. 'You'd just lost your dad; I didn't want you to have to deal with me too.'

Mina thought about all the time she'd spent over the last twelve years thinking about this: lying in bed at night; sitting in meetings about brand strategy; staring at blank Word documents, willing herself to write. She'd played out every conceivable scenario: Elaine was too sad. Elaine was too anxious. Elaine couldn't do it alone. Elaine was weak. In some of them, Elaine was the villain. In all of them, Mina was the victim. She had always suspected love was the reason but never like this. Never this complicated, never this strange. Never this.

'What makes you think I haven't been dealing with you every single day?' She finished her drink and reached for the bottle, poured another, leant with her back against the arm of the sofa, her legs pulled up to her chest. 'Okay,' she continued, 'so why now? What changed?'

'I ran out of time,' Elaine said, and Mina watched the tears well up and over, falling gently down Elaine's cheeks. She watched her mother wipe one cheek with the back of her hand, the other with the fleshy part below her thumb. She held her hand there as though pressing an open wound, trying to stop the bleeding.

'What do you mean?'

'He's sick,' Elaine said. 'He's –' The tears came properly then, between big sobs that banged in Elaine's throat. 'He's dying.'

'Mum,' Mina said and took Elaine into her arms. She held her mother and let her cry, let her tears seep into the shoulder of her pyjamas, already damp from her wet hair.

'Kira didn't say anything.' Mina thought back over all their conversations of the last week.

'She doesn't know,' Elaine said. 'None of them know. He was only diagnosed two weeks ago. He won't tell them and you can't either.'

'Oh my God.' Mina felt a surge of pain, a knife in the guts, when she thought of Kira. Of Valerie. Brendan and Lottie. Of what lay in store for them.

'So when you leave the house . . .' Mina said, prompting her.

'I've been going to the pharmacy for him sometimes to get his medication. He keeps it here so Valerie won't see it. When you saw us today, he just needed to talk.'

'How long has he got?'

'Six months.'

'I wish you'd told me sooner,' Mina said.

'Do you really?' Elaine asked her.

'No,' Mina conceded. 'I don't know. I don't know anything anymore.'

'That's not true, now you know everything,' Elaine said. The tears had slowed and stopped. She pulled back, sat upright, looked at her daughter.

Mina looked back. She had always thought of secrets as things that broke people apart, but maybe they were really what held them together.

When the phone rang it startled them both. Elaine disentangled herself from Mina and jumped up from the sofa. She answered the phone by saying the last four digits of the phone number, the way she'd always done.

'Hello, George,' Elaine said and turned to look at Mina.

Mina's heart jumped, her eyes widened in panic.

'Yes, this is the right number. I'm her mother.'

Mina ran over to her, shaking her head, mouthing exaggerated NOs. She made a cutting motion across her throat.

'Yes, she's here, but it seems as though she's not that interested in talking to you,' Elaine said, and then, 'I see.' She nodded, sighed comically to Mina. 'I agree, that does leave you in a bit of a pickle, yes.'

Mina's guts churned. She tried to get Elaine to give her the phone but Elaine held her hand up. Standing beside her, Mina could hear the posh lilt of George's Oxbridge accent slither down the phone as he tried to charm Elaine. Mina jiggled up and down on the spot, desperate to know what he was saying, desperate for Elaine to hang up.

'Well, Mr – George, yes.' She tried to answer him in stops and starts; Mina knew George was interrupting her, wouldn't let her get a word in. 'George, please listen to me. For all the reasons you've just mentioned, I can understand why my daughter no longer wishes to work for your company. This is a pickle entirely of your own creation. You will accept her resignation and you will not call us again.' She nodded at something he was saying. 'Yes, thank you. Goodnight.' She hung up the phone, triumphant.

'Thank you,' Mina whispered and put her arms around Elaine, held her tight.

'He said you were having a tantrum because someone got a promotion over you.' Elaine stroked her hair and Mina pulled back from her embrace.

'He's not just anyone. He was my creative partner. We've been a team for a year,' Mina said. 'He has three years' less experience than me, I did all the work. I even did his timesheets for him, Mum.' She shook her head. When she said it out loud it seemed so obvious. How could she have been so blind? 'I did twice the amount of work and *he* got the promotion over me. That job was mine. It should've been mine.'

Mina remembered all the men at her first job getting promoted over her, getting the best briefs, how hard she had to fight just to get in the room. Even ten years ago, there weren't just glass ceilings but walls too.

She had taken the job in London, at Peach, because George made promises. About diversity and quotas. About her talent and career path. She could see now more than ever that the world was made up of layers of lies, half-truths, secrets, empty promises.

Mina looked at her mother standing there in the hall by the phone, at the way she held her arms in front of her body as though she was protecting herself from something.

'I've spent so much time trying to work this whole thing out. I kept wondering what I did wrong, what else I could've done to help you or to fix you,' Mina said. 'But I realise now it had absolutely nothing to do with me.'

'No,' Elaine said quietly.

'I wish it had,' Mina said. 'I wish at some point when you decided that this love you felt for him was worth staying for, you'd considered me. What about the love you felt for me? What about what I needed? Did it not occur to you that a consequence of you staying was that I would leave?'

Elaine breathed slowly, deeply, as she processed what Mina was saying, the answers she needed.

'I –' Elaine started, then stopped.

Mina waited, gave her ten, fifteen, twenty seconds to continue, but she didn't.

'I have to go to bed,' Mina said, and she turned and walked away.

MINA CLOSED THE door of her room, lay down and stared at the ceiling. She tried to line the facts up in a row, to take stock of everything she knew and work out how she felt about it.

She'd always imagined that knowing the truth would be like opening a valve, that it would provide instant relief. But now she just felt like she'd been emptied of one gas and filled up with another, more flammable one. How could she face Kira knowing what she knew? Face Valerie, face Arthur, Brendan, knowing that she had the power to set everything alight?

She had seen for the first time that her mother was a whole person. It was easy to forget our mothers weren't born with us. That before they were mothers, they were women with pasts, with secrets, desires, needs; that being a mother didn't cancel that out, didn't wipe the slate clean. It all came along with them.

Mina imagined young Elaine trying to find her place in the world, trying to understand what it was to love, knowing she needed more but not knowing how or where to get it. She thought about Jack, about what she'd done for him, what she would've done if he'd asked, how long she would've waited for him.

Elaine had spent so many of her fifty-seven years wanting. She was always hungry but never full, never satisfied. Mina worried that was in her too.

Mina picked up her phone. She scrolled through five missed calls from George. The tone of his text messages ranged from surprised to angry to desperate. She deleted them all.

While you might not be able to choose who you loved or explain why you loved them, you could choose how you loved them.

There were three messages from Jack.

Just spoke to George.
WTF?
I thought youd be happy for me.

She deleted those messages too.
There was one from Kira:

Sorry, just finished. Are things okay with you and Elaine? Call me if you need or I can come over. I love you.

She texted Kira back.

I love you too.

Twenty-three

WHEN SHE WOKE UP, IT took her a few seconds to remember. That Arthur was dying, that her mother . . . her mother was what? Mina always imagined this day would be sunny, deep blue skies with all the promise of the early days of summer, that she would jump out of bed refreshed, renewed. That she'd feel lighter, be thinner, prettier. That people would notice the change in her. 'You look different,' they'd say. 'Have you had your teeth whitened? Cut your hair? You're taller!' She felt stupid for putting so much faith in the truth.

She rolled over and looked at the time. Seven-thirty, the sky outside the colour of ash. She could hear Elaine moving around in the next room.

She got up and knocked on her mother's bedroom door. 'Let's go for a walk,' Mina said and didn't wait for an answer. She got dressed and waited for Elaine by the door.

She emerged from her room, dressed. Wearing shoes. Mina took Elaine's keys from the hall table and put them in the pocket of her jeans. The two women stepped out into the cool morning.

Mina stole glances at Elaine in the daylight. There were new lines around her eyes, a little grey flecked in her eyebrows.

'Stop looking at me,' Elaine said sheepishly.

'You were a stranger to me until last night,' Mina said. 'I'm going to look at you.'

They walked past the low brick walls, the white picket fences that lined the footpath.

'Feels like rain,' Elaine said and pulled her cardigan closed across her chest.

'How do you even remember what rain feels like?' Mina asked.

'There are some things you never forget,' Elaine told her.

They crossed the road, walked down the alley to the trail, along the creek, in step together. Mina wondered if Elaine felt lighter (prettier, thinner, taller), if a problem shared . . .

'Is that Brendan?' Elaine pointed at a man doing push-ups in the middle of the oval.

Mina watched him, his arms shaking as he lifted his body up from the ground. She remembered the taste of him, the smell. She shuddered. He jumped back up to his feet, punching the air as though fighting an invisible opponent.

Brendan stopped boxing and squinted at them, jogged towards them. Mina felt her whole body tighten.

'Hey, Elaine,' Brendan said, a little out of breath. 'It's nice to see you. You too, Mina.' He smiled at them both.

'And you, Brendan,' Elaine said. 'Sorry to hear about you and Kylie.'

Brendan shrugged. 'She's just going through some things,' he said, as if it was no big deal. 'We'll work it out.'

'I'm sure you will,' Elaine said.

'You should come by later if you get bored,' he said to Mina.

'Got my hands pretty full with this one,' she said, hoping Elaine wouldn't notice the colour of her cheeks, know what she'd done. 'We'd best be off.'

They walked up along the creek. Mina stopped in the middle of the rickety wooden bridge. It wobbled violently as a middle-aged man jogged across it, his face pulsing Mars-red.

'Thank you for not being mad at me,' Elaine said.

'Who says I'm not mad at you?' Mina laughed but she wasn't sure at what. Nothing about this was funny. 'I've been angry for so long, I'm exhausted.'

Below them the creek bubbled, the dirt-brown water parted around a rock, came back together. A few drops of rain pattered, darkening the green-painted railing.

They walked back through the green of the park, past all the gum trees, the air thick with the smell of eucalyptus.

'Will you show me how to cook with that Moroccan thing?' Elaine asked her when they were halfway back up the hill. 'I want to be able to use it once you've gone.'

'Sure,' Mina said. 'Although I might not be going anywhere for a while.'

Elaine stopped walking and stared at her. 'Don't you dare stay here for me,' she said.

'It's more that Peach were sponsoring me,' Mina said and kept walking. 'So, after early December, I won't have a visa.'

'Oh, Jasmina, no.'

'It's fine. I have options. I can get a new job. Or live somewhere else. The world is my oyster.' Mina skipped ahead a little then turned to watch Elaine walk towards her. 'And maybe I *want* to stay here a bit longer.'

Twenty-four

THE NUMBER 11 TRUNDLED DOWN St Georges Road. The rain had cleared, there was sun behind a cloud somewhere. Mina watched the houses pass, the blur of Edinburgh Gardens, the new leaves budding and unfurling. She sat heavy on the green-and-gold-patterned seat, weighed down by all the things she had to keep to herself. Elaine was in love with Arthur; Arthur was going to die. Her and Brendan in the basement. She couldn't tell Kira any of it. Mina opened her phone and scrolled through Instagram, pulled it down and down, looking for something new. She looked at Jack's profile. He'd posted. She sat up in her seat and looked at it, his new business card: *Jack Adams – Creative Director.* Her lip curled into a snarl. If he had a business card already, they must've known of the promotion for weeks. *Weeks.* He knew when he let her do all the work for the pitch, he knew when she went to his house, when he unzipped his jeans. Mina felt humiliated about all that longing, all those feelings. She pulled the cord, a bell rang.

The old pair of bathers she'd found at the back of her closet wedged themselves further and further up between her cheeks as she crossed Alexandra Parade, jogging to make it across all the lanes while the walk signal flashed red. She stood outside the pool and waited, the sun, out now, warming her face, her arms.

'I'm sorry.' Kira ran up to her, squeezed her arms, kissed the top of her head. 'I'm late. I don't even have a good excuse. I just couldn't get my legs to move.'

'It's fine, I was enjoying the alone time,' Mina said and squeezed her back.

'You're a liar but I appreciate it.' Kira laughed. 'Just two swims, please,' she said to the guy with a pockmarked face behind the desk. 'My shout.' She swatted Mina's money away. 'I just got paid.'

The concrete change room was sludgy in the corners from years of damp and it reeked of chlorine. A woman in her fifties emerged from the shower and dried herself off at one of the benches, her clothes hanging on hooks like colourful ghosts. Mina loved seeing the bodies of the older, every-day swimmers, their tans etched into their skin over decades. They always walked around naked, not one of them caring about their body hair, their excess skin, their cellulite.

'Remember the time I was on the train and saw someone scrolling through your Instagram?' Mina said as she pulled off her jeans. From her spot standing in the aisle on the seven-fifteen train to Liverpool Street, Mina had watched the woman zoom in on different parts of Kira's body in about ten different photos, as if she didn't believe it was real. Mina took a video of it on her phone; Kira would never have believed her otherwise.

'That still creeps me out,' she said. 'Do you think she'd zoom in on a photo of this?' Kira asked, and Mina turned to see her in a training suit, full swimming cap and goggles.

'That's the thing, you idiot,' Mina said, laughing. 'You still look beautiful.'

'Oh, shut up.' Kira flicked her towel at her.

They headed out the frosted-glass door that divided the pool from the change room. The concrete was wet out on the deck too, cold under their feet.

There were a few dedicated swimmers gliding up and down the fast and medium lanes, bodies sexless, ageless in the light blue water. A guy in a tiny red Speedo lay out on the concrete steps even though the sun had disappeared again, hiding behind the thick clouds rolling in from the west.

Mina lowered herself into the Aqua Play lane. Steam rose off the water and disappeared into the grey sky. She watched Kira lap in one of the fast lanes, pounding the water so fast a man three times her size, all shaved chest and big muscles, swapped out to a slower lane to get out of her way.

Mina floated on her back and watched the sky, rolled to her front and back again. She put her feet on the pool floor and sank down until the warm water covered her shoulders. She heard two men arguing at the end of the next lane over.

'Can you not swim in the middle of the lane, mate?' one of them said.

'Piss off,' the littler, balder one said. 'I'm a runner and I can barely swim. I'm doing my best.'

They stood so close together, their naked chests all puffed up.

It looked for a moment as if they might start hitting each other, but they didn't. One of them pulled himself out of the pool, everyone kept swimming. Mina imagined them together in the change room later. Maybe they'd jostle a little, their bare chests, wet bodies touching, rubbing, and the fighting would turn to kissing, their little swimsuits peeled off, lying in puddles on the floor.

'Oi,' Kira said as she ducked under the lane ropes after her swift kilometre, ten up and ten back. Her cheeks were a little flushed but she wasn't out of breath. Mina wished she could tell her that her dad was sick, that she didn't have much time left with him, that Elaine loved him, *loved* him, enough to wait for him forever. The weight of the secrets made it harder for her to float.

Kira peeled off her silver swimming cap and dumped it on the edge of the pool. She launched herself off from the side, her black hair spread around her head like seaweed, an oil slick. Mina sat in the water like a crocodile, eyes and nose on the surface, the rest of her body submerged in the warm blue.

Kira flipped over onto her stomach and disappeared into the water, surfacing next to Mina. She smoothed her hair back and crouched, keeping her long neck above the surface.

'How was the rest of the shoot?' Mina asked.

'It was okay.' Kira moved her hands under the water like a synchronised swimmer.

'Just okay?'

'I guess I thought I'd be doing better than this by now.'

'But you're working, you're getting paid to do what you've always wanted to do. That's amazing.'

'I also make a lot of coffee. I'm a thirty-two-year-old barista. I just thought I'd be doing something more meaningful, or important, just something *more* by now.'

'Panty liners are very important. Otherwise we'd all just bleed right into our undies.'

'You know what I mean.' Kira dunked her head under the water again, stayed down for ages. Bubbles rose around her as she surfaced.

'I do, you're right. I'm sorry. This is a good stepping stone, though. You never know what's next.'

'Maybe I'll move up into tampons.' Kira squeezed the water out of her hair. 'How is . . . everything?'

Mina wanted to say: *I had a fight with Shelly and sucked off your brother. Then I quit my job. My mum's been in love with your dad for thirty-something years. Your dad is dying.* But she knew not every story in the world needed to be told; that there was rarely kindness in the truth.

She settled on the safest talking point. 'I quit my job.'

'Whoa!' Kira swam closer to her. 'That's huge. What happened?'

'Remember how I took the job because they had this whole career path mapped out for me?' Kira nodded, winced, waiting for the reveal. 'Well, they lied. Or they changed their minds. Either way, they screwed me over.' She took a mouthful of water, spat it out like a fountain. 'God, I always thought I needed to have this big life, to be out in the world doing things. But it turns out I've just been running away from my life here.'

'You've only just realised that? Mate.'

'Why didn't anyone try to snap me out of it?'

'Oh sure, because you Gordon women just love to be told what to do. The apple doesn't fall far from the tree.' Kira laughed.

Mina let the revelation sink with her to the bottom of the pool. She opened her eyes; the chlorine stung. Everything down there was a murky version of real life, but to Mina it looked clearer than ever.

'So does this mean you're staying here?' Kira asked when Mina resurfaced. 'Please say yes.' She rested her arms on the edge of the pool, kicked her legs.

'At least for a little while,' Mina said and slid in next to her.

Kira dropped her head onto her arms and looked at her. A few drops of rain started to fall on the surface of the pool, creating little ripples everywhere.

'So here's another thing,' Kira said. She took a deep breath. 'My period's a few days late.'

'Not Hillary Clinton?' Mina asked.

Kira nodded.

'But it's too soon.'

'That night of the party wasn't the first time,' Kira said. She shivered. 'But I think he might be a good guy. Maybe it would be nice?'

'I hear it's a good way to curb your existential crisis for a few years,' Mina said and put her arm around her friend, kissed the top of her bare, goosebumped shoulder.

'You and I could raise it together.' Kira joked, but she looked scared.

'Let's go. We can buy a test. We'll work it out.' Mina said, and they pulled themselves out and up and into the rain.

They showered next to each other in silence, wrung out their bathers over the drain, changed next to each other. Mina dried herself with a threadbare beach towel from her childhood. She used one of the hairdryers that looked like something out of an eighties sci-fi movie and watched the hot air blow her hair around. She rubbed at it a little with the towel, left it mostly wet.

'I just need the loo, I'll meet you out in reception,' Kira yelled, and Mina walked through the chlorine-filled corridor. She peered in through the window to the spa as she waited. It was mostly full of men with their doughy torsos exposed, tufts of hair growing in strange places. Mina watched two women sitting in the corner. They were in their late sixties. One of them had excess skin that swung back and forth as she gesticulated wildly, the other was lithe, all sinew and bones.

'Hey, it's us in thirty years,' Mina said as Kira emerged from the change rooms. They stood and watched them together; the sinewy one cackled as she laughed. Mina smiled at her friend.

'I just got my period,' Kira said and put her arm around Mina's shoulders.

'Back to the drawing board, I guess.' Mina slipped her arm around Kira's waist and squeezed her tightly. They let go of each other and fell into step, walked through the gates, out through the sliding doors and into the wet afternoon.

'Fancy some company up north? I'm due a visit,' Kira said, and they walked towards the tram stop together.

As the tram rumbled north, they sat opposite each other in a comfortable silence, their hair wetting their backs and the backs of their seats. The faint goggle impression around Kira's eyes faded slowly.

'I really like having you here,' Kira said as they passed the bowls club. 'I feel like I've got my legs back.'

Mina squeezed one of Kira's knees between hers and they sat like that, their legs entwined, until the tram turned down Miller Street and Mina stood to reach for the bell.

Twenty-five

MINA WANDERED AROUND THE CHENGS' living room, looking at it with new eyes. In the family portrait, she noticed Arthur's long neck was Kira's neck too. His high cheekbones. She could see that he was handsome. How had she not known? She tried to recall him and Elaine together, if she'd ever noticed any eye contact, any hands touching, but there was nothing that sent up a red flag; in thirty-two years, nothing. She noticed a photo she hadn't seen in a long time, from an Easter long weekend the two families had shared down in Rye. The Gordons and the Chengs standing in one long line, Loretta in her underwear because Valerie forgot to pack her swimsuit again. Mina remembered how she and Kira had eaten all their little Easter eggs then filled them with bits of tissue and taped them back up, offering them to Loretta as she sat on the top bunk reading. They ran away laughing as she opened them. She noticed Lottie on the edge of every family photo, looking like she'd rather be anywhere else. Now she was: she had a good job in New York, was living with her girlfriend in Brooklyn.

She thought about her getting the call about her dad, the long plane rides home, a worried layover in LAX. Poor Lottie.

Mina looked closely at the holiday photo. In it, Elaine and Arthur were standing next to each other, their forearms touching, just slightly. On either side of them their spouses stood smiling. Bill had white zinc across his face, a big wide smile beaming out of his beard. Mina missed him, missed how his laugh seemed to come from his stomach and fill a whole room. On the other side of him, Brendan stood flexing in red board shorts, the hint of a six-pack showing on his stomach. Mina wondered what other secrets lay between these people, wondered if maybe every family was built on an intricate web of lies, or at least things people chose not to tell each other. She'd learnt that not every truth deserves air: some truths were better smothered, extinguished before they could take hold and burn everything to the ground.

She heard Valerie and Kira in the kitchen and walked through the house the way she used to, as if it was hers too.

Valerie was holding Kira in a long hug. 'Mummy's so proud of you.'

'Stop it, Mum.' Kira pulled back and out of Valerie's arms. 'Where's that deadbeat brother of mine?' she asked.

Valerie pointed down to the floor and then scrunched her hand and shook it up and down, the universal sign for wanking. Mina shrieked with laughter, Valerie looked proud of herself. Kira looked horrified.

'Brendan Andrew Cheng, I'm coming downstairs so you'd better stop whacking off,' Kira said with a glint in her eye as she disappeared down into the basement. Mina heard his voice through the floor, the low rumble of a few terse words.

'Hey, Valerie,' Mina said, moving to stand beside her. 'I don't know if I've ever said this before, and I'm sorry if I haven't, but thank you for everything you've done for us.'

'Oh, baby girl.' Valerie reached over and pulled Mina into a hug. 'You're family,' she said, as though that cancelled it all out. Mina let herself relax into Valerie's arms. 'I love you and I'm proud of you too,' Valerie said, then released Mina from her embrace. 'Never forget that.'

Kira's feet plonked back up the stairs and she raised her eyebrows suggestively at Mina, as if she had a secret now too.

'Hey, Mum, we're just going over the road to Mina's for a bit. I'll be back for dinner.'

'You should all come for dinner, your Mum too,' Valerie said. She swatted gently at Mina's arm as if she'd made a great joke.

'I'll ask her. You never know.' Mina smiled, still uneasy about this new reality. She felt like she'd just settled on the moon, a parallel universe.

Outside, the rain-darkened bitumen was drying in patches, lightening in splotches. When they reached the street, Kira pulled a fat joint from the back pocket of her jeans.

'My brother may be a depraved moron,' she said, running it under her nose, 'but he has the best hook-ups.'

Mina thought about the force of his hand on the back of her head.

'How long's he going to stay here?' Mina asked. She could taste the sourness of him.

'Don't you dare,' Kira warned her as Mina opened the front door. 'Don't even think about it.'

'Ew, as if.' Mina grimaced cartoonishly but she hadn't stopped thinking about it.

'Hey, Elaine,' Kira said as she drifted down into the living room.

Mina followed and saw Elaine's face light up at the sight of Kira. She stood and hugged her quickly, smiled at Mina.

'Mum invited you over for dinner now that you're' – Kira paused – 'you know.'

Elaine looked over Kira's shoulder at Mina, as if asking for her permission. Mina nodded enthusiastically. She wanted to watch her mother and Arthur together, to see it with her own eyes.

'That would be nice,' Elaine said nervously. 'I'll make something for dessert.'

'Good idea,' Mina said and Elaine disappeared into the kitchen.

'She's going to come, just like that?' Kira whispered and they heard the white noise whirr of the oven coming to life.

Mina shrugged and motioned to the garden.

The long, wet grass soaked their socks, the cuffs at the bottom of their jeans. They stood under the dripping branches of the wiry gum. Kira pulled the joint and a lighter out of her pocket. She lit it, and the end smouldered as she inhaled. Two puffs, just like her brother. She passed it to Mina.

'Remember that party we were at when Mum called about your dad?' she asked through a cloud of smoke.

'You were planning to have sex with that guy, Joe.'

'Joe Daniels,' Kira said with nostalgic lust. 'I remember being so angry.' She laughed. 'Until we got to the hospital, obviously.'

Mina put on a voice: 'This better be a fucking emergency.'

'After that, I was mostly mad at your mum,' Kira said.

'It wasn't her fault you never got to fuck Joe Daniels,' Mina said, and she felt the high hit, felt the distance between her brain and her thoughts growing and growing.

'I did fuck him. I went over to his house a few days later. He lived in that gross share house with Ben for a while. Who asked me about you.'

'Don't you think it's weird that Ben wanted to go out with me so soon after my dad died?' Mina took a drag, coughed a little.

'God, he was so in love with you,' Kira said. 'No one's ever loved me like that. It was so' – she paused looking for the right word – 'pure. Did you see him before he left?'

'Yeah, we had a drink and I watched him do karaoke and then we had a fight,' Mina said, and above them the clouds swirled like just-stirred coffee. 'It was a hoot.'

'What did you fight about?' Kira asked.

'He told me the chip on my shoulder is boring and I should get over it.' Mina exhaled.

'Mmm, maybe he has a point,' Kira said, smiling.

'Shut up,' Mina said and whacked her arm.

'What did he sing?'

'"Kokomo".'

'Kokomo's not even a real place.' Kira rolled her eyes, wiped a drop of water from the wet leaves of the gum tree from her shoulder.

'Well, it's –'

'A city in Indiana, yeah. Also a resort somewhere, I think. But it's not the tropical island the Beach Boys made everyone think it is.'

'Exactly.'

'And what kind of lyrics just list place names?' Kira put on a deep voice. '*Bundoora, St Kilda, ooh I wanna do ya.*'

'*Tecoma, Altona, come on, baby mumma.*' Mina giggled, Kira too, and then they were laughing loudly together, the laughter turning to tears.

'That's not even how it goes,' Kira managed to choke out.

'You think the lyrics are actually *ooh I wanna do ya*?' Mina retorted as she wiped the tears from her eyes with the crook of her finger. 'I hate that song.'

She looked back at the house, lit up against the last light of the day. She could see Elaine pottering about in the living room; she'd showered, put on a nice dress.

'I'm here whenever you're ready to tell me what's going on there,' Kira said, looking at Elaine too.

'I know,' Mina said. 'Thank you. *I just wanna get away from it all*,' she crooned in an off-key falsetto.

Kira snorted, stubbed the joint out on the trunk of the tree, buried it in the dirt and followed Mina back into the house.

AS FAR AS Mina knew, Elaine hadn't been inside the Chengs' house in twelve years. Maybe Elaine and Arthur knew differently. Just one more secret tucked into their shirt pockets, stuffed down the back of the sofa.

'It looks just the same in here.' Elaine walked around the room. She picked up some photos from the mantelpiece and looked at them lovingly, studying them as you would the cover of a favourite book you've not read in years.

'We got new cushions,' Valerie said, giving Elaine the guided tour of anything that was different. 'We got my beautiful baby boy back.' She pointed at Brendan as he walked into the room.

'Hi, Elaine,' he said and kissed her on the cheek. He put one hand on Mina's shoulder and kissed her too, she felt his hot breath, the wet of his lips drying on her cheek. He stepped back but didn't take his eyes off her. 'Shall I get some wine?'

'Does the Pope shit in the woods? Get the white,' Valerie said and ushered Elaine towards the kitchen. Brendan hung back.

'I believe this is yours,' he said and pulled a hairband from his pocket.

Mina cringed. Took it from him, put it on her wrist, felt it there, a constant, strangling reminder.

'Come on,' Valerie called to Mina from the kitchen, and she stepped around Brendan and left him standing in the hall.

In the kitchen, Arthur (*Arthur.* **Arthur.** <u>Arthur</u>.) was at the stove with three saucepans on the go. Kira was leaning over the bench watching him work. Mina stepped in beside her and knocked her gently with her hip.

'I'm still high as a kite,' Kira whispered.

'Me too.' Mina laughed. 'It's the only thing stopping this from blowing my mind.'

They turned around to watch Valerie fuss over the cake Elaine had brought, sticking her finger under the lid to taste the icing. She rolled her eyes back in her head in the throes of exaggerated ecstasy. Mina turned back to Arthur.

'What's for dinner?' she asked.

'Crispy whole barramundi, garlic greens and coconut rice,' he said. He stirred and tasted the sauce, threw in some sugar.

'I keep telling him he should go on next year's *MasterChef*,' Valerie teased. 'They always have one old guy on there.' She joked. Mina winced. She knew he probably wouldn't be around long enough for that. She tried not to catch his eye, not to let on. He said nothing, just kept stirring, adding.

Brendan emerged from the basement with two bottles of wine. He opened one and lined up glasses on the bench. He filled Mina's first, glancing at her while he did. She let herself look back, just for a second, before taking the glass, swirling it, smelling it.

Arthur pulled the fish from the oven and carried it to the table, made a second trip for the greens, a third for the rice. Brendan handed wine to everyone, they sat.

Mina watched the way Arthur and Elaine moved around each other. She wanted a sign that Arthur loved her back. But they didn't look at each other, they didn't talk, not directly. There was no touching, no spark, nothing she could see. They'd been performing this routine for years, a dance so perfectly choreographed no one even knew it was happening. Mina wondered if Arthur really did know or if this was a fantasy orchestrated solely by Elaine. What if Elaine had spent most of her life unpicking the truth then sewing it back together in a different way, until she had something that fit? Maybe that's what we all do, Mina thought. Maybe that's what love is: the refashioning and remodelling of the truth until it fits the lies we've told ourselves.

Mina looked at the fish in the middle of the table: its little fish face, its mouth burnt open in a grimace. Arthur took his knife and fork and started pulling big chunks of flesh away from its skeleton, stripping it bare. Mina could see its tiny teeth; she looked into its crisped-up, dried-out little eye.

'I'd like to make a toast,' Kira said, banging her knife on her wineglass dramatically. 'To family,' she said and raised her glass into the air.

'To family,' Mina said, Elaine said, Valerie. Brendan let his legs fall open and his knee rest against hers, just for a second. They all clinked glasses.

Mina knew things were going to get bad soon. She watched Arthur move the food around his plate, not wanting to eat, not able to. He wouldn't be able to hide this for much longer, this sickness that was eating him from the inside out. Lottie would come home, Brendan would stay. The two women who loved Arthur Cheng would care for him, watch him waste away and then mourn him together. And then what? What would happen to Elaine? What would happen to all of them?

Mina tried to think about something she wanted as much as Elaine wanted Arthur. She wanted to be taken apart and put back together, a kettle filled, boiled, emptied and refilled again. She wanted this. This new understanding that love was never everything you wanted or needed it to be. It was uncontrollable, it misbehaved. It tethered you but helped make you free.

Kira sat down and raised her glass to Mina, Mina tapped it against hers, leant over and crooned in her ear in her best falsetto, *'This is where we're gonna beeee.'*

The two girls cackled, Kira dribbled wine onto her plate. Brendan shook his head. Mina looked over at Elaine just in time to see her smile.

This troubled and imperfect thing. This.

Acknowledgements

This book is dedicated to my friends whose kindness, humour, good looks, patience, love, enthusiasm and unwavering support shapes, buoys and motivates me. I have so much to thank so many of you for but to start: Amy Vuleta (this book/I wouldn't be here without you), Meredith McHugh, Christian Best, Joy Chen, Marieca Page, Jazz Feldy, Caro Cooper, Meg Madden, Daniel Stephensen, Kate Cooper, Liesl Pfeffer, Libby Noble, Khaleda O'Neill, Nikola Errington, Tess Braden, Jessica Stanley, Matt Shurgold, Sarah Fitzpatrick, Chloe George, Kira Cook, Nicolas Greiff, Alice Bishop. I will be forever grateful to Amy, Caro, Meg, Dan, Amelia Marshall and Sean Wilson for your time, input and guidance early on. And to Kathryn Savage, Nabeeha Mohammed and Briony Barr for your friendship in strange lands and beyond.

To Hannans 1–3, thank you for your support, for letting me prioritise this, for teaching me that humour is both possible and necessary when times are tough. I love you.

Thank you to dear Robert Watkins, Louise Sherwin-Stark, Fiona Hazard and the entire Hachette team for your support, passion and ambition. I'm still floored by how much you believe in this book. Thank you to Rebecca Allen, Ali Lavau and Rebecca Hamilton for your close reading and keen eyes, and Tessa Connelly for being the best publicist.

To Pippa Masson, I don't know how I would've navigated this strange new world without you. I'm so grateful you're on my team.

To the Victorian Premier's Literary Awards, Elizabeth Flux, J.P. Pomare and Jaclyn Crupi. You changed my life and I'll never stop saying thank you (and crying in front of you) for it. Sorry for all the crying.

This novel was written at and with the support of:
Casa Na Ilha, Brazil
All That We Are, Tasmania
Gullkistan Centre for Creativity, Iceland
Jacky Winter Gardens, Victoria